# Beyond the Sea

# Also by Keira Andrews

## Contemporary

*Honeymoon for One*
*Beyond the Sea*
*Ends of the Earth*
*Arctic Fire*
*The Chimera Affair*

### Holiday
*Only One Bed*
*Merry Cherry Christmas*
*The Christmas Deal*
*Santa Daddy*
*In Case of Emergency*
*Eight Nights in December*
*If Only in My Dreams*
*Where the Lovelight Gleams*
*Gay Romance Holiday Collection*

### Sports
*Kiss and Cry*
*Reading the Signs*
*Cold War*
*The Next Competitor*
*Love Match*
*Synchronicity* (free read!)

### Gay Amish Romance Series
*A Forbidden Rumspringa*
*A Clean Break*
*A Way Home*
*A Very English Christmas*

### Valor Duology
*Valor on the Move*
*Test of Valor*
*Complete Valor Duology*

# Beyond the Sea

BY KEIRA ANDREWS

*Beyond the Sea*
**Written and published by Keira Andrews**
**Cover by** Dar Albert
**Formatting by** BB eBooks

# Acknowledgements

Thank you to Anne-Marie, Becky, Jay, Jules, and Mary for your invaluable beta reading and friendship. Thanks as well to Liz for sharing my fascination with aeronautics and spending many a Saturday watching documentaries on YouTube.

Finally, to Rachel for your honesty, kindness, and unwavering support.

# *Chapter One*

T HE STRAW THAT broke the camel's back was shoved up his little
brother's nose.

Quads still burning from his workout and run up to the top floor,
Troy watched Tyson where he knelt on the floor in his boxers, shirtless
and snorting a line of white powder off a hand mirror on the coffee
table. The door to Tyson's suite swung closed, and Troy stood there
dumbly in his sweaty workout gear. Even if he'd been able to manage
words that weren't screamed curses, the Rolling Stones were blasting too
loudly for anyone to hear.

The curtains in the living area were drawn tight, blocking out the
sun and any telephoto lenses. Glasses and bottles cluttered every surface,
the stench of cigarettes and pot thick in the air. A few girls in short-
shorts and crop tops sprawled on the suite's couches with Nick, a
passable singer and the band's best dancer. It was a cliché VH1 docu-
mentary brought to life.

The fact that one of the women at this secret party was Troy's girl-
friend sent a fresh flare of rage burning through him. He'd thought
Savannah didn't do more than drink or take a toke, yet here she was.
The betrayal churned his stomach, hurt and anger warring.

One of the groupies lifted her head and stared at Troy with glazed
eyes, a discarded needle on the floor near her dangling fingers. Savannah
followed her gaze, leaping to her feet so quickly her boob popped out of
her halter top, her long, dark curls flying. Her pupils were too big, blue

1

eyes too bright. She wore makeup as usual, but her lips somehow seemed unnaturally red.

"Troy!" She hastily straightened herself while kicking Nick, who was completely out of it with his head back and mouth wide open. His shaggy blond hair was matted and skin sallow in the artificial light of the room's lamps.

Nick's partying had increased dramatically on this tour, and *fuck*, Troy should have done something about it. Nick was Ty's best friend and worst influence, and Troy should have known this was coming. He should have gone to Joe, because that's what managers were for. But he hadn't wanted to cause trouble. He'd taken a page from his mother's book and stuck his head in the sand.

But the shitty truth was that Joe and the label knew. Between the crew and all the staff who worked on the tour, *of course* they knew. The members of Next Up couldn't sneeze without the entourage around them taking notice. They knew, and they hadn't done a damn thing either.

Nick grunted and muttered something, and Troy wanted to rip him apart with his bare hands and then get his stupid, reckless ass into rehab along with Ty.

Savannah lunged for the iPod stereo dock on the cluttered bar, jabbing a button. In the sudden silence, Tyson's head jerked up, and he stared at Troy from the floor, still holding the straw.

Tyson was like a mirror of Troy's former teenage self. They shared the same wavy dark hair that Troy cropped close now and Ty let curl cherubically since every band member had to have a different style. Their dark brown eyes and tan skin were the same, faces a similar round shape down to the little cleft in their chins. But Tyson was a good four inches shorter than Troy's five-ten and fifty pounds lighter. At twenty-two, he was still the pretty boy baby of the band, an unthreatening pinup for young girls around the world.

Troy wanted to haul him over his shoulder and take him home. Lock him away.

Tyson licked his lips, and his voice cracked. "Hey, man. We're just…it's no big deal, BT."

Short for "Big T," Troy's fan-coined nickname that the band had co-opted. He stared down at his little brother. Cocaine dusted Tyson's nostril. Savannah reached out to Troy, and as her red-tipped fingers settled on his wrist, he realized his blunt nails were close to breaking the skin of his palms where he clenched his fists. He shook her off with a sharp exhale.

She breathed shallowly. "I thought you and Tomas had to do that animal sanctuary ribbon cutting thing?"

"Greg wanted to see the koalas, so he went instead. I grabbed a workout. Thought maybe we could all hit the pool. Obviously you guys had other plans."

Ty scoffed defiantly. "Chill, dude."

"*Chill?* I can't fucking believe this," Troy grated out like his throat was lined with broken glass. "You promised." He stared at his brother. "You *swore* to me."

Ignoring Savannah's protests, he stepped around her and yanked Tyson to his feet with one hand, sending the remaining cocaine through the air with the other. Gripping his brother, he stared into his enormous pupils. They looked all wrong in his baby face. Roughly, he examined Tyson's arm, looking for the track marks. He squeezed hard when he found them. "*Heroin?* Are you kidding me? With a coke chaser to bring you up for the concert?" Glaring toward Nick, he added, "Was this his fucking idea? I bet it was."

Tyson swallowed audibly, his curls waving as he shook his head. "We're just…it's not…" He looked to Nick still slumped on the couch. Help was clearly not forthcoming. "It's good stuff! It's not dangerous like street shit is. It's just for fun. It's safe."

"There's nothing safe about heroin! Or coke for that matter! It doesn't matter how pure it is."

Puffing up, his brows drawing together, Tyson tugged his arm free. Familiar righteous indignation took over. "You're such a killjoy. You're supposed to be my brother, not my father. Fuck off."

"Are you seriously bringing up Dad right now? If he was here, he'd have been first in line for the smack. He's the fucking reason you can't go near this shit." He glared at Savannah. "Either of you."

"God, she's having fun." Ty waved dismissively. "She's sick of you being so fucking boring."

It shouldn't have hurt, but it did. Troy's breath came hard and fast, an iron band around his lungs. He shot his gaze to wide-eyed Savannah. "Is she? Good to know."

*I've been bored of her for months*, a little voice hissed. She was Next Up's opening act, and as the endless tour ground on, they had fewer and fewer things to say to each other. He knew they weren't right together, so why was he coasting along? Sure, she was beautiful—twenty-three and gorgeous with small tits and a huge voice. But he wanted more.

"Of course I'm not!" Savannah's voice rose several octaves, her words tripping out as she reached for him. "Troy, you know I love you."

As he stood there in a crazy expensive hotel room on the other side of the world from home, Troy didn't *know* anything anymore. Fury left pinpricks as it faded, leaving the cold truth behind. "You don't, actually. And I don't love you either."

Jerking, Savannah blinked. Her eyes filled with tears, and guilt slithered through him. He tried to soften his voice. "I'm not saying that to hurt you. It's just the truth."

"Jesus, Troy. Why are you such an asshole?" Tyson's face twisted. "Don't be mean to her because you're pissed at me."

"Is there more blow?"

They all looked to the redhead, who stretched her legs over Nick's lap and snapped a piece of gum.

She shrugged blearily. "If you want him to make it to the show, you'd better get some."

Pointedly not looking at Troy, Savannah cleared her throat. "Okay, let's just handle Nick. We can deal with the rest of it later. We have a show to do."

"No." It was a simple word—*no*—but Troy couldn't remember the last time he'd said it to Tyson and meant it.

Jesus, it had probably been five years ago at Troy's twenty-first birthday party in Vegas when he'd refused a lap dance and Ty had bought him one anyway, not caring that people were taking video on their phones. Not caring that he was too young to be in a strip club in the first place. They'd just won video of the year at the MTV Awards, and Ty had been let in everywhere.

Because no one said no to him.

"No," Troy repeated, testing the word on his tongue.

All eyes but Nick's swiveled to him, since the asshole was still passed out and snoring now.

Tyson's bravado faltered. He tried to smile. "Look, we'll work this out, BT. Like Savannah said, we have a show to do. This is our last night in Sydney."

"No." Troy inhaled deeply, purpose and determination filling him. "No," he repeated. "*You* have a show to do. I'm not going to enable you or Nick another minute. I quit."

"Whoa." The other groupie hanging off one of the couches who'd been watching and giggling, high as a kite, stopped smiling.

"You can't quit!" Savannah sputtered. "Next Up can't do the show without you. There are thousands of fans coming. You can't just leave with no notice!"

"I gave my notice that night in Perth." He addressed Tyson, whose eyes went wide, the whites bright in contrast to his dilated pupils. "I told you! Mess with drugs again and I'm done." A memory of hauling their father's dead weight up the stairs filled his mind. All those nights he'd taken care of him, protecting Ty and Mom from the worst of it.

All those nights he should have said no.

"I won't watch you piss your life away, Ty. I won't help you do it. Won't stick around and play my part like the good little soldier while you lie to me."

Tyson's lips flattened into a thin line, and he lifted his chin. "Fine.

Go. We won't miss you. We don't need you. Greg can sing your parts." Shaking, he spat, "You were only in the band because you're my brother!"

Troy flinched. It was the truth—when their father had orchestrated the five-guy band and pitched them to the label, Tyson was the star and Troy was part of a package deal. He inhaled and exhaled, struggling to keep steady. "I know. I love you, Ty. Call me when you're ready to get help."

"I don't need you!" Tyson screamed. Whirling, he picked up a chair and threw it into a mirrored piece of art on the wall.

As the glass shattered, Troy wanted to stay and pick up the pieces. But it would only make things worse. Another flash of their father hijacked his mind—bleary and slurring, making promises, telling lies, lies, lies.

Troy had tried so hard to fix their dad. He'd always been there to haul him up and drag him to bed. Mom slept in another room because she said Dad had restless leg syndrome. So it was Troy who'd take off his shoes and help him puke into a bucket. All the while pretending nothing was wrong. Pretending it was just a bad night, and it would be better tomorrow. Never saying a goddamned word until it was too late.

And he'd done it again in Perth a week ago when Ty had gotten fucked up on booze and coke, bouncing off the walls before crashing. Ty had made his promises, so familiar that Troy could see their father, his blond hair sticking up and dried vomit on his collar.

Guilt and sorrow and icy hot resentment compelled his feet to move.

It was time for a new approach. If he quit, Joe and the label would have to do something. They wouldn't be able to ignore this.

Bruno, one of their massive security guards, barreled in as Troy reached the door. Bruno had done four years with XP, a drug-crazed rap group who'd torn up the charts like they did hotel rooms. There was nothing he hadn't seen.

"Everything okay?" he asked tonelessly.

Nodding, Troy shoved past him into the hush of the hallway. Two more security guards at the end of the corridor started toward him. His stomach clenched, and he leaned a hand on the textured beige wallpaper. *Oh fuck. Fuck, fuck, fuck.*

Could he really do this? Would it help? Was he abandoning Ty when his baby brother needed him most? No. He had to take a stand. He had to do something dramatic. If he stayed now, Ty would know his threats were empty. Troy would go home and get their mother. Wake her up to the truth she hadn't been able to face with his father.

He was going to puke.

"Baby?"

He reeled away from Savannah's touch just as the guards approached. He barked, "We're fine!" Like he'd waved a magic wand, they retreated, their steps silent on the plush carpet.

Arms crossed, she looked up at him with glistening blue eyes. Her feet were bare, and without her usual heels she was barely over five-two. "You can't walk out. What about the fans?"

He shoved away the sticky swell of guilt. "The fans will be a hell of a lot more upset when Ty and Nick OD. They need help, and I need to force them to get it. Force the label to do something."

"Okay, after the tour's over—"

"No! Now! There's still a whole leg left in Japan and Korea. I can't wait. I won't."

"But you have a contract. You're in the biggest pop group in the world! The most popular boy band since One Direction and Backstreet put together. They won't let you quit."

"They can sue me. I don't care. I'm not going to stand here with my thumbs up my ass while Ty kills himself. While he and Nick pull you into this shitshow too. Are you shooting up now? Jesus Christ, Sav. You're smarter than this. Don't throw your career away. Your *life*."

She shook her head vigorously. "I just did a little coke. I was keeping an eye on them, Troy. Making sure they stayed safe."

"Spare me!" His nostrils flared as he breathed through the surge of fury. "Making sure they were safe would have meant making sure they didn't do any of that toxic shit."

Savannah opened her mouth and then closed it and pressed her too-red lips together, apparently unable to argue.

Troy wasn't going to let her off the hook. "You know how I feel about this stuff. What we went through with my dad. What *I* went through. I can't do this again. For years I've tried to protect my brother. I've tried to do all the right things and make everyone else happy."

Her face softened. "I know, baby. That shit with your dad growing up was horrible. Ty needs you now more than ever."

"So I can enable him? No. I'm done. With all of it."

Her lips trembled. "Even me?"

"You don't need me. You'll be fine."

"No, I won't!"

"Come on. We don't have anything in common. We fuck, and we watch TV, and we—it's all...fine. Nice. But it's not *real*. What do we even talk about?"

She scoffed. "Hello? Music, for one. We have a million things in common! We hit it off the day we met."

"Yeah, the day Lara and the PR flacks introduced us? They orchestrated our relationship from the get-go. Ohhh, the strong, silent, mysterious bad boy is finally settling down, falling for the opening act with the voice like honey. Savannah Jones tames Troy Tanner and wins his heart."

She clenched her jaw, but then fresh tears spilled over her pale cheeks, streaking her mascara. "Didn't I? Or did you never actually care about me at all?"

He sighed, guilt returning in a rush. "I do care about you. Of course I do. I want you to be happy. But I don't think I'm the one. Hell, you know I'm not the mysterious bad boy who barely talks. I'm not who they manufactured. So how can I be the right guy for you when I don't even know who the fuck I am?"

"So it's not me, it's you." She swiped at her eyes. "Right. Okay. I hope you can find yourself and all that shit. Have a nice life." Spinning on her heel, she stalked down the hall. At her room, she rattled the door handle. "Someone fucking open this!"

As one of the security guards hustled to comply, Troy hesitated. Even if he didn't love Savannah, he didn't want it to end this way. She was a good person and hella talented, and she deserved someone who really wanted to be with her. He took a step, but then she was gone, the door slamming and the security guard returning to his post.

Someone cleared his throat, and Troy turned to find Bruno in the entryway of Tyson's room. "Everything okay, BT?"

*No. Everything is a fucking disaster.* But Troy simply nodded. "Thanks. Sorry for all the shit you guys have to deal with." He stuck out his hand, and Bruno shook it, a frown appearing on his meaty face.

With a deep breath, Troy turned to the private elevator and jabbed the call button. He could do this. He *had* to do this. He'd failed his father by not taking a stand, and he sure as hell wasn't going to make that mistake again.

"YOU KNOW—THE BROODY one in the black leather jacket. Never says much in interviews."

"This presupposes that I've ever had occasion to watch an interview with…what are they called again?"

Slouched in a chair at the Sydney airport after midnight, Troy studied the reflection in the large window looking out on the tarmac. The pilots stood several feet behind discussing him quietly. The private jet he'd rented was flying out of a small terminal separate from the main three, and he'd fortunately been able to shuffle in without being noticed. The only other people in the terminal had been businessmen who surely couldn't have cared less who he was even if they'd recognized him.

He'd stuffed his stupid leather jacket in his enormous suitcase and worn a gray hoodie instead, which was clearly a smart choice. He tugged his baseball hat lower on his head. There was a wide pole behind his chair, and it seemed the pilots thought they were alone.

The woman sipped from her paper cup of coffee. "Next Up. Are you sure you don't live in a cave? Is that why you've never invited me round?" She looked Filipina to him, short and pretty like his mom. Her accent sounded like the ones he'd heard in New Zealand—"next" came out like "nixt."

Troy glanced around the deserted terminal. It was unnerving to be completely by himself; he couldn't remember the last time he'd been truly alone in public. Shit, he was hardly ever alone in private either. There was always someone there, whether it was a girlfriend or Ty or one of the guys in the band, or the seemingly endless stream of record label staff.

Troy had never minded too much since he liked being with people, and especially since when he was alone, he started thinking. When he started thinking, he wondered how the hell he'd gotten to twenty-six without making any decisions about his own life. His father had made them all until he died, and the label had picked up where he'd left off.

Troy floated along in the current, and what did he have to complain about? He was a millionaire. So what if Next Up's music wasn't the kind he wanted to do?

He could hear his father's voice even now: *Be grateful for everything you and your brother have been given. This is the American dream!*

Rubbing his hands over his thighs, Troy tried to calm his pulse. Was he throwing it all away? Was he ruining everything for Tyson too?

The male pilot opened a file folder. "Aren't you a little outside their target demographic, Paula?"

Paula flipped him the bird. "I'm barely thirty. Okay, so I'm a *little* old for boy bands. But hey, thirty's the new twenty."

Groaning, the man muttered, "Terrific. Living through my twenties once was bad enough." His accent was American, surprisingly.

Troy had lucked out in finding a private jet to go international on short notice, and he glanced at the terminal doors, expecting the cavalry of Joe and assorted minions to charge in any moment. They likely didn't think he'd actually leave the country, but he should still get moving. Yet he was rooted to the spot as the pilots continued talking.

Paula said, "This is going to be a huge scandal. Their world tour isn't over yet. They still have Asia to get through."

"You really do know an alarming amount about this boy band." The man spoke with mock solemnity. "Captain, you know we have a strict policy against sexually harassing our passengers. Just for the record."

Going up on her tiptoes, she mimed pouring her coffee over his dark, neatly trimmed hair, garnering a low chuckle. They both wore the standard uniform of navy pants and jackets over white shirts. Troy wondered where their hats were as his mind whirled with half-formed thoughts.

God, it really was going to be a scandal. The band might be on the other side of their popularity peak, but they still had millions of fans. Before he'd turned off his phone to avoid the cavalcade of texts and voice mails—from everyone but Tyson, Nick, and Savannah—his Twitter had blown up with get-well messages. Apparently Ty had announced from stage that Troy had the flu, but that excuse wouldn't hold up for long.

Before shutting down, he'd texted the same message to Joe, Greg, and Tomas:

*Ty and Nick are addicts. If they don't get into rehab, I'm quitting the band for good. Ask Savannah if they won't tell you the truth. She knows the score. I'll talk to you soon.*

The guilt at bailing on the concert roiled his empty stomach, but he undoubtedly had the label's attention now. There was a week before their next show and the start of the Japanese leg. Troy would go home, get his mother, and bring her to Tokyo to confront Ty. He'd call Nick's parents too and see if they could do a group intervention.

Next Up would have to postpone the Asian concerts, which really sucked because they had so much family coming to see them in Manila, but getting clean was way more important.

"I wonder if something happened with his girlfriend. You know,

Savannah Jones? Has that song about texting that gets stuck in your head for days."

"I haven't had the pleasure."

"She's a stunner. Great looking couple. He's never been with a girl this long before—more than a year. He was so heartbroken after Delia Tate dropped him for James Franco, the poor thing."

Troy resisted the urge to snort. He'd dated Delia for a couple months, and it had been fun. But when she'd fallen for Franco, Troy had wished her well. Lara the PR guru had created a fiction about Troy's broken heart, which of course appealed to all the women in the world who wanted to kiss it better. Troy had been quieter than usual in public, wearing sunglasses everywhere, even inside. He'd felt like such a douche, but he'd done as he was told.

"Okay, we should be ready to go." The man snapped the folder shut. "As soon as our passenger and his entourage show up."

"Right here." Troy stood and turned. "No entourage, I'm afraid." He ignored Paula's reddening cheeks and extended his hand with a smooth smile. "It's nice to meet you." He'd played the role so many times over the years it was second nature. Always polite, but never revealing too much. Staying quiet and letting Ty have the spotlight.

Clearing her throat, she took his hand with confidence. "Captain Paula Mercado. A pleasure to meet you. This is my first officer, Brian Sinclair."

"Thanks for doing this on such short notice." Troy turned to the other pilot. The slim man was roughly mid-thirties and a little taller than Troy, probably just over six foot. He had a firm handshake and the calm, in-control demeanor Troy associated with pilots.

Paula said, "Happy to help. It's just you tonight? We assumed you'd have a few people with you. Let's take care of your baggage and get going."

"So we can leave now? They said they weren't sure..." *Thank God.* By morning he might have lost his nerve or been busted by Joe.

"No curfew on jets this small, so you don't have to wait. We just needed to rustle up a first officer since it's a long hop." She motioned toward Brian. "Lucky for us, we've got the best in the business. Far too talented a pilot to play second fiddle if you ask me, but he never does."

Brian ignored her teasing before leading the way with a polite nod to Troy. Troy followed them through the back corridors of the terminal and across the tarmac to the private jet. It was far too much money for him to spend, particularly since he'd just lost his source of income and would likely be sued by the label for breach of contract, but the thought of flying commercial to LA was unbearable. All the questions and photos would be too much. He had to get home under the radar and talk to his mother. Calling her wouldn't work—Troy had to be there so she couldn't hide from this.

They climbed a little staircase up to the small jet, and he got settled in the large lounge area. There were padded chairs with seat belts in groups of two along the sides of the airplane. He'd asked for the smallest plane they had, and this one sat eight. When the record label footed the bill, he'd flown on private jets plenty of times, but it felt a little ridiculous and stupidly extravagant to have the whole plane to himself. But he couldn't back out now. He chose a seat by a window, watching the hint of orange on the horizon as the sun disappeared.

The cockpit door was still open, and Paula called back, "All buckled up, mate?"

"Yes. Thank you."

"Won't be long now." She closed the door.

As the jet powered up and taxied the runway, Troy gripped the armrests. He was really doing this. He was leaving the band. Leaving Tyson. Savannah. The press were going to eat him alive. Fuck, was he doing the right thing?

This was the first time he'd made an actual decision about anything more important than fries or a baked potato. He hadn't protested when they'd cut his hair and dressed him head to toe in black. He hadn't argued when he wasn't allowed to go bowling because it wasn't cool or mysterious enough. When they insisted to the media that his dad's death was a heart attack, he toed the party line.

He'd drifted along, performing like a trained seal. It was time to take control of his life.

Over the years, he'd ridden a hundred planes. Probably a thousand. But this time, Troy paid attention, savoring the little details as the wheels left the ground—the whir and *clunk* of the landing gear as it retracted into the plane's belly, the little dips of turbulence as they rose, the lights of Sydney receding as home beckoned.

"Can I get you a beverage? Something to eat? We have quite a few selections."

Blinking, Troy turned away from the oval window where he'd pressed his forehead, watching the world go by even though it was black outside. Brian stood by his chair with a bland, vaguely pleasant expression—not a smile, but not a frown. Troy recognized it as the mask he often wore so he wouldn't look unhappy or pissed in paparazzi photos. It'd taken a couple of years to train himself out of his resting bitchface.

"No thanks. Not right now." He should probably eat something but didn't know if he'd keep it down.

"Are you sure?" Brian's expression didn't change, but he lowered his voice a notch. "You look like you could use a drink."

"Thanks, but I'm good." Troy supposed since he'd said he didn't need a flight attendant, the copilot was stuck doing the job.

"Please let us know if you need anything. We'll be stopping briefly in Honolulu to refuel on the way to LA. Can I give you a tour of the plane? There's a sleeping area, and of course a bathroom, shower, and—"

"I'm good. Thanks, though."

With a nod, Brian disappeared back into the cockpit and closed the door behind him.

After a while, Troy chugged a bottle of water and ate a package of cookies that sat in a basket in the little kitchen. Normally he watched TV shows or movies on his iPad on planes, but after trying three different episodes of *Modern Family*, some terrible CW show about teenage sea creatures that Savannah had told him he "must see," and a movie about a space disaster, he gave up and changed into track pants and a T-shirt before settling into one of the sleeping berths and pulling the curtain.

He normally only drank beer, but maybe he should down a couple little bottles of vodka to knock himself out.

A memory of the gust of alcohol on his dad's breath filled his senses. A few extra drinks every night had started it all. No, he'd stick to beer.

Closing his eyes, Troy tried very hard not to think about anything at all.

HIS HEART SEIZING and a gasp on his lips, Troy crashed back down to the mattress. There had been some turbulence for a little while, but nothing like this. As the plane shuddered and took another dip, adrenaline-fueled fear evaporated the cobwebs of the dumb dream he'd been having about not being able to go down a staircase. He reached for the curtain, tearing the fabric as he tumbled out, jolted to the floor.

*Seat belt. Seat belt! Fuck.* As the plane veered from side to side, shaking and creaking, he crawled to the closest chair and dragged himself up. Fingers trembling, he braced his bare feet and yanked the seat belt around his waist, struggling with buckle. He couldn't quite—

Troy slammed onto the carpet. Pain radiated from his cheekbone, and he scrabbled for something to hold. The plane bumped and jumped like an old car speeding over potholes, and he swallowed a scream. Another violent rattle tossed him to the foot of another chair. He hauled himself up, his whole body seizing and bile rising in his throat.

He was screaming now as he searched for the seat belt. Troy's fingers closed over one end of it, and he bit his tongue, tasting coppery blood as he fumbled for the other half. Panting, he realized he wasn't screaming after all—it was the shriek of alarms beyond the cockpit door.

Troy's ears popped. The plane was descending. No, more than that, it was *nosediving*. Muffled shouts from the pilots joined the ear-splitting sound of the alarms. His heart was going to explode. He couldn't breathe.

*Get it, get it, get it!*

He barely heard the *click* as the belt finally locked around his hips. Tugging on the strap, he made it so tight his legs tingled. He whapped his forehead against the window, squinting desperately in the early dawn light, breath coming in little gasps.

He could only see gray, an awful metallic screech filling his ears as they plummeted. *Going to die!*

Squeezing his eyes shut, visions of family tore through his mind. Mom the last time he'd seen her, pinching his cheeks and saying he was too skinny: *"Payat payat ka, no? Kain na tayo!"* Auntie Gloria and Uncle Jojo giving him the guitar his father had later taken away. Dad on a good day, driving up the 101 with the top down and the Stones blasting. And he saw his baby brother, shrieking with laughter and gripping his arm as they reached the top of an old wooden rollercoaster.

*I'm sorry, Ty. I love you.*

The air felt paper thin, his lungs not working. The plane shuddered, making an ungodly sound. Alarms wailed. As they plunged back to earth, he did the only thing left.

"Our father, who art in heaven…"

# Chapter Two

*M*OVE. *MOVE!*

Blinking, Brian lifted his head. He could only see a wall of thick gray rain in the gloom of dawn. The wind howled, vibrating through the fuselage. In a sickening rush of adrenaline, it all came back. The plane was on the ground. They'd made it. They'd managed to land on the beach on the speck of an island. They'd—

He turned to reach for Paula on his right, but his hand scraped across a rough rock face where her seat should have been. Brain spinning, he stared. His neck screamed as he turned to look behind him. More unforgiving stone and ripped metal.

*Oh God, no. No!*

The beach had been their only shot, but it hadn't been long enough. It narrowed at the end, where a cliff towered over the sea.

A cliff that had sheared off part of the plane as if it was a tin can.

"Paula." It was little more than a croak. He flattened his palm on the wet stone as if he could push it away and reveal her. There was something pale on the floor, and he reached down—

Gasping, he dropped Paula's arm and retched all over the yoke and dashboard. He wiped his mouth with the back of his hand, bile and puke putrid on his tongue. Something was dripping down his face, and his fingers came away red, but he wasn't sure whose blood it was.

He stared at his hand, then back at the rock where Paula had been minutes—*moments*—before. But she was gone, and there wasn't a goddamn thing he could do about it. He wanted to curl up and die, but he had to get the passenger out.

*Move!*

Brian fumbled for the radio, but it was dead. The electrical cables had surely been cut when the plane… He stared at where Paula had just been, forcing himself not to look down.

An acrid smell filled his nose. He bolted up, grappling with his seat belt. The heat singed his hair, fire tearing through the plane—

Except it wasn't. Chest heaving, heart about to burst through his ribcage, Brian blinked at the remains of the cockpit door. Why was there no fire? Why hadn't the fuel blown?

"Hello? *Hello?*"

Relief soared through him. "Yes! I'm coming. Stay where you are. Don't move." But when he pushed against the door, he heard a muffled grunt from the other side. He squeezed through the opening and found his passenger on his hands and knees, rubbing his nose. "I told you not to move," Brian said stupidly.

"I was already moving!" Tom—no, that wasn't right. Tim? *Troy.* Troy peered past Brian. "What about…?"

Grief seized him, and Brian could only shake his head and grit out, "She's gone. Get off the plane. Get clear of the aircraft." He pulled the emergency lever on the door and shoved it open with a grunt. The wind whipped so forcefully he staggered back, the plane rocking as water spilled over their feet. "Can you swim?"

With a jerk of his head, Troy nodded, his wide eyes locked on the violent waves.

Life vests. They needed life vests. He squeezed past Troy in the ruined remains of the fuselage and reached beneath the nearest seats. Distantly, Brian registered that he was in shock and likely had a slight concussion, because his brain simply wasn't operating efficiently.

Now he was in the position he'd never, ever wanted to be in again: the captain. He was in charge. In control. Get the passengers out. Or passenger, in this case.

Water sprayed violently at the door as they jammed the life vests over their heads. Brian swallowed salt as he tugged on the cords to inflate Troy's vest and then his own. Squinting into the swirling storm as it hammered the tiny island, he got his bearings. The sandy beach was to the left, only ten feet out of reach, maybe fifteen. But they could be swept away in a blink.

*Rope. Emergency kit.*

"Stay back from the door," Brian shouted as he returned to what was left of the cockpit. He exhaled sharply as he spotted the red heavy-duty backpack. An orange nylon cord was coiled on the side of it, and he managed to unhook the carabiner before strapping on the pack. Metal screeched on the rock as a powerful wave crashed into them.

"Holy fuck!" Troy yelled.

Brian staggered back, bracing as the fuselage quaked in the onslaught of wind and water that bit into his skin. Somehow, his fingers managed to clip the carabiner to his belt at one end and wrap the cord around Troy's waist. He knotted it twice. "We're going left. Not sure how deep it is."

The water was surprisingly tepid considering the frigid rain, dousing Brian with another wave as he sat on the edge of the open door. Gripping the ledge, he reached out with his feet. He couldn't feel—

With a blast of wind and sea, he was under, swallowing saltwater. The soles of his leather shoes jolted against a rock, then he stumbled in sand. He pushed with all his might, gasping as he broke the roiling surface. The rope tugged at his waist, and he blinked at Troy in the doorway, his feet planted as he strained to pull Brian back to the plane. Brian felt like he was ankle-deep in quicksand but forced his legs to move.

"This way!" He reached up for Troy, taking his hand and digging in to the sand, his thighs burning as he angled them toward the safety of the beach. Troy clenched his fingers so tightly Brian thought they might break.

Heads down, they staggered through the surf. Thank God it was shallow enough to stand. They were practically horizontal, blinded and choking on briny sea water as the beach got nearer inch by inch.

They crawled the last few feet. Brian coughed, his lungs burning as he spit up water and more bile. The sand was almost mud as the relentless rain plunged down and waves crashed over them. Still clutching Troy's hand, Brian urged him farther up the beach to the tree line. Palms leaned precariously, bowing in the wind's fury. But they usually withstood cyclones, so Brian parked Troy against the closest trunk and unhooked the carabiner.

"I'm going back for supplies! Stay here."

"What? No fucking way!" Troy swiped water from his eyes. "Are you crazy?"

"We need water!" He wavered, the wind almost pushing him off his feet.

Troy was on his knees, hooking the carabiner back onto Brian's belt. "I'll stay on the beach and pull you back if I need to."

Arguing wouldn't help anything, and leaving his passenger alone to fend for himself wouldn't either. Brian tugged off the emergency pack and undid the straps before hooking them securely around the tree. "You *stay on shore*! The rope should be long enough."

Pushing back into the waves was even harder than reaching the beach. For every gasping, choking step he took, he was shoved back three. His limbs burned, using every ounce of strength he had to make it to the point where he could dive below the surface and approach the wreckage, skimming along the sandy bottom with his hands out-stretched.

With a gasp, he came up just under the wing, nearly thumping his head. He managed to reach the door, and before he could contemplate how the hell he was going to heave himself up high enough, a booming wave swept him inside.

Brian was literally at the end of his rope, the nylon cord taut and digging into his waist. He thought about unhooking it as the plane lurched, metal screaming on rock over the din of the storm, but Troy might panic and come after him.

Stretching his arm as far as he could, shoulder straining, he reached for the closet behind the cockpit, his fingers just able to brush the door handle. *Damn it!*

Another wave blasted him, but it carried him an extra few inches so he could yank open the door. His suitcase rocketed toward him, smacking into his chest. The kitchen had been obliterated, but they kept an extra case of water in the closet. Fortunately, it *thunked* out as another wave pounded the wreckage.

With surprisingly steady hands, he opened the suitcase and shoved in as many bottles as he could. He tucked them into the front pockets and unzipped the expander. When he was done, the small suitcase weighed a goddamned ton, but they needed water. Needed supplies. He dragged himself into the closet, reaching around for anything else they could use. His fingers grazed the stack of blankets, and he stretched to grab as many as he could, snagging the cotton flannel. He shoved three blankets into the straining suitcase and used one knee on top to get it zipped again as water flowed higher.

The pressure remained on the rope, which meant Troy was still okay. That was the most important thing. "Okay. Get back out there." He was breathing too fast and could barely hear his voice over the storm's clamor, his words vanishing into the wind.

With the suitcase handles in both hands, he plunged back into the sea, sputtering as he went under. A sharp pain tugged on his waist, and he thought he might get ripped in half as another wave barreled into him.

He realized Troy was hauling him to the beach, and it was a damn good thing his passenger clearly spent a lot of time in the gym. Brian could barely see, salt stinging his eyes as he pushed against the sandy bottom. Crawling onto solid ground, he saw Troy on his back, his heels dug into the sand as he wrenched Brian to safety. With a muscular arm around Brian's waist, he helped drag the suitcase to the palm tree.

"We need to take shelter!" Brian jerked his head left and right, ignoring the pain that shot down his neck and made his eyeballs almost explode. He squinted at what was left of the plane. It looked like nothing more than a child's broken toy against the towering cliff face.

*Hell, Paula. Should have been me.*

Brian blinked. The passenger was talking. He tried to focus, staggering in the gusting wind. Rain streamed from Troy's brown hair and over his tanned face. His teeth were very white and straight, and wait, he was still talking. Brian shouted, "What?"

Then he was flying, actually lifted off his feet. The air slammed from his lungs as he hit the sand, tasting grit and blinking it from his eyes. He threw out his hands, grabbing hold of Troy's bare foot.

They clutched each other and the suitcase, crawling. "It's getting worse! Holy fuck!" Troy yelled. With shaking hands, he nudged Brian along. "Over there?" He jutted his chin toward the base of the cliff. Hyperventilating, his chest rose and fell rapidly.

Brian nodded, which sent a fresh knife of pain through his skull. They needed shelter against something solid, or surviving the crash would be moot. With the emergency pack and suitcase, they crawled along the tree line and then beyond it into the jungle, hoping it would be safer away from the shore.

Sticking close to the jutting cliff that apparently extended across the end of the island, they found a little cave where the rock seemed to be cleaved in two. The cave barely covered their heads, but they were able to jam themselves and their cargo into the crevasse. Knees to their chests, they huddled together. Troy trembled, his teeth chattering. The uneven stone ground dug into Brian's ass, and Troy's elbow was jammed against his ribs.

But his passenger was alive, and Brian closed his eyes, bone-deep grateful that he hadn't failed in that, at least.

As the wind grew from a howl to a scream, they both shivered. He heard Troy muttering a prayer over and over, and hoped it would be enough for both of them.

JOLTING AWAKE, TROY jerked his head from his knees. He blinked at a world of green—nearby trees and vegetation. A jungle.

The memories stormed back, explaining why he was hideously uncomfortable and more tired than he'd ever imagined he could be. Why he ached, starving and soaked, wedged next to a stranger in an opening in a rock wall. His sodden sweatpants clung to him, and he pulled at the damp cotton of his T-shirt.

Thirsty. Fuck, so thirsty. He reached beneath his collar for the plastic water bottle he'd shoved down his shirt to keep it from being blown away. After gulping down the rest, he realized it had not only stopped storming—it had stopped raining too.

It was quiet.

After the relentless howl of the storm, the relative stillness was eerie. Water dripped from leaves. Birds chirped. Beyond the bent and ragged tops of the palms and leafy trees he couldn't identify, the sun was a diffuse light low in the sky behind a wall of steel cloud. But the terrible darkness seemed to have passed. The storm was over.

Troy turned to Brian beside him, their arms sweaty where they were squashed together. "Hey—"

Heart plummeting, he inhaled a jagged breath, scrambling out of their little hidey hole. *God. Please no.* Mind reeling, he stared at Brian's open hazel eyes and the vacant expression locked on his face.

*Fuck, he can't be dead. He can't be dead! Don't leave me alone!*

"Dude, are you okay?" His voice scraped out of his raw throat. "Brian?" He touched his trembling fingers to Brian's bare forearm. His skin was cold and clammy, and he didn't move. *"Brian?"* This time he shook Brian's arm, expecting him to topple over stiffly, his eyes still wide.

Slowly, Brian blinked and turned his head. He didn't seem to actually register Troy, but he was alive. Brian ran a hand over his short brown hair, wincing. *Thank fuck.* For a minute, Troy simply breathed in and out to calm his racing pulse. He cleared his throat. "Brian? You okay, man?"

It was a stupid question, because no, Brian was clearly light years from okay. He was in shock, and the bruise on his forehead had deepened to a purplish red. *Shit.* Troy couldn't handle this. He needed Joe and Lara and the minions to tell him what to do and how to do it. He wanted to squeeze back into the crevasse and close his eyes until this was all fixed.

*Time to man up.*

After a few deep breaths, he prodded at Brian's limbs. He didn't think there were any major injuries. Troy ached all over but didn't seem to have any big injuries either. Poking through the backpack, he found a shiny square that unfolded into an emergency blanket. He tucked it over Brian. "I'm going to check things out, okay? I'll be back soon."

Brian barely blinked. Shit, maybe Troy shouldn't leave him, but he had to see what was left. They'd need as many supplies as they could get from the wreckage. They'd need to…what? He racked his brain, taking far too long to come up with building a fire so rescuers could see them. And getting warm would be awesome too. Even though the temperature had to be seventy degrees, the rain had been icy, and Troy had shivered for hours. He hoped the sun would make it out from behind the clouds before it got dark.

Gingerly, he picked his way along the side of the cliff face back to the beach, wishing he'd thought to grab his shoes after the crash. But he hadn't been thinking of anything aside from getting out alive.

Sticks and rocks and whatever else covered the jungle floor scratched his bare feet, and his mind raced through all the possibilities for snakes and spiders and whatever the hell else lived on tropical islands. Each step was a victory, and it was glorious to have the sand between his toes again, even though it was wet and clumpy.

The palms lining the beach listed wildly, but most still stood. Fronds, plants, and small trees littered the sand and entrance to the jungle. Troy's legs burned as he picked his way around the base of the cliff, his whole body bruised. The ocean was calmer, powerful waves rolling in, but no longer violent. Although there was still a gray cast to the world, it seemed the immediate danger was gone.

And so was the plane.

Staring, Troy bunched his toes in the damp sand, willing the battered plane to appear again at the base of the cliff. But it had vanished, swallowed by the sea. He stared at the sand narrowing to a collection of black rocks, and up at the stone wall, swallowing thickly. Brian had said the other pilot was dead, and if there had been anything left of her, it was gone now.

The cliff face had been washed clean, and the pieces of sheared metal and debris left amid the rocks at the base didn't seem like much. Most had apparently been swept away. The murmur of the waves and a bird's distant cry filled the air.

He bent in two, his knees hitting wet sand as a sob choked him. He wanted to go home—he wanted to go *anywhere* that wasn't...this emptiness. Turning left and right, Troy searched for any signs of life. Did anyone live on this island? Was anyone going to help them? Surely they would have seen the plane go down, even in the swirling storm?

"Hello?" His shout was swallowed by the heavy sand and growing humidity in the air. "Hello? Hello?" Terror clawed his throat as he stared at the empty horizon.

Breath coming in quick bursts, Troy tore back across the sand and into the jungle, not caring about the scratches and jabs to his feet. On his knees again by the crevasse, he panted. Brian was exactly where he'd left him, eyes still open and unseeing.

"Brian!" Troy yanked off the silver blanket and gripped Brian's shoulders, the black and gold stripe decorations of his pilot's uniform digging into Troy's palms. "You need to snap out of it. I know you probably have a concussion or something, but talk to me. Say something. Please." He needlessly added, "I'm freaking out."

Brian barely blinked.

Swallowing the urge to scream in his face and shake him, Troy took a deep breath. "Dude, look at me. Can you hear me? Please. I need your help. Help me. Help!"

As if a light had flicked on, Brian's focus snapped to Troy. "So much smoke. Get out. The fire's coming. Get out!"

*Whoa.* Sitting back on his heels, Troy smoothed out his grip, awkwardly petting Brian now. "It's okay. There's no fire. We're fine. We're safe."

Brian closed his eyes, shaking his head. "Have to get everyone out."

"We're out. It's okay. Just rest."

He closed his eyes, muttering something Troy couldn't make out.

With a sigh, Troy tried to make himself comfortable. He drank more water and settled in. Listening to Brian breathe as the day faded, he whispered another prayer.

"HELLO?"

Amid the buzzing insects and the jungle's chirps and mysterious exhalations, Brian's voice was like a gunshot. Troy yanked his head up and tried to smile even though it was pitch black. *"People can hear the smile in your voice."* His father's baritone echoed through his mind. Troy said, "It's okay. I'm here."

"Where? Who?" Brian was rigid.

"Um, it's Troy Tanner? I was your passenger on the plane. We crashed on an island this morning. I know, it's crazy dark now. Still cloudy, I guess." He'd wanted to examine the emergency pack to see if there was a flashlight, but he'd left it out of reach on Brian's other side and he'd been too afraid to venture out even a few feet. Afraid of what jungle creature his outstretched hands might encounter.

"How do you feel?" Troy asked. "You need to drink some water. Here." He felt for the full bottle at his hip and pressed it gently into Brian's hand. "Can you hold it? Let me take the top off."

Troy listened to Brian swallowing. He hoped the concussion was mild and tried to remember how it was supposed to be treated. He'd once seen a football movie where the hurt player had been asked memory questions. "What's your name?"

"Brian Sinclair."

"And what do you do?"

"I'm a pilot."

"Okay, good. Where do you live?"

"Sydney."

Troy assumed that was true. He urged the bottle back to Brian's lips, wishing he could see. "Uh, who's the president of the United States?"

"Barack Obama. Not for much longer. Too bad about term limits."

Troy smiled. "Yeah. Not loving the other options." At least Brian sounded more awake and with it. "Drink a bit more. Does your head hurt?"

"Doesn't tickle." He was silent a moment. "The rain stopped." He brushed against Troy as he sat up straighter. "We need to get back to the plane."

"We can't. It's okay, just rest."

"How long has it been?" Brian's voice was clearer, and it seemed the fog was definitely lifting, thank God. "It's so dark."

"I'm not sure. I'm hoping it's at least midnight. Been dark for a long time." The night felt like a living thing, keeping them prisoner in the jungle. Troy longed for sunrise. "Is there any food in the emergency pack?"

"Yes. But we need to check the plane first."

Troy sighed. "It's gone."

There were a few heartbeats of silence. "What is?"

"The plane. The storm got worse after we got off the beach. Must have washed it away. I went out and checked earlier." Troy listened to the hum of insects, waiting for Brian to say something else. Finally, Troy asked, "Do you think anyone lives here?"

More silence. A mosquito buzzed near his ear, and Troy slapped at it. "Brian? Are you still awake?"

"Yes, sorry." It sounded like Brian took another swig of water, his arm brushing Troy's as he swallowed. "We'll make sure, but no. I don't think anyone lives here."

Acid bubbled in Troy's belly. "How do you know?"

"We changed course for Kiritimati. Christmas Island is another name for it. There's an airport there. We're west of it. At least a thousand miles."

"A *thousand miles?*" He couldn't even visualize how far that was. Blood rushing in his ears, Troy willed himself to wake up safe in his bed. This couldn't be real. It couldn't. "But…but there are other islands, right?"

"Phoenix islands to the west are closest. Six, seven hundred miles. Atolls and coral reefs. Uninhabited, I think. This whole area is."

Troy dug his fingernails into his palms to keep from screaming or crying or both. "We're just out here all alone?"

"Dumb luck to find this island. We'd be dead otherwise." He shuddered, his shoulder trembling. "Not just her."

Troy didn't know what to say to that. He hadn't even seen Paula after the crash. She'd just been…gone.

*Maybe she was the lucky one. We're going to fucking die out here.*

Panic squeezed his lungs like a python, and Troy saw little bursts of light in the blackness. After concentrating on his breathing for a good minute, he got up the nerve to ask the only question that really mattered. "They'll find us soon, right?"

Brian was quiet for too long. Finally, he said, "I don't know."

"But there was a black box thingy, right? Those have a beacon or whatever?"

"Yes."

Exhaling, Troy smoothed his palms over his knees. "That's good."

"Sorry, I meant yes, they have a beacon. Activated by immersion in water and sends out pings. But we didn't have a CVR or FDR. They're only required on commercial aircraft. Most private planes don't have them. Too expensive." Brian spoke flatly, as if he was reading from a manual.

*Fuck. Fuck, fuck, fuck.*

Troy had to take a few breaths to ease the pounding of his heart. Brian was quiet, and Troy barely resisted the urge to poke him and yell to stay awake. *Stay with me.* "What's...FDR? CV...what?" Not that it mattered, but he needed to focus on something other than the barbed-wire panic.

After a few moments, Brian answered, "Flight data recorder." His voice was still flat like he was reciting facts in his sleep. "Cockpit voice recorder. We don't really call them black boxes. The media does. They're actually orange. Easier for searchers to find."

"Oh. So there's more than one?" Needed to keep Brian talking. Otherwise it would be nothing but darkness and the sounds of the jungle breathing around them, and Troy couldn't handle it.

"FDR records things like airspeed and altitude, vertical acceleration. Technical specs. CVR records all noises in the cockpit on a two-hour loop. Pilots talking, radio transmissions, any other sounds that might occur."

"Why on a loop?"

"Don't need the whole flight. In a crash..." He went quiet.

"What?" Troy prompted after a few moments.

Brian barely whispered, "It usually happens fast."

Out of useless questions for the moment, Troy closed his eyes and concentrated on getting his breathing back to normal. Hugging his knees, he counted his inhalations and exhalations. They'd be rescued. *Of course* they would. It didn't matter that there was no black box or whatever those things were called.

*The plane isn't even here anymore. Must have sunk. Could be miles and miles away. How will they find us?*

His lungs constricted. "They'll look hard for us, won't they?" He seized Brian's arm blindly. "Won't they?"

Brian was still and calm in his grasp. "They'll look, but here in the Pacific...it's a vast area."

Troy shivered, nausea rolling through him. "Like when that Malaysian Airlines plane went missing."

"Yes. Over the Indian Ocean."

"But with us, they know the general spot we went down." He dug his fingers into Brian's warm skin. He was holding on too hard but couldn't stop.

"They know we changed course for Kiritimati due to extreme weather."

"That's good. So we were on their radar, and they'll see where we crashed." He exhaled, but the relief was short lived. Troy's pulse kicked up again as the silence stretched out. *"Right?"*

"We were too far away for radar."

"What?" As adrenaline pumped through him, his voice rose. "What are you talking about?" He realized he was still gripping Brian's bicep when Brian's hand covered his and gently pried his fingers loose. Troy tried to catch a breath, crossing his arms tightly over his chest. "Shit, sorry. But what do you mean there's no radar? How is that possible?"

Brian didn't answer at first. Again, the need to hear the rumble of Brian's voice felt as necessary as air to Troy. He needed the distraction and comfort even if he didn't actually want to hear what Brian was saying. He asked again, "Dude, how is that possible we weren't on radar?"

Brian's voice was low and calm in the darkness, the only thing keeping Troy grounded, along with the warm press of his shoulder. "Radar doesn't cover the whole planet. Only two, three percent. If you're more than two hundred miles away from land, there's no coverage."

Troy's jaw dropped. "Are you fucking serious?"

"I'm afraid so."

"So we've just…disappeared. In the middle of nowhere."

Brian shifted, clumsily patting Troy's arm with his damp palm. "I'm sure they'll find us." His voice seemed to snap into a commanding tone. "Yes. Don't worry. We'll get organized in the morning. Do everything we can. It's going to be okay."

"I…" Troy gulped some water, blinking away tears. "Okay. Yeah." A thought jolted him. "Wait, do you have your phone? I didn't think to grab mine. Shit, that was dumb."

"Mine was in my jacket. It doesn't matter anyway. We got soaked, and we're nowhere near a service area."

He deflated. "Right. Duh."

"We're going to be just fine."

Brian sounded more and more alert. Troy wasn't sure how he could sound remotely confident after being practically catatonic earlier, but shit, he'd take it. The fog of shock seemed to dissipate the more Brian drank. Troy asked, "We should eat, right?"

"Right." Brian moved, hissing.

"You okay?"

"Yeah." Brian moved again, and Troy heard a zipper. A flashlight beamed on, startlingly bright in the blackness. The bruise on Brian's forehead was a mottled shadow. "I'm going to take some Advil. Do you want any? Are you in pain?"

"I'm okay." Well, truthfully his cheek twinged where he'd hit the floor of the plane and he ached dully all over, but they should conserve their medicine.

*What if they never find us? What if I never see Mom and Ty again? What if I die here?*

"Troy?"

He was screaming in his mind, and he blinked a few times, trying to smile. "I'm fine."

In the glow of the flashlight, Brian stared skeptically. But after a moment, he nodded and dug into the pack. He muttered as if to himself, "Need to get organized. Stay calm." Louder, he said, "There are protein bars in here. We have enough water for now, but if it rains again, we should fill our empty bottles."

"Okay." It was a relief to be able to sit back and follow instructions. They ate gross bars that tasted like chalky peanut butter, but after the first bite, Troy realized just how hungry he was. He had a second bar and drank more water.

God, what he wouldn't give for a hot shower and to change out of his dirty, damp sweats and tee. What he wouldn't give for shoes. And underwear. But Brian gave him leather flip-flops and a spare pair of socks, so that was something, even though the socks were wet and the thong between his toes pulled at the cotton.

"How did this happen?" The question popped out of its own accord as they sat in the dark again, now with a mosquito net from the emergency pack draped over them. Troy was tempted to ask to have the flashlight back on, but knew it was dumb to waste the batteries.

Brian's shoulder against him hitched, then slumped. "I'm sorry."

"It's not your fault."

"But…"

"Dude, I'm not blaming you." Troy nudged Brian's shoulder. "You saved my life. That storm was intense."

Brian sighed, a whisper that fluttered the net. "We checked the weather reports. They were calling for rain, but nothing we couldn't handle. Nothing out of the ordinary." He was quiet for a few moments, and then swore under his breath. "Wet season is supposed to be over. It's May! Goddamn global warming. I don't know where the hell that storm came from. Seemed like a full-out cyclone. The wind was too strong, and we changed course to land and wait it out. And then… Hell, I can't believe the rain came down that fast."

Brian almost seemed to be talking to himself now. When he didn't go on, Troy asked, "But planes fly in rain all the time, right?"

"Yes."

"So what was different?"

After a few moments, Brian said, "Huh? Sorry."

"It's okay. You should rest." The net brushed against him, and Troy jumped a little before adjusting it. It was claustrophobic in the blackness to have the net on his head and around him, but he could hear mosqui-toes whining. He was usually catnip to the little fuckers, so the net had to stay.

"No, I'm fine." Brian cleared his throat. "In torrential rain, when a high volume of water falls too quickly, a film develops on the wings and fuselage. It becomes like…waves almost."

"Okay. Why is that bad?"

"The friction builds, dragging on the aircraft. The wings lose lift." His elbow brushed Troy's. "I guess you can't see what I'm doing with my hands. Anyway, it's a bad thing."

They sat in silence in the utter darkness, the humidity stifling, the buzz of insects making Troy's skin crawl despite the net. It was all so *much*. He hated it, and his heart raced, and he was going to freak the fuck out. He'd tried to be calm before, and now he was going to lose his shit.

"Keep going," he begged Brian. "About the wings. Or anything! Just talk. Please?"

"Yeah. Okay." Brian leaned his shoulder against Troy's a little more. "I was telling you about the wings losing lift?"

"Right." Troy clung to the distraction, to the low melody of Brian's voice in the blackness.

"So when there's too much friction, the lift is compromised, and the stall speed increases. The engines flamed out. We dove but couldn't restart them."

"But why would you dive? Isn't that just bringing us closer to crashing?"

"It's like… Imagine you're driving uphill and your car stalls. If you keep trying to go up, you won't get anywhere. There's no momentum. No speed. You need to go downhill. The velocity restarts the stalled engines. Assuming the flameout wasn't due to fuel starvation."

"Huh. Okay, that makes sense. But it didn't work?"

Brian sighed. "The engines might have ingested too much water. I can't say for sure. But the bottom line is that the engines were gone."

"So basically we were fucked."

"Yeah. Without the rain and wind, we could have tried gliding to the airport."

"*Glide?* I mean, I know it was a small jet, but seriously?"

"You'd be amazed what aerodynamics can do. Transat two-thirty-six heavy glided across a big chunk of the Atlantic to the Azores in 2001. Three hundred people on board. They had a fuel leak, and the pilot soared her in. Some of the best damn flying in history. Granted, they fucked up the fuel transfer, but hindsight's twenty-twenty. They saved all the souls on board." He was silent a moment. "That's what matters," he added quietly.

Troy thought of Paula and didn't have a clue what to say. He fidgeted in the oppressive darkness, fiddling with the net. He cast about for something to say or ask. Anything other than: *Just how fucked are we?* "What does that mean, when they call a plane 'heavy'? Is it just like, literally big?"

"Huh?" Brian sounded distant again.

No. Troy needed him here. He asked again, "Why do they call some planes 'heavy'? Is it just big?"

"Right. It's a plane capable of a hundred and thirty-six tons MTOW or more. Sorry. Maximum takeoff weight. So yes, when a plane is designated 'heavy,' it's literally heavy."

"Okay, so why do they say that?" *Please keep talking. I can't take the quiet.*

"Because of the wake turbulence. If a smaller plane got too close, it could flip over. ATC—air traffic control—makes sure a heavy jet gets a wider berth, and other pilots hear the call sign 'heavy' and know to stay clear. Does that make sense?"

"Right, I get it. You know a lot about flying." He laughed softly. "Duh. Which is obviously good since you're a pilot and all. You must really love it, huh?"

Brian was silent so long Troy thought he might have fallen asleep or gone catatonic again. But he finally answered, "I did."

Troy frowned. "You don't anymore?"

Brian sat rigid, and Troy could practically feel the waves of tension coming off him. "I want to. That probably doesn't make sense."

"No, it's cool." *Time to change the subject.* "Hey, why is it a 'cyclone' over here, but a 'hurricane' in the States?"

"Dunno." Brian seemed to relax a bit and took another drink. "As far as I know, it's the same thing."

"Have you ever seen one whip up that fast?"

"Not anything close to this level. But with climate change, all bets are off. Weather has always had fluctuations, but it used to be much more predictable."

Troy briefly stretched his legs out beyond the net and smoothed the foil wrapper of a protein bar on this thigh, making it crinkle in the darkness. His damp sweats stuck to him.

*How is this real life? How is this my life?*

He tried to choke it down, but he had to ask, "We'll be okay, right?"

"Absolutely." Brian repeated it with more force. "Absolutely."

Troy could almost believe him when he sounded like that—large and in charge, Troy's mom would have called it. He breathed through the pang of longing for her and tore a strip from his wrapper, circling it around his finger. "Okay."

"Besides, we've got one thing going for us most people in this situation wouldn't."

"What's that?"

"From what I hear, you're a pretty popular young man. A rescue crew of teenage girls will probably show up in the morning."

The laugh wasn't huge, but it was warm and good. "The paparazzi will be close behind. It's impossible to keep those fuckers away."

"I'm going to land an exclusive interview and be able to retire. Too bad there's no camera in that pack. I could sell shirtless desert island pics and make a mint."

Brian's tentative teasing was like a warm blanket wrapped around Troy. They were hungry and banged up and probably going to die alone in the Pacific, but they were together. As the night wore on, they kept talking to fill the darkness, and Troy could breathe easier.

And that was something.

# Chapter Three

**"W**HAT WAS THAT?"

Heart thumping, Brian wondered the same thing. He forced his lungs to expand as he listened intently. The sound had been utterly foreign, and undoubtedly emitted by some kind of living creature. A tree or a plant had not made that *screech*. He squinted into the black void of the jungle but couldn't even make out the outline of Troy huddled beside him beneath the mosquito net.

They were still sitting wedged into the crevasse. Even with a flashlight, traipsing through the jungle at night was unwise. Especially when Brian's head had spun wildly when he'd tried to stand. He'd slept a little, and the Advil had made a minor dent in the dull pain throbbing from his shoulder blades up through his skull. He should have been hungry, but he'd had to force down the protein bar.

Mosquitoes whining set his teeth on edge, and Brian wished the jungle would just *shut up*. The emergency blanket tucked over him and Troy crinkled as he shifted his numb butt on the unforgiving rock.

This night was never going to end.

At least he wasn't alone. Troy brushed against him, warm and alive, his bulk a comforting presence. It was a reminder of why Brian couldn't zone out again even though his brain seemed wrapped in gauze. No, he had to stay focused. Stay present. It was unacceptable that he'd been so out of it earlier. Troy shouldn't have had to go out on his own.

Although, for a rock star, Troy wasn't what Brian had expected.

He'd seemed distracted and stressed during their brief conversation on the plane, but not arrogant or spoiled. And he'd certainly held his own after the crash. Brian wondered what had prompted him to suddenly quit his band. In the cockpit, Paula had mentioned a few theories involving people whose names he didn't know, but they'd always kept idle talk to a minimum, even at cruising altitude. She'd said—

He closed his eyes through the deep pang of grief and guilt at the memory of her lilting laughter. Choking down a swell of nausea as he remembered the sensation of her arm in his hand—her flesh still warm—Brian tried to clear his mind. He'd felt so guilty earlier, joking with Troy about fans rescuing them. Joking about *anything* when Paula was dead. When it should have been him.

But he had to be in control. Be comforting. Humor could help put the passengers—passenger—at ease and ensure their safety.

Brian cleared his throat. "It's amazing, the noises tropical birds and frogs can make." He listened again but heard only the steady drone of the night insects he assumed were cicadas or something similar. The buzzing nocturnal chorus was constant. "At least that shriek didn't sound like a polar bear."

Troy's warm breath brushed Brian's face. "Huh? A polar bear?"

He worked on a light tone. "Please tell me *Lost* is not *that* old already? Or that you're *that* young?"

Troy chuckled. "Oh, on TV. I remember it, but I didn't have time to watch. Our show had a tight schedule, and we had schoolwork too."

"Your show? Concerts?"

"Wait, you mean you didn't watch *Rock 'n' Roll Academy*?" He mock gasped. "I'm insulted."

Brian's smile was real. "Sorry, must have missed that one. So you're an actor too?"

"Not really. I'm okay, but Tyson was the star. My little brother."

That rang a bell. "Oh, is he in your band too?"

Troy was quiet for a few breaths, and when he spoke, his voice was tight. "Yeah. He's always been super talented. Even when he was ten, he was a star. Had his first hit single—the theme song to the TV show."

"Wow. When I was ten, my biggest accomplishment was sweeping up hair at my Grandpa's barber shop and winning the fifth-grade spelling bee. You must have been young too?"

"I guess so. Fourteen."

"At fourteen I was still sweeping up hair. I did win a local model airplane design contest. My spelling skills were untested since there was no bee in high school." He took a gulp of water. It hurt to talk, his throat rough and head a cement block on his neck, but it was better than listening to the mystery noises of the jungle in the darkness. "What was the show about?"

"We played brothers at a boarding school. I started a band with my cool middle-grade friends, and Ty was my genius little brother who skipped a bunch of years and also sang better than anyone else. So, of course, we had to let him in our band." He snorted. "It was so dumb. But it paid really well and ran for five years. Oh, and I'm twenty-six, for the record, so not that young. How about you?"

"Thirty-nine." The shriek rattled them both again. "It could be a monkey, but I think I read that they're not native to the South Pacific. Humans introduced them on some islands, but unless they're *really* good swimmers…"

"I don't think it's a frog either," Troy whispered. "Doesn't sound like a 'ribbit.' I'm going to go with bird. Must be a bird, and not a…what else lives on these islands?" He tensed, his elbow jerking against Brian's arm. "Could there be tigers here? We're not in the right place for that, are we?"

"No tigers. They're on Sumatra. Many miles away."

"Okay, good. But what else could be here?"

"Well…" Brian tried to think of the least frightening species that could be surrounding them that very moment. "Birds, obviously. And frogs. Turtles. Fish."

The mystery shriek vibrated through the humid air. "Loud and angry birds?"

"Apparently." He stretched his legs out from under the net, his stiff muscles screaming. His dress socks and leather shoes were sodden, but bare feet in the jungle wasn't appealing. At least the temperature hadn't dropped much. "I think there are bats here, but that's good for us since they eat insects. Maybe there could be wild pigs, but I don't think so? We'll have to see how far we can walk around the island. It didn't look big."

"How small?"

Brian tried to imagine it, but all he could see was gray driving rain and the red and yellow of the flashing dashboard. Paula gripping the yoke as he calculated their landing speed. "I'm not sure. Our attention was on the beach. We could barely make out the sand."

"Right, of course." Troy was silent for a few moments, and when he spoke again, his voice was hoarse. "I'm so sorry about the other pilot. Did I say that before? She seemed really nice."

Flexing his wet toes in his shoes, Brian's throat was so tight it burned. "Thank you."

*Nice.* A pathetically inadequate word. Paula had made such an effort to be friendly and welcoming. The other pilots hadn't seemed to know what to make of him. They'd been polite and professional, but he knew they couldn't understand why he'd only fly as first officer now, and how he could give up a career flying commercial.

And how had Brian thanked her? By turning down her invitations to the pub, or a BBQ on the beach when her parents were in town from Auckland. God, what were their names? He'd met them at the terminal one day. Her dad was…a mechanic?

*I should know this.*

Troy muttered miserably, "If I'd stayed, she'd be fine. We wouldn't be stuck here. Fuck. I wanted to fix it, but I made everything a million times worse."

"You didn't do anything wrong. Don't blame yourself."

"Did she… That side of the plane was gone." Troy swallowed audibly. "Do you think she felt it?"

"No. It was too fast." Bile rose in Brian's throat, prickly and hot. It was true, at least. There would have only been a second or two before oblivion. The rest came out before he could stop it. "It should have been me."

Troy's voice rose sharply. "What? But it was an accident."

He pushed the words past his throat. "Captain usually sits on the left. First officer on the right. But Paula liked it the other way. I never argued. Controls are the same on both sides. Figured it didn't matter."

"It's not your fault. That was luck. You didn't know this was going to happen."

It was true, but Brian still wanted to vomit.

"If it wasn't my fault, it wasn't yours either. I'm sorry. I know she was your friend."

She was, and he'd been too shut off and stuck in his own world to be any kind of real friend back. Brian's eyes burned. That he could never thank her or tell her he was sorry was one more regret to lock away.

After a few minutes of silence, Troy asked, "Are there snakes here?"

Brian was grateful for the change of topic, even if thinking about snakes while sitting in a pitch-black jungle made him shiver restlessly. "Probably."

"Poisonous ones?"

"In all likelihood. And maybe pythons, I imagine. I think we should just assume that all snakes and spiders and various insects are dangerous and to be avoided."

Troy shuddered. "Ugh, spiders." Brian could hear Troy's nails scratch over his skin. "I don't like creepy crawly things."

"I confess I'm not a huge fan myself. Let's hope we can set up camp on the beach and avoid them. Although we'll have to be careful in the ocean. Sea snakes are deadly."

"*Sea* snakes? Jesus."

"Not to mention eels and jellyfish and God knows what."

"Okay, so the jungle and ocean are a shitshow. But the beach should be okay?"

"Definitely." He didn't mention that insects surely lived in the sand as well.

Leaves rustled nearby, and they both froze. Troy hissed, "Maybe we should go out there now."

"We could get turned around," Brian whispered. "Even with the flashlight, it's damn dark."

"Right. Okay. I'm sure that was nothing."

"Whatever that was, we scared them off." Brian didn't know if that was true, but it's the kind of thing his grandfather would have said. He smiled in the darkness at the thought, then winced. Shit, his head hurt. The headache sent tendrils of pain and tension down his neck and spine. He was pretty sure it was only a mild concussion, but Advil wasn't cutting it.

He shifted, no spot on his ass now that wasn't numb. Anxiety flapped as he blinked in the blackness, and he stretched his hands out as if to make sure the crevasse hadn't magically closed around them. Maybe they should try for the beach after all.

But no, there was no sense in getting lost. The tide had to be out, because he couldn't hear any waves. Best to wait for dawn. Here in their mini cave, they had shelter and were reasonably sure there were no dangerous insects or animals with them in the crevasse.

Of course, for all he knew, a python was stalking them from the treetops, waiting to drop down and strangle them. Or a tarantula was scuttling across the jungle floor, about to crawl right across them. He yanked his legs back in and tugged the net tighter.

Troy spoke hoarsely. "So. Um, are you married? Kids?"

"No. Was married out of college, but it didn't last."

"What was her name?"

"Alicia." Brian wondered how she'd feel when she heard the news. Last he knew, she was living in Seattle with a daughter from her second failed marriage. He hoped she knew he'd truly loved her once. God, it was all so long ago. Another life.

There had been Alicia and later Rebecca. The guys from his dorm in university, the other pilots and crew he'd been so close with back in the States. They were all from...before. He wondered if they'd mourn him.

An intense pang of yearning hollowed out Brian's chest. He wanted another chance. He wanted to tell them he was sorry. How strange to think he hadn't spoken to his friends in years now.

But he'd stopped answering texts and messages, and eventually they'd stopped trying. Not that he blamed them. When he thought about it—which he usually avoided at all costs—it was hard to believe how easy it had been to exit so many lives. To just...fade away.

Troy said, "I dumped my girlfriend right before I left. Fuck, I was an asshole. Now she'll think I'm dead, and I can't say sorry. Not that I'm sorry we broke up. But...I'm still sorry in general. You know what I mean? I dunno. I'm rambling."

He could feel Troy shivering where their shoulders touched. It was humid and mild, and they had the emergency blanket, but their clothes were still damp. God, they just needed this night to end. "We should really try and sleep."

"Right. Sorry. I'm just—" The shriek rattled through the trees. "Just feeling wired now. Go ahead and rest. How's your head?"

"It's okay." He checked his watch, which was fortunately waterproof and had a light.

"What time is it?" Troy gazed at him anxiously in the faint glow of the watch.

*Oh, hell.* "Not quite midnight."

Troy groaned. "Morning is never going to come."

It really, really wasn't. As much as he didn't want to get lost in the jungle, he needed to stretch out and sleep, and so did Troy. To hell with it. He groped in the pack for the flashlight. "You went back to the beach earlier. You know the general direction?"

"To our right. I think if we stick close to the cliff, we'll be fine."

Brian hadn't thought of that, and the risks of tripping or getting lost in the darkness now seemed insignificant compared to the need to reach the open expanse of the beach. "Okay, I'll take the pack." He turned on the flashlight and handed it to Troy before carefully folding their blanket and mosquito net, blinking in the glare. "Can you manage the suitcase?"

The light shone up at Troy's face, illuminating the cleft in his chin and a bruise darkening his cheek. "Uh-huh. Let's do this. Can't stay here."

Brian took the light and scanned the trees and around the jungle. The beam hardly penetrated the dense foliage, but at least he didn't see any eyes reflecting back at them. He had no idea which snakes actually lived on this particular island, and he didn't want to find out. Ever.

Troy was already on his feet, and Brian pushed himself up, leaning on the cliff face. Everything spun, and he stood still, clutching the flashlight as his stomach rebelled.

"You okay, man?" Troy squeezed Brian's shoulder, his hand firm and grounding.

"Yep. Just need to get the pack on."

"It's cool. I got it." Troy shouldered it.

Brian wanted to argue that Troy shouldn't have to carry the pack and drag the heavy suitcase, but just standing and walking was enough of a challenge. He led the way, keeping his right hand on the cliff wall where the jungle abruptly ended. But for the odd vine, it was just rock, worn smooth in some places and jagged in others. He swept the light over the ground in front and then behind so Troy could see where he was walking too. "Get out of our way, poisonous things," Brian muttered.

"I second that motion," Troy whispered.

It was odd, feeling like they had to keep their voices down. They were surely the only humans on the island, so they could have shouted. But even though the light only picked up leaves and greenery, sweat prickled the back of Brian's neck, his hair standing up on end as though dozens of unseen eyes tracked their progress.

The salt in the humid breeze intensified and the jungle disappeared, the flashlight now cutting a swath through open air. When they both had sand under their feet, Brian switched off the light. For a few moments, they stood there. Clouds still obscured the stars, but without the jungle's umbrella, there was enough ambient light reflecting off the sand to see their way.

The tide was indeed out, and aside from the steady hum of chirping from the jungle behind them, the night was silent. "Let's keep away from the trees. There are probably coconuts up there, and we don't want any falling on our heads," Brian said. *Please let there be coconuts.* Even though food was the last thing he wanted at the moment, he knew the protein bars wouldn't get them far.

"Good plan."

Troy dropped their baggage far enough away from the tree line, and Brian spread the silver blanket on the sand, keeping his head up as a wave of dizziness washed over him. "Should be another one." He fumbled in the pack. "Here you go."

Troy exhaled loudly as he unfolded the blanket, his teeth flashing as he smiled. "Feels good to be out of there."

"Definitely." Brian gingerly stretched out on one half of his blanket before wrapping the other side over him. The sand was a featherbed compared to the stone crevasse. His head hammered like a drum, and every muscle and tendon ached. "My kingdom for a hot tub. Or a Swedish massage. Or a massage of any nationality."

"For real."

A cool breeze sailed over the sand, and the mosquitoes didn't seem as prevalent. He had no idea if mosquitoes carrying malaria or other diseases could be this far from civilization, but there was no sense in risking it. At the very least, bites were itchy and annoying. "You ready? We should...let me get the net out."

Troy shifted closer on the sand, stopping a few inches away. His white tee looked bright against his tan skin as he removed the flip-flops and peeled off his wet socks. He wrapped himself loosely in his blanket and wiped a hand across his sweaty brow. "This good?"

"Yep." Brian draped the net over them and settled back down, closing his eyes. *Okay. Sleep now.*

Of course his brain refused to shut off despite his exhaustion. The minutes ticked by as he fidgeted, images unspooling like the worst movie ever. The wall of rain, the flashing lights as alarms screamed, the merciless cliff wall where Paula should have been, the pale mystery of her arm at his feet.

The net grazed Brian's cheek, and he shoved it away, his heart beating too hard.

Troy whispered, "I can't believe this is real. You know?"

Brian's throat tightened again, and he pushed away an image of Paula's teasing smile. "Yeah."

"Do you think they know yet? That we're lost?"

"Yes. The airline will have contacted our families." He stared up at the dark sky, barely able to make out the shapes of clouds. "Well, your family. Paula's." *What were their names?*

"You don't have any family?"

"Not anymore." He missed them so much, but at least his grandparents wouldn't suffer, worrying for him. "The authorities will be investigating. The coast guard launching a search."

"Do you think...will they think we're dead?"

He wanted to tell a pretty lie to make Troy feel better, but what was the point? "Yes. Over water, there are rarely survivors."

"God. My brother's going to..." He muttered something under his breath. "Fuck, why did I do this? Ruined everything."

"You couldn't have known."

Troy was shaking, his voice thick. "I should have called my mom before I left. And Ty... The things I said."

Troy's eyes gleamed, and Brian reached out to awkwardly pat his arm. "It's not your fault."

Gripping Brian's wrist, Troy whispered, "I need to talk to them. Even if it's just one more time. It's not fair."

"I know. I'm sorry." The bone ached where Troy squeezed, but Brian didn't pull away.

With a shuddering exhale, Troy let go. "Sorry. I'm freaking out.

They're going to be so upset, and I won't be there to help."

"Don't be sorry." Brian gave him another pat before curling his hand to his chest.

Troy was quiet for a minute, aside from forceful breathing. Then he asked, "What happened to your family?"

"I was raised by my grandparents, and they're gone. My grandmother lasted to eighty-four. She passed five years ago."

"I'm sorry." He exhaled sharply. "I just...I feel like I'm going to wake up in that bunk, and we'll be landing in LA. How did this happen? I was sleeping, and then it was so bumpy, and my ears were popping. It was so fast. I can't..." He shook his head. "Sorry. I know you told me how it happened."

"It's okay. Your brain's processing. I keep seeing it happen again too. Repeating over and over."

"They'll find us soon. Won't they?"

In that moment, Troy sounded unbearably young. Brian hadn't been able to protect him in the air, but he wouldn't fail him now. Even if no one found them, he'd keep Troy safe. He put every ounce of confidence and hope he had into his next three words. "We'll be okay."

It must have convinced Troy, because soon his breathing evened out. Brian stared at the few stars starting to inch their way through the shadow of clouds.

Normally he hated sleeping next to someone. Even with Alicia, they'd had a king-sized bed so there was plenty of room to stretch out. But he didn't mind feeling the heat of Troy's body, listening to the sighs and hitches of his inhalations and exhalations. They could have been the last two people in the world, and unless rescue miraculously came, they were.

"JESUS FUCKING CHRIST!" Troy shot up, pawing at something stuck to him, his heart pounding. The honks filled the air, and he turned his head left and right desperately. *What? Who? Where the fuck—*

It was real. He was actually stranded on a desert island. It hadn't been some fucked-up nightmare.

Gut twisting, he forced a breath and managed to kick off his silver blanket and get free of the mosquito net without tearing it. Brian was blinking and muttering beside him, and Troy turned to find the creators of the hideous honking cries that sent shivers down his spine. Rubbing his eyes, he focused on the moving swarm of color in the trees in the pale light of dawn.

"What the..." Groaning, Brian pushed himself up to sitting and dragged the net over his head, balling it in his lap. The crisp white of his uniform shirt was dull with dirt. "Are those...?"

"Parrots," Troy answered. "They look like parrots." The loudest freaking parrots in history. As the sun rose, it was apparently breakfast time, and they clustered in the trees, eating God knows what. Very enthusiastically.

Brian groaned again, wincing. The red mark on his forehead had darkened to a purple bruise. He gingerly stretched his neck side to side. "That's some wakeup call."

"Yeah. How's your head?" He peered closely, relieved to see Brian's pupils looked normal in his hazel eyes.

"Hurts. But I'll live." He rubbed his face. "Got some sleep, at least. You?"

"A few hours, I guess." Troy gazed around. The sky had cleared, and it looked like it would be a hot day. The sun was rising on the other side of the island, so their beach was facing west. Not that it mattered, since they were in the middle of nowhere. "So...what do we do now?"

Brian stared at the parrots, barely blinking.

Shit. Brian was in no condition to be doing anything. *Okay. Be logical. What do we need first?* "I should look for water. We still have some full bottles, but they won't last long in this heat. There must be fresh water on the island, right? A stream, maybe? And we need something to catch rain when it comes."

At least Brian snapped out of it. "Yes. Sorry, I'm a little...fuzzy. Water is the priority. We should see what food we can find as well. Explore the island. But first do an inventory on our supplies. I'm not even sure what's in this emergency pack."

Turned out to be a surprising number of things. Waterproof matches and a magnifying glass. A heavy duty orange laminate sheet that was a blanket or perhaps...something for camping? It had grommets on each corner, which confused Troy. He'd never camped a day in his life, but he'd watched some Bear Grylls. Now he *really* wished he'd paid more attention. "Orange seems to be the color of the day," he noted as he unfolded two ponchos and bandannas.

"Good for being seen from above," Brian said, unzipping a little kit. "Oh, thank God. Fishing line and hooks. Lures. This is important."

They cataloged the remaining protein bars and took two more. There was also a Nalgene water bottle, water purification tablets, a first aid kit, the orange rope and carabiner, and a thick roll of duct tape.

Troy unzipped a small rectangular soft case. "A mirror? With a star in the middle?" He flipped it over to find instructions on the other side. The mirror was about the size of an instant camera and encased in solid plastic. "Oh, for signaling."

"We'll have to keep that handy."

"One more thing in here..." Troy tore open the Velcro closure of a little black pouch and tipped out a coil of metal with thick material handhold straps on each end. "This looks like...a bike chain? With sharp edges?"

Brian glanced up. "Chainsaw. We can cut through branches to make a shelter. Firewood."

"Oh!" Troy eyed the teeth on the chain and carefully coiled it into its pouch. "Cool." He watched as Brian unsheathed a knife from a leather case, about six or seven inches. "Whoa. That's serious business."

"It is indeed." Brian slid it back into the sheath and buttoned the clasp before examining small tubes of sunscreen, lip balm, and mosquito repellent. "These won't last long. We have to be careful."

"Right." Troy tried to smile. *Fake it until you make it.* "But we won't be here very long. They'll already be looking."

Brian seemed to be thinking as he checked his watch. "Yes, the searchers could be heading out this morning. They would have had to wait until the storm cleared. It depends on which direction it went, and the level of resources available. Regardless, we should start a signal fire."

Troy sipped a bottle of water and finished his protein bar. His stomach still rumbled. "I guess we can use this chainsaw thing to cut logs?" He glanced around the beach. "There's a tree down over there. That's as good as any."

Brian was staring out to sea. After a few moments, he blinked and looked at Troy. "Sorry? Yes, yes. That tree's good."

"I'll get started on it." Troy hopped to his feet, attempting to appear as capable and confident as possible. "You drink some more water and rest."

"No, I'm fine." Brian pushed himself up, then swayed.

Troy grabbed his arms. "You hit your head. Just sit, okay? You can supervise."

Brian opened his mouth before closing it again with a sigh. "Okay." He obediently sat back down on the sand.

"Now where should we light this fire?" Troy gazed around, peering up at the cliff towering above this end of the island. "Up there would be great, but I dunno if there's anywhere to climb. We should probably start one here on the beach first, I think?"

"Definitely. We can explore later, but for now we should set up here." Brian stared at the rock face. "We almost made it," he murmured. "She did such a great job getting us down at all. But we had too much speed coming in. Nowhere to go. She…"

In the silence that followed, Troy swallowed hard. "I'm really, really sorry. I'm so grateful to her for saving my life. So grateful to both of you."

"No," Brian bit out sharply. He shoved items back in the pack, arranging and rearranging. "I didn't do anything. Paula was the pilot. She saved us."

"From where I'm sitting—well, standing—you did a hell of a lot. So thank you." Before Brian could argue, Troy squared his shoulders. "Okay. Where should we put the fire? If we're too close to this end with the cliff, it'll be hard to see the fire from that direction. Maybe we should move down the beach?" He didn't add that it would be good to get away from the place the plane had crashed.

It was incredible what little sign there was left of it. The waves had been so violent, and the storm had sent so many trees and plants scattering. The tracks the plane must have made in the sand had been wiped clean. It was like he and Brian had simply been dropped there.

Brian looked left and right. "Yes. We'll move down. Not too far— the cliff might give us some shelter if there's another storm."

They shifted their gear, and Troy made sure Brian was sitting again before he took the chainsaw pouch and set off across the sand. It was warm and fine between his toes, almost white.

Being careful of the chain's ragged teeth, Troy took the strap handles in each hand and sized up the small tree that lay on the beach. It wasn't a palm and had several branches. There were others down the beach, as well as a ton of fallen palm fronds that would probably be good for...he tried to remember the word. Right—kindling. They'd be good for kindling. He hoped everything would be dry enough.

"I can do this," he muttered. "It'll be like CrossFit or some shit."

He bent and went to work sawing through the first limb, yanking the chain back and forth. At first he didn't keep it taut enough, and the teeth got stuck in the wood. But after a few tries he started to get the hang of it and removed a limb a few inches thick.

The fact that he was actually on a desert island in the Pacific like someone in a movie was so beyond weird he couldn't really wrap his head around it. He'd survived a plane crash. And now he was going to build a signal fire and look for water. He was *on a desert island*. It was too freaking crazy.

As he sawed, sweat gathered on his brow and dampened the collar of his dirty tee. He rolled up his sweatpants to his knees. His throat was dry and arms aching by the time he finished. The trunk of the tree was too thick, but he sawed the limbs and branches into smaller pieces and tried to think of the last time he'd done manual labor. He came up blank.

Carrying an armload of wood, he returned to where Brian sat, the sand becoming uncomfortably hot. Troy slipped on the flip-flops. Brian had taken off his dress shoes and socks, and poked through his suitcase.

"This is as good a place as any, I guess?" Troy asked.

"I think so." Brian motioned to the trees about fifteen feet away. "Far enough that we won't risk a forest fire, but still away from the tide. Here, let me help."

Troy wanted to say no but had a feeling Brian would protest more strongly this time. "I'll bring the wood, and you can arrange it. Do you know anything about making fires?"

"We went camping most summers when I was growing up. I was a Boy Scout too." He half smiled. "Pretty sure I got my fire badge. I'll dig a pit."

Once they had a good pile of wood and palm fronds in their shallow pit, Brian got out the magnifying glass. The sun was clear of the trees now, bright and powerful.

"Let's try this. Save the matches." Biting his lip, he held out the glass, moving it until he was satisfied with the angle.

They knelt there, watching and waiting.

And waiting.

And waiting.

"Maybe we should use a match," Troy whispered. It felt like if he spoke too loudly, he'd somehow jinx the fire.

"One more minute. I think it's close."

It was more like five minutes, but finally a thin line of smoke rose from the pile of fronds. It was barely anything at all, but slowly it thickened. Then, with a soft *whoomp*, the dry leaves ignited.

"Yes!" Troy pumped his fist.

With a grin, Brian kept the glass steady and leaned over to blow gently on the burgeoning flames. They watched as the fire spread, finally catching the wood and not just the palm leaves. Gray smoke trailed into the sky, and Troy said a quick prayer that it would be spotted soon.

A swell of optimism filled him. Maybe they'd be rescued in a few days! Sure, they were a needle in a haystack, but the sky was so clear someone would see the smoke. They could have a nice shower and hot meal, sleep in comfy beds. He watched the smoke and daydreamed.

Then his stomach growled.

Right. Not rescued yet. They needed to try fishing. And maybe... Troy gazed at the brown lumps scattered near the tree line and went to grab one, turning it over in his hands, the husk dry and rough on his skin. "Hungry?" he asked Brian.

Brian glanced up, poking the fire with a stick. "Oh, good. You know how to open one?"

"No clue. You?"

"Uh-uh. I've drunk coconut milk and eaten macaroons, but I've never bought an actual coconut."

"Me either. I've never really cooked. I can heat stuff and make toast or whatever. But my mom still brings us a ton of food when we're home, and on the road we have catering for...well, for everything." He'd wanted to take control of his life, and here was his chance. He would feed himself, damn it.

The good thing about coconuts was that they appeared to be plentiful on the island. The bad thing about coconuts was getting the freaking things open. Even with the knife, Troy had a feeling he was more likely to lose a finger than get inside to the milk and juicy flesh.

He hefted the coconut and shook it. There was definitely liquid sloshing around inside, which he assumed was a good sign. On one end of the coconut, there were three little indentations. "I guess this is the top? Or the bottom."

Turning the fruit, he found a natural seam around the middle and poked at it. He gently dug in the knife and tried to cut. No dice. The knife sawed through a bit of the husk, but he had to use all his strength just to make a tiny bit of progress. "Man. This is hard. Maybe I should try to peel the brown stuff off?"

"Can't hurt." Brian shifted logs around. "I think you can crack coconuts? In half."

"Like, with a rock or something?"

"Worth a try."

Troy peeled off as much as the husk as he could. The coconut was a pale brown now, with the three distinctive dents on one end, presumably from where it had been attached to the tree. He found a good-sized rock just inside the jungle. After propping up the coconut in the sand, he raised the rock. "Here goes nothing." He slammed it down, aiming for the seam.

Nothing.

Grunting, he tried again.

Nothing.

Just when he was ready to accept defeat a few minutes later, the coconut gave way an inch. "I think I'm getting somewhere," he muttered. Yes, there was definitely an opened crack. He turned the coconut a bit and hit it again. Using the knife, he tried to pry it open. "Jesus, this thing is tough." He cracked it again and pried. "Holy shit!" The coconut split neatly in half, splashing his hands with pale liquid. Quickly, he held up both sides so no more would spill.

"Nicely done!" Brian grinned.

It didn't smell particularly inviting. Not sweet, like he'd expected. "I guess this is coconut milk? Looks more like water. Oh, that's a thing too, isn't it? Coconut water."

"I guess we should try it." Brian took half the coconut and sipped. He screwed up his nose. "Ugh. Kind of tastes like... I don't know what."

Troy sipped from his half shell, grimacing. "Dirty water?"

Brian laughed, a low rumble that somehow eased the sharp edges of tension in Troy's chest. Troy found himself smiling, wanting to hear that laugh again.

"Well, we know it's locally sourced," Troy said. "Totally organic.

Could probably make a fortune selling these at Whole Foods."

Brian did laugh again, his shoulders rising and falling and a smile tugging his lips. "Sounds about right. They probably add a shit ton of sugar to the bottled coconut water. But the meat inside doesn't look rotten, and it smells okay. I think it's fine. There are nutrients, so we should drink it."

Troy took another mouthful, grateful most of it had splashed out. Using the knife, he awkwardly carved out some of the white meat and passed that side of the coconut to Brian, taking Brian's half and carving it up too.

Brian waited until he was finished to put a chunk into his mouth. He chewed thoughtfully and swallowed. "It tastes like…"

After chewing his own piece, Troy said, "Soap?"

That low, deep laughter was music to Troy's ears. Brian took another bite. "It's not terrible, though. Maybe if we cook some later, it'll taste better."

"At least it's fattening. Lots of calories in coconut. It's on my trainer's list of fruits I'm not even allowed to look at." Troy ate a bit more and read the instructions on the signaling mirror. "Hopefully we'll only be here a few days, and then we can have our coconut with sugar again."

"Yeah." Brian bent his head and ate more, the laughter gone.

Troy gazed out to sea, shielding his eyes with his hand. All he could see was a world of blue, broken only by the distant horizon.

# Chapter Four

PUSHING UP THE wide brim of his fisherman's hat, Brian tipped his head back and squinted. The cliff wasn't quite a sheer face where it rose out of the jungle, but it was close. The dull throb of a headache that wouldn't go away spiked behind his eyes. His sunglasses had been in the cockpit, lost now.

At least he was out of his dank uniform and into cargo shorts and a fresh shirt. He wore a white tank top the Aussies would call a singlet and Americans an undershirt. The other black tank top he'd packed stretched across Troy's broad chest. He'd only been planning to spend a day in LA, but always packed a few extra clothes in case.

Troy was a little shorter than Brian, but muscular and more defined. The navy board shorts Brian had given him were a tight fit, but they'd do. *He'll lose weight soon enough*, he thought grimly.

He'd volunteered for search and rescues a few times since he'd moved to Australia, and he knew how hard it was to actually spot anything from a search plane. The ocean was a frighteningly big place, especially when you were lost in it. At least they were on land and not a life raft. That was a huge advantage.

"There's no way, man." Troy shook his head, the bandanna almost blinding in its orangeness. "No way."

"I did some abseiling in the Blue Mountains, but this is way out of my league. Also, we don't have any ropes."

"Some what?"

"It's another word for rappelling. That's what they called it."

Brian scanned the rock for hand and foot holds. After failing in a quest to find a fresh water supply in the area near the beach, Brian had napped while Troy kept an eye on the fire. Despite his headache and the glare, Brian was feeling better, so they decided to see if it was possible to get on top of the cliff and light a fire up there.

Chirps and rustles and the odd squawk filled the silence, the jungle a living, breathing thing, smelling of earth and sweet moisture. From the corner of his eye, Brian could see Troy anxiously looking left, right, and behind them regularly.

Brian gazed up again. They didn't want to stray too far from the beach, and there seemed to be no end to the steepness of the cliff. No sloping hill that led to the top. It was as though the rock had exploded violently from the earth, jutting up stubbornly. From what he knew about the formation of volcanic islands, it probably had.

"What was that?" Troy asked sharply. "There's something on the ground." He lifted his feet, left and then right, repeating the little standing dance as he stared at the fallen leaves and twigs and jerked his head around. He wore Brian's flip-flops, the only other shoes Brian had packed. They were good quality at least, not cheap plastic. Still, he had to admit he felt more secure in his leather shoes, which had been a size too tight for Troy.

Brian peered down. "I don't see anything. Just walk carefully." He winced. "Sorry, I know that's terrible advice."

Troy snorted. "Thanks for these, though. Much better than being barefoot and wearing my smelly stuff."

"Of course."

"Good thing we got your suitcase off the plane." He smiled teasing-ly. "And you've got that stylish hat."

Brian grinned. "I sure do. My grandfather's Tilley. This thing is damn near indestructible." He took off the worn khaki hat and spun it in his hands. "A good hat is a must in the tropics."

"Your grandfather's? That's cool."

"Yeah." Brian suddenly thought of their last camping trip. He could almost taste the s'mores all these years later; smell the campfire and hear the old songs he could never sing well, but still knew by heart. Shaking it off, he plopped the hat back on his head. "We've gone pretty far. I don't think this cliff is climbable. We should get back to the beach to check the fire and use the signaling mirror."

Troy gazed around again nervously. "Good idea. I like the beach better."

Brian led, pushing back the leaves and generally making a racket he hoped would send anything scurrying out of their way.

"Hey, should we write something in the sand? Like, SOS or whatever?"

"Absolutely. Great idea. We can search for rocks." At the very least, it would keep them busy. Brian wanted to curl up in the shade and sleep until his headache subsided, but the early hours and days of a search and rescue were vital. They had to do everything they could to attract attention if they were lucky enough to have search planes in their quadrant.

His stomach churned. They were so far away. The odds of being found were astronomical. He tried to shake the thought loose. *We're alive. Take it one day at a time.*

At the beach, they added more wood and leaves to the fire, creating as much smoke as possible. Brian eyed their meager collection of worldly items. "We need something to catch rain. I guess my carry-on is the biggest container we have."

Troy peered at the clear blue sky. "Doesn't look like there'll be rain today."

"I think it usually comes in short bursts this time of year. I guess we'll see."

"Hopefully they'll find us soon and we won't have to worry about it."

It was good Troy was so optimistic, even if Brian didn't share the feeling. "I'll get the suitcase emptied out just in case." They still had several plastic bottles of water that he'd grabbed from the plane, but he really hoped it rained soon. Drinking rainwater was far preferable to straining and purifying river water if they were lucky enough to find any.

Since his suitcase had been soaked, the contents were still damp. The tanks and shorts he and Troy wore had dried quickly in the heat after they'd put them on, but now he looked for somewhere to hang the sodden flannel blankets he'd grabbed. The listing palm trees along the edge of the jungle of course had no branches, but he used the orange rope as a clothesline, tying it between two trees.

"I'm going to find some rocks."

"I'll help you. I—" Brian straightened from where he'd been bending over and stumbled, his head spinning.

"Whoa!" Troy was there, gripping his shoulders. "I think you've done enough. Sit. You can do the mirror."

Brian wanted to argue—he shouldn't let his passenger do the hard work—but the headache pulsed behind his eyes. "Okay. Be really careful with rocks. Might be spiders or something living underneath them. Don't go far into the jungle. I really should come with you. I'm—"

"You're sitting down." Troy pushed gently, but there was iron underlying his grasp. "Come on. Not too close to the fire."

As Brian sat and crossed his legs in the sand, he had to admit it felt good to be off his feet. "I'm sorry. I don't know what's wrong with me."

"Um, you have a head injury? That's a good place to start." Troy handed him the mirror. "I was thinking of those rocks over there, by the end of the island."

Brian gazed to his right. He hadn't really noticed the smaller black volcanic rocks that dotted the beach's end; his attention had been focused on the cliff face, and whether... He shook off the macabre thoughts. *Paula's dead. It was over in a heartbeat for her. Nothing can change it now.* "Good idea. Still be careful."

"I will. Make sure you keep your hat on." Troy squinted at him uneasily, looking as if he wanted to say more. Finally he added, "It's hot."

"Uh-huh. I'm fine."

Although he didn't appear entirely convinced, Troy went off toward the cliff. It really was damn hot, eighty degrees if not more. They'd need to build something for shade in the next few days.

Brian pulled out the signaling mirror and read the instructions on the back, which had a round indent in the middle of the plastic about the size of a nickel. A little star-shaped pinhole for sighting sat in the center of the indent.

After lifting his hand and reflecting sunlight onto it with the mirror, he slowly lifted the sighting hole to his eye, finding the bright dot. It felt like needles pierced his brain, but he had to suck it up. Now he was supposed to aim this dot at his target, but not having a specific plane or ship in sight, he panned back and forth across the horizon as suggested by the instructions. A few times he had to start the process again and find the dot.

"How's it going?" Troy asked as he passed by with a rock in his hands.

"Getting the hang of it, I think."

After ten minutes, his head throbbed too powerfully to ignore, and he swallowed two more Advil. After closing his eyes for a few breaths, he forced them open so he didn't fall asleep. Focusing on Troy hefting up a rock by the cliff, he watched.

Troy really wasn't at all what he'd expected. He'd gotten the call to copilot the overseas flight and hadn't given any thought as to passengers until Paula had indulged in that giddy little smile in the terminal and leaned in with eyes shining, almost bouncing on her toes.

He had to squeeze his eyes shut at the thought, bracing through a wave of nausea and sorrow. The storm had cleaned the stone of Paula's blood and remains, but he could still feel the solid flesh of her arm in his hand.

Why hadn't he been a better friend? She'd asked him for drinks repeatedly, insisting he'd be a great wingman so she could pick up hot chicks. He'd disagreed, but had actually been tempted a few times. Paula had teased and cajoled and made him smile for real. While he knew he'd never love flying again, he'd liked it with Paula, and that was more than he'd had in a long time.

As Troy went back and forth, undoubtedly working up a hell of a sweat, Brian realized he'd actually talked more to Troy in the past...how long had it been? Shit, he wasn't sure. Uncapping a plastic bottle, he drank. This was the second day. Right. They'd crashed yesterday morning. Maybe they could use one of the stones as a calendar and scratch the days on it.

But yes, he'd spoken to Troy more than he'd spoken to anyone in too long. The only time he spent this many hours with someone was on a long flight, and that was different. Now Troy was all he had.

Impossible questions simmered in his mind. How many days could they survive? What if it didn't rain? What if they got sick? What if—

"You okay?" Troy called.

Blinking, Brian refocused. Troy stood by his growing collection of black rocks. "Yes."

"Maybe you should lie down in the shade."

"No. I'll start on the first 'S.' I'm feeling better."

Acquiescing, Troy went for more rocks, and Brian pushed to his feet and approached the pile. The rocks were heavier than he expected. Troy certainly didn't seem to be afraid of hard work. As he returned, Brian asked, "Aren't rock stars supposed to be spoiled?"

Laughing, Troy dropped his load. "I'm not a rock star."

"Okay, pop star. Teen idol. Whatever. I thought the rich and famous had people to do everything for them."

"You wanna be my assistant?" Troy grinned. "I think you're the only applicant. You're a shoo-in."

"How's the pay?" Brian picked up a stick from the scattered foliage still left on the beach.

"Pretty shitty. Do you take coconuts?"

"As a matter of fact, I do."

They laughed even though it wasn't that funny, and Troy went off again. Using the stick, Brian started tracing the SOS in the sand, stopping and starting several times. When Troy returned, he stood there, feet visible beyond the top curve of the letter Brian was digging. Brian glanced up, his heart leaping into his throat when he saw what Troy was holding.

"I thought we could use some pieces? They'd be shiny." Troy gazed hesitantly between Brian and the two-foot piece of wing in his hands.

Brian stood straight up, his heart racing. "Don't cut yourself. It's dangerous." He wanted to grab the metal and hurl it into the sea.

"I'm sorry. I didn't mean to upset you. I just thought it would be a good idea."

"I'm not upset." The stupid lie hung there in the hot air. He stared at the metal, hearing the shriek of it as they'd collided with the side of the cliff. "Is there a lot of it over there?" he asked hoarsely.

"No. The storm washed most of it away. I guess there might be some in the water beyond the rocks. Metal and...stuff."

"Debris." Brian's mouth had been dry, but now saliva flooded it, his stomach clenching. He forced himself to look up at Troy, who watched him with kind eyes as he licked his lips nervously. "Yes, we should use it in the letters. Good idea." He rubbed his face. "Just be careful with the metal. It really can be sharp. I should be the one to pick up the pieces."

"Just work on tracing the letters. I'd suck at that. I'll be careful, I promise." Troy cautiously put the metal in the sand next to the rocks. On his way back to the cliff base, he gave Brian's shoulder a wordless squeeze.

Brian was sure he could feel the heat where Troy's hand had been, and it was strangely comforting. He went back to work after gulping more water. "Writing giant sand letters is harder than I thought," he said as Troy returned.

"Hauling rocks is pretty much exactly as hard as I thought."

They laughed, and Brian breathed more easily. As far as being stuck on a desert island with a stranger went, he could have done a hell of a lot worse than Troy.

"I THINK 'SO' will have to do for now." Plopping down on the sand, Troy pulled off his sweat-soaked orange bandanna and gulped from one of the plastic water bottles. He grimaced at the taste of the warm water, swatting at a fly. The flies left itchy bites he tried not to scratch.

Brian sat beside him with a soft groan and drank as well. He closed his eyes. "It'll be a philosophical statement."

Troy wanted to ask Brian if he was okay, because he clearly had a killer headache, but he knew by now Brian would insist he was fine. The vivid bruise on his forehead was stark against his skin. "Like, 'So what?' Maybe we should do a dot-dot-dot instead of the second S tomorrow."

A faint smile lifted Brian's lips as he rubbed his temples. "Sounds like a plan." He opened his eyes. "Oh, the mirror."

"I can do it."

"It's all right. You did all the hauling." Brian took the mirror from one of the big pockets in his cargo shorts and aimed the reflection before sweeping it side to side in a slow pan. He'd been doing it regularly, and now the sun was getting low in the sky, faint pink streaks beginning to appear.

"They really didn't come," Troy said before he could bite his tongue. He shook his head. "I know it was stupid to think they'd find us the first day." But in the back of his mind, he'd been hoping.

"Not stupid. Optimistic. Nothing wrong with that."

"I guess."

As he'd hauled the rocks across the sand, deep down he'd expected to hear the drone of an engine. But there were no planes or ships or anything but chirping birds and the gentle lap of the returning tide. It was beautiful, but God, when he looked out, there was just *nothing*.

Troy tried to ignore his thumping heart and push away the panic. "I'm a mess. Want to rinse off? I'll take my chances with the possibly deadly creatures of the deep."

"Water's so clear, we'll see them coming." Brian returned the mirror to his pocket, buttoning it closed carefully.

Troy glanced down at the board shorts and tank top he'd borrowed. "Do you usually swim in these shorts?" His sweaty junk had been rubbing against them since he didn't have underwear.

"I do, but don't worry about it." Brian got to his feet, and Troy tensed, waiting for him to sway or stumble. But he seemed secure as he unzipped his shorts. "We have so few clothes that we should save them for land."

"Okay, cool. But first…" He felt his cheeks get hot. "I need to go to the bathroom. Um, number two."

"Right, right." Brian turned to the jungle. "I believe the standard outdoor method is to dig a little hole, do your business, and cover it up again."

With a shudder, Troy looked at the trees. "In there?"

"I know, it's not an appealing thought."

"What if…" It was so stupid, but he had to say it. "What if something bites my butt?"

Brian kept a straight face for a few seconds before shaking. Then he winced. "Ow. It hurts to laugh."

Troy couldn't help but smile too, wanting to hear more of Brian's rumbly, reassuring laughter. "That's what you get for mocking my extremely valid concern."

"My apologies. I'm sure it'll be fine. Just…"

"Poop fast?"

"Indeed." Brian smiled again, a dimple creasing his cheek. "At least we can piss by the trees or in the ocean. But shit floats, and…ugh."

Troy grimaced. "Yeah, that's super gross. Dig a hole it is. Even though I really don't want to." He poked through the storm debris by the tree line and found a big stick. "Three days ago, I was at the Hilton."

"'First Up singing sensation shits in the woods, inspires back-to-nature craze.'"

Troy bit back a laugh. "It's *Next* Up, thank you very much. Also—" He cut off as a thought occurred. "Oh God, what do we use for toilet paper?"

"Well…" Brian shrugged and nodded toward the trees.

"What if the leaves are poison or something?"

"Hmm. Good point." Brian joined him at the jungle entrance and examined the wide leaves of a plant. He tore one off and rubbed it over the back of his hand. "See if I get a rash. Better here than…there."

"Definitely."

After they both tested a patch of skin on their hands and waited ten minutes with no ill effects, Troy headed about ten feet in with a fistful of leaves, wearing Brian's flip-flops. He beat the bushes with his stick, then dug out a little hole. Feeling extremely awkward and exposed, he squatted.

And waited.

"Come on, come on," he mumbled. "You know it's time. Let's just get on with it!"

He finally willed himself to relax enough, and when he was finished, he covered up the hole with a grimace and practically ran back to the beach. Troy really hoped he wouldn't have to get used to *that*.

Brian had taken off his clothes and waded in the sea. He was in good shape, tall and lean, and Troy idly wondered if pilots were required to work out. Boy banders sure as hell were. He could imagine their trainer now, glaring that he wasn't doing his push-ups and planks.

Troy stripped and walked into the calm water, inhaling the briny air deeply. The bottom was perfectly soft and sandy, the startling clear turquoise water just cool enough to be refreshing. He sighed as he dunked his head, the ocean floor just out of reach of his toes. "Oh yeah. This was a good idea."

"Amen." Brian ducked under and came back up, slicking his thick, short hair.

Troy took a few deep breaths, hearing the mantra his annoyingly zen yoga instructor constantly repeated. *Be present. Be in the now. There is only now.* They floated lazily, the sun arcing closer and closer to the horizon, pink-rose light washing over them.

"Is that one of the band's songs?"

Troy realized he was humming softly. His cheeks went hot. "Oh, no. Just a little melody I wrote. It's nothing."

"Sounded good to me."

"Well…thanks." He thought of his old guitar and the day he'd come home from dance rehearsal to find it gone and his father utterly unrepentant.

*"No time to waste on that kind of music. Folk doesn't sell."*

"You know, I thought rock stars were supposed to be arrogant assholes."

Shoving away useless memories, Troy paddled his feet, rolling onto his belly. "Sorry to disappoint. I can throw a hissy later if you want."

"I'd appreciate it. If you don't pull a diva routine daily, my tell-all exposé won't sell. Although I suppose I could make it all up."

Troy smiled. "As long as we split the profits. Not that I need the money. You know, it's ironic. People would pay a fortune for this. White sand beach, crystal clear water. Complete privacy."

Brian chuckled. "I guess they would."

"I haven't skinny dipped since I was a little kid. Always have to be careful. Never know where the paparazzi are hiding and how long their lenses are." The water washed over him, caressing his skin. He could feel it between his ass cheeks and around his balls. There was something strangely freeing and sexy about it.

"I'd go crazy never being alone."

"Yeah. Sometimes it's the worst." His mother's voice echoed in his head. *Don't complain about the American dream, Bongbong. People would murder for this!* Closing his eyes, he gulped down a swell of longing. He needed to see her again. Stoop down and feel her little arms around him, hear his silly Filipino nickname on her tongue.

"So being a rock star isn't all hot chicks and limousines? Free stuff and adoring fans?"

"Well, it is those things too, which is why I sound like a total douche if I complain. Wah, wah, my life is so hard. My father forced me into this mega-successful band and I have a stupid amount of money and millions of people love me. Also, my diamond shoes are too tight."

Brian laughed softly. "Too bad we couldn't grab those shoes. They'd be great for crushing spiders." He was quiet a moment. "So your father forced you into it?"

Troy hadn't talked about his father since he'd first started dating Savannah and she'd asked and asked until he gave in. But in this beautiful purgatory with someone he'd just met, floating in the sea as pink and red streaked over the cloudless blue sky, what had happened seemed like a different life on another planet.

"It sounds worse than it was. My father was..." Troy hesitated, searching for the right words. "He was a cowboy. Not literally, but he had that kind of personality. Big and broad, filling the room. Six-two, blond hair and blue eyes. Square jaw. Ty and I got the cleft in our chins from him. He grew up a foster kid in Texas. No family. Came to LA and married my mom. She's Filipina. Barely over five feet. Immigrated in her twenties and worked her ass off. Dad was this American hero to her."

Troy drew circles in the water with his fingers, his chest tight as he thought about his parents. He continued, "Dad loved showbiz. He could sing and act, but his real talent was in management. Promotion. So my brother and I became his business. He pitched the idea of the TV show to all the networks. Was an exec producer. When it went off the air, I thought maybe I'd go to college, but he'd already dreamed up the boy band idea. Ty was clearly the star out of the two of us, but Dad convinced me the older brother figure was important. Not that I really argued. What Dad said went."

"And the rest is history?"

"Yep. Like I said, I shouldn't complain. I have a good life. Had one, anyway. I guess we'll see what happens." His pulse kicked up, a tangle of questions snagging his mind and dissipating his calm.

"You talk about your father in the past tense. He's not alive?"

"No. Died just after I turned twenty."

"I'm sorry."

"Yeah, it's… It sucked." And now he was leaving Tyson and his mom and the rest of the family. Why had he thought it was a good idea to rent a plane? He should have slept on it. Come up with a better plan. Who would look after Ty now? His heart hammered.

*Be present. Be in the now. There is only now.*

Troy put his face close to the water, peering down at the sandy bottom. "It's so clear." Although with the sun setting, it was becoming hard to see. "What was that you were saying about sea snakes?"

"Don't worry. We're still close to land. I was told they stay farther out, near the reef. We should be careful around the reef. Make sure we don't touch it and cut ourselves. Reef cuts are nasty."

"Good to know." Troy ran his hand through his cropped hair. "Don't suppose you had any shampoo in your suitcase?"

"Sadly, no. I usually use whatever the hotel stocks. Didn't pack any soap either. I heard once that sand works." Brian swam in closer to shore, and Troy followed.

When they were in waist-deep water, they bent and picked up handfuls of sand. Troy scrubbed it over his body. "People would probably pay a fortune for this too. Exfoliator straight from the pristine beaches of the South Pacific."

"Maybe we should bottle it." Brian scrubbed his chest, working the wet sand through the dark hair there.

"God, it feels good to get clean." Ducking his head, Troy worked it through his hair and rinsed. His stomach rumbled. "But I really need to eat."

Brian gazed around. "Maybe we should try fishing."

The idea of fish to eat made his stomach growl louder, but the thought of sea snakes or eels or jellyfish or *whatever* sent a chill down his spine. "In the dark? No, we can have protein bars and cook some coconut. We could use the shell. Like, just crack it in half and cook it like that?"

"Worth a try. There are dozens of coconuts on the beach and more in the trees, so if we ruin them we can just do more."

As the moon rose over the trees and the stars blinked into sight in the darkening sky, they walked ashore, sand sticking to their feet. Troy contemplated it. "We should have a bigger signal fire by the SOS, and a campfire here."

"Good idea. We can do that in the morning. Should keep them both burning all the time if we can. Helps keep the bugs away."

Still naked, Troy went to work on cracking open a coconut, waiting until he was dry to get dressed. Fortunately, the water evaporated quickly. It probably should have been weird to be naked around someone he barely knew, but unlike in the gym, here he didn't have to be afraid Brian was trying to take sneaky pictures of his junk.

"I did pack some extra boxers. Never know when flights might get delayed. They're clean." Brian had changed into a red plaid pair and held out others.

"Cool, thanks." Troy took ones with green and purple checks and stepped into them. "Haven't worn boxers in years. Usually do briefs. But I didn't have anything on under my sweatpants the other night, so…" He shook his head as he gave the coconut another whack. "Weird, isn't it? Only two days, but being on the plane feels like a million years ago."

"It does," Brian agreed quietly. "Completely surreal." He looked toward the cliff, his face creasing.

Troy hesitated. "Did you want to…we could do a little service for her? Say a prayer or something?"

Brian turned away. "It's okay. But thank you."

Maybe Troy would say his own later. It would make him feel better. "I'm sorry. I wish…" Acid swirled in his empty belly. "This wouldn't have happened if it wasn't for me. She'd still be alive."

Shaking his head, Brian focused on Troy. "No," he said forcefully. "It's not your fault. It was me who—" He shook his head again.

Troy tried to smile. "If it's not my fault, then it doesn't get to be yours either. Remember?"

Brian's lips lifted briefly. "Touché."

Troy went back to the coconut. Before too long, he had the two halves cooking near the base of the fire. He didn't want the meat to burn, so tried to keep the husks out of the flames. "Wow, I'm actually cooking something. My mom would be so proud." His smile vanished as he imagined what she was going through. His aunties and uncles and cousins, and God, Ty... His throat tightened.

*"I don't need you!"*

Ty's angry shout echoed through his mind. What if those words were the last they ever said to each other? At least Troy had told Ty he loved him. That was something. Still, tears stung his eyes, and he inhaled sharply.

"You okay? Did you burn yourself?" Brian appeared beside him, his brow furrowed.

"No. I was just thinking." He swallowed thickly. "About my brother. The big fight we had."

"Ah."

"The thought that I might never see him again is..." He blinked rapidly. *Get it together. Be in the now or whatever the fuck.*

"Right. I get it."

Troy concentrated on the coconuts, prodding with a stick and testing the meat. When he thought they were cooked, he let them cool and scraped out the meat with the knife, leaving it in the half shells. The little bit of juice in each half had cooked as well, making it all tender. He handed Brian his half. "We can use them like bowls. Coconuts are pretty handy."

He cracked open another coconut and put it on the fire, because a protein bar and one serving of fruit wasn't going to make a dent in his aching hunger. Brian had spread out one of the flannel blankets from the plane, and they sat cross-legged.

Brian poked at the white meat, which was a little brownish in places. "This is great. Thank you."

"Well, let's see how it tastes. Don't thank me yet." Troy picked up a piece and took a bite, chewing thoughtfully. "Better, yeah? Not so soapy."

"Mmm. It is better."

They ate for a few minutes, and Troy took a deep breath. He had the feeling he always got from a day in the sun, sand, and saltwater—tired but satisfied. And shit, *hungry*. "Can you imagine how good a burger would taste right now?"

"Well *now* I can. Thanks for that." Brian glared jokingly.

They ate quietly, starting on their second coconut before long.

"Is that why you left the band?" Brian asked.

"Huh? Oh, you mean the fight with my brother. Yeah. Well, not the fight exactly, but what caused it."

"I see."

After a few moments, Troy raised an eyebrow. "You're not going to ask what the problem was?"

Brian shrugged. "I figure you'd tell me if you wanted to. It's none of my business."

"Huh."

"What?"

"Most people would ask."

"I've been on the receiving end of invasive questions, so I know what it's like. Not anything on the scale you deal with, but public curiosity can be…daunting."

Of course, now Troy wondered why Brian would have garnered public attention, but if Brian wouldn't pry, he couldn't either. "Daunting's a good word for it. I'm used to it after so many years, but people ask the most inappropriate shit you can imagine."

"Well, I'd ask if you wear boxers or briefs, but I guess I already know the answer."

Troy laughed, a wonderful calm spreading in his chest. "I guess you do. You can devote a chapter to it in your tell-all."

Brian laughed too, that low, warm sound. "I could call it *A Rock Star Wore My Underwear*. Wait, what's the band called again?"

"Next Up." He actually loved that Brian didn't know.

"Would be good if I could work that into the title somehow.

Hmm."

"I'm sure the publisher will have a million ideas."

"I'll hold out for the one that comes up with the punniest title."

"Good plan." Troy's stomach still rumbled. "Guess I'll throw on another coconut." He went about cracking it, aiming the rock for the seam and bashing it repeatedly.

"We definitely need to fish tomorrow."

"You know anything about fishing? Because I don't."

"A little. My grandfather loved it. It's been years, but I know enough. We can find a good piece of wood for a pole and tie on the line. Use a hook and lure. Put it in the water. That's basically all there is to it."

"Cool." Sweat dripped down Troy's temple as he finally cracked the coconut and put it on the fire. "Fish would taste amazing right now. When they rescue us, I'm having the biggest burger with the coldest soda. And ice cream. Definitely ice cream."

Brian smiled softly. "Sounds good."

The fire crackled and sparked, the stars bright overhead now as night wrapped around them fully. The push and pull of the waves hummed beneath it all. He stared up, trying to recognize any of the constellations. The stars were remarkably bright.

When he was finally full, Troy picked up the stick and poked the fire. "I'll get some more wood on here."

"I think I'm going to turn in. We should really work on a shelter tomorrow." Brian unfurled the mosquito net and one of the other flannel blankets several feet away, then unfolded the two silver emergency blankets. "I can sleep through anything, so don't feel like you need to sleep right away too. It's still early." The face of his waterproof watch lit up. "Not even eight p.m."

"It's okay. I'm beat. And yeah, a shelter." Maybe they wouldn't even need one. Yes, they'd be rescued soon, and sleeping under the stars wasn't bad at all. The sky was clear for miles.

Brian unzipped a toiletry bag. "Good thing I didn't bring my electric toothbrush." He shot Troy a guilty look. "I don't have an extra, though."

"Don't worry about it." Troy waved his hand dismissively. Truthfully, his teeth were coated with a layer of grossness, but they'd had so much else to deal with that he hadn't given it much thought.

"You can just use mine when I'm done. I don't mind." Brian squeezed a tiny blob of toothpaste onto his brush and took a swig of water from a bottle.

"You sure?"

Brushing and pacing around, Brian nodded. When he was finished spitting into the scrub edging the jungle, he rinsed the bristles and put on another blob of paste before handing it to Troy.

*Sweet Jesus.*

Troy moaned softly, possibly never so glad to brush his teeth in his entire life as he was in that moment. The mint tasted incredible, and his mouth felt so fresh and alive. It was kind of weird using another guy's toothbrush, but they were on a desert island and he'd take what he could get. Troy was sure to rinse it as well as he could without wasting too much water when he was done. He passed it back.

"Thanks, man."

"No problem." Brian poked through the rest of his bag and pulled out a washcloth. "We've got one little towel, at least." He sighed. "Definitely no soap in there. Sorry." He put his things away and got settled under his blanket, which crinkled as Brian fidgeted.

After slipping under the netting, Troy curled up with his blanket a foot away. "Well...good night."

"Night," Brian murmured.

Brian soon snored softly, but it didn't bother Troy. He'd always liked the sound of someone sleeping nearby, the heat of a body next to him. It was one of the best things about being in the band—he never lacked for company. He thought of Savannah with a sigh. What was she thinking now? Did she hate him?

Flicking through memories like the pages of a book, he thought of his old girlfriends. They'd all been fun, nice girls. He'd had good times with them, and the breakups had been made easier by Next Up's endless touring. Probably made easier too on his part because he'd never loved them. He'd come closest with Savannah, but when he imagined his life and the person who would fill his heart and make him complete, it wasn't her.

He snorted to himself. He'd been singing sappy ballads for too many years. Did love really fill anyone's heart or make them complete? His parents had loved each other, but it hadn't stopped his father from self-destructing. Troy wasn't sure the kind of love he imagined—passionate, strong, and peaceful too—actually existed.

Brian rolled toward him, mumbling in his sleep. His silver blanket had slipped down, and Troy eased it up over his shoulders again. Brian's mouth was slack, and the furrows in his brow were smoothed out. Troy hoped the headache would dissipate soon. The bruise on Brian's forehead was still an angry purple shadow in the darkness. He said a quick prayer that it would heal soon.

Flattening out on his back as Brian breathed deeply beside him, Troy watched the stars, giving the unfamiliar constellations new names.

"WHAT?" TROY ROLLED over and opened his eyes, kicking the blanket. Wet splotches hit him, and he blinked at the sky. The stars had vanished. "Shit. Shit!"

As the sudden rain intensified, Brian bolted up. "Water. Quick, the bottles." He tugged off the net.

Troy shook the cobwebs from his mind, made easier by the surprisingly cold rain now pouring down. Brian had left the suitcase lid open, and water splashed into it. They'd also collected all their empty plastic bottles, and now burrowed them upright in the wet sand.

"What time is it?" Troy asked.

"Just after eleven."

"Is that all?" It felt as if it should have almost been morning.

"Afraid so. You want your poncho?"

"A little late now."

"Indeed. We definitely need to work on a shelter."

"Maybe they'll come in the morning." Troy wiped water from his face, shivering.

A minute or so later, the rain stopped as if a giant faucet had been turned off. They screwed the caps back on all the bottles, and Brian zipped the suitcase, which was almost full. With the fire extinguished and the stars and moon blotted out, it was dark when they crawled back under the dripping net.

Shivering, they huddled closer together, only a few inches separating them. As the night wore on, Troy wished the stars would return.

# Chapter Five

"YOU KNOW HOW to make a teepee?" Brian looked up at Troy from the slender, downed trees they'd dragged from the mouth of the jungle. After a few moments, he pushed up his hat and raised an eyebrow, waiting.

"Oh, that wasn't rhetorical? No, dude, I don't know how to make a teepee. You were the Boy Scout, remember? I was too busy taking tap lessons." Troy swatted away a fly and scratched his bare, mostly smooth chest, yawning widely.

They'd walked the length of the island at dawn after being rudely awoken by the honking, squawking parrots. It was about two miles or so long and half the width. Squinting into the distance, the other side of the island had appeared virtually identical and just as deserted.

To sea, there was nothing on that side either—not even a blip in the line of the horizon as the sun rose in the cloudless sky. Not wanting to exert themselves too much with a limited food and water supply, they'd returned, hauling any wood that looked useful. They'd swim around the cliff end of the island and walk down the other side another day. First, they needed to spend their energy on shelter and food.

And before that, Brian needed to sit for a minute. He rubbed the back of his neck, stretching his head left and then right. The headache had eased, although dull pressure still throbbed against his eyes. The sun's glare was merciless.

"Tap dancing? Really?"

Troy smirked. "Yep. Tap, jazz, ballet, hip-hop. Not to mention voice and acting lessons. Mom and Dad were obviously total stage parents. Dad had a vision."

"Did you want to do it?" Brian asked.

"Sure. I liked it. But it wasn't as if I had a choice. It was just what we did. It was our normal. Especially once Ty got started and they saw his potential. He was such a little ham." Troy smiled fondly, his gaze going distant. "I was pretty good—worked hard and followed instructions. But Ty had that spark. Star quality, even back then."

"Did the other kids at school give you a hard time?"

Troy scoffed. "In LA? They were jealous, especially when Ty and I got the TV show. Then we got tutored on set anyway, so it didn't matter what anyone thought."

Brian couldn't imagine it. His upbringing with his grandparents in Western New York was positively quaint in comparison. The most exciting thing he did was an annual Buffalo Bills game with his grandmother. He smiled softly. Grandpa hadn't cared for sports one way or the other, but Gran had been a football fanatic.

"A teepee's a triangle, right?" Troy asked. "Are these trees tall enough?"

"As long as we have enough room to sit up comfortably, it doesn't need to be super tall. Probably better if it isn't. Less liable to blow over." Brian sized up the trees. They were four or five inches in diameter, so should be sturdy.

They collected armfuls of palm fronds and spread them out far enough from the tree line that falling coconuts wouldn't be an issue. A ton of fronds had ripped off during the storm, which was fortunate, since Brian didn't enjoy the idea of climbing up a palm tree to cut some down.

"Sure you're feeling up to this?" Troy asked.

"Yes, but thanks. Better today." The pain *was* better, that was true. His head didn't feel normal, but he kept that to himself as he reached up to take off his hat and poke at his forehead. "How's the bruise?"

"Turning into a sick-looking yellow. Getting better."

Brian hesitated after putting his hat back on. "Sick as in cool, or sick as in sickly? Not sure what the kids are saying these days."

Troy laughed. "The second one. Although it is pretty badass. Looks like you punched someone with your face."

"Thanks." With a smile, Brian checked his watch and took out the mirror to do a sweep of the horizon. The sky was clear, perfect blue again. Not a cloud—or a plane. But he told himself it was only the second day the searchers would be out. There was still hope.

Faint, faint hope.

The silver emergency blankets were orange on one side, and they'd spread them out farther down the beach beyond the SOS, which they needed to finish. They put smaller rocks on the corners of the blankets. There was hardly any breeze to speak of, but they couldn't afford to lose any of their supplies.

"Okay, now what?" Troy asked. "You're the teepee expert. If you need me to do a little soft shoe, I'll be right here."

"Well, *expert* is overstating it greatly, but it's a pretty basic principle. Stand the logs up in a circle and lean the tops together in a sort of triangle. Tie them with part of the rope, then cut off the rest so we still have a clothesline to hang wet stuff."

"Right. And how do we stop from getting wet ourselves?"

"I'm thinking once we have enough wood for a solid base, we put the big orange blanket over the top. Use duct tape to secure it to the sides of the teepee. And we need to keep a space empty for a doorway. Won't be perfect, but should keep the worst of the rain off."

"Sounds good. Worth a try." Troy scanned the heavens, his hand shielding his eyes as he turned in a slow circle. He refocused on Brian. "Let's do it. Doesn't sound too hard."

Half an hour later, Brian wiped sweat from his eyes and peeled off his tank top. "You jinxed it," he grumbled.

They stood on the fronds, trying to get the logs to stay put and lean against each other. Brian's arms shook as he struggled to hold two of them. "Okay, lower—right there."

Of course as soon as they let go, the logs tumbled over. They sighed in unison. It was going to be a long day.

After much cursing and sweating, they assembled their teepee frame and lashed together the tops of the wood with duct tape and the cut piece of nylon rope. They draped the orange blanket over it, and of course it wasn't even on all sides. But it would have to do, and they adjusted it as best they could before going around and taping down the edges to the frame.

Troy passed Brian the knife after cutting off another length of tape. "Did you always want to fly?"

Brian rolled his neck to ease the sudden tension. "I suppose." He cringed internally at the lie and cleared his throat. "Yes, actually. Ever since I can remember. I loved model planes and anything to do with flying. When I was little, I wanted to be an astronaut, but I wasn't smart enough."

"Really? But you must have to be smart to be a pilot."

He shrugged, slicing off more tape. "Smart enough. I got my degree in aeronautical engineering, then went to flight school. Started off with a regional airline and worked my way up."

"Have you ever flown the big jets?"

Brian inhaled and exhaled. "I have."

"Really? Cool! What's that like?"

Images of blackened metal and white foam flashed into his mind. He wiped his forehead beneath his hat, sure that it had suddenly just gotten hotter. His skin prickled. "It was fine."

"How'd you end up in Australia doing private planes? You didn't like working for a big airline anymore?"

"Just wanted a change. Slower pace."

"Do you miss it? Flying jumbo jets?"

Brian didn't have to lie this time. "No."

"Have you ever had any emergencies happen? Before this one, I mean."

Brian sliced through a few inches of tape—and right into his thigh. Sucking in air, he bit back a gasp. "Shit." The cut was just above his knee and below the hem of his cargo shorts, which had hiked up. "It's fine, it's fine."

"Let me see." Troy was at his side. "Not too deep, I don't think. I'll get the kit." He scrambled up.

"Don't know my own strength," Brian joked lamely. He pressed his hand over the cut, which was a few inches long. "That knife is amazingly sharp. For the record."

Troy returned with the first aid kit. "Once the bleeding stops, we should put iodine on it. Let me see." He bent his head and peered close at the cut before putting a small piece of bandage over it and pressing down. "Should be okay."

Troy's palm was hot, his fingers against Brian's knee. "It was a careless mistake."

Deepening his voice, Troy scowled. "You can make a mistake once. Do it twice and you're walking home." He laughed ruefully. "That's what my dad used to say. I was in a local production of the *Wizard of Oz* when I was a kid. I was the Tin Man. Totally went up on my lines when I met Dorothy and stood there like a deer in the headlights. In the car after, Dad told me his little mantra. I never missed my lines again."

"Your dad was pretty intense." Troy still pressed his hand firmly, and it was sweaty, but Brian didn't mind.

Troy laughed. "That's one way to put it. Hey, how'd you end up in Sydney?" Leaning over, he checked the cut, his breath tickling Brian's skin.

"Seemed like a good place at the time. Nice weather. Seafood. Rugby on TV." The other side of the world from everyone he knew.

"When did you move there?"

"Three years ago. I rent a tiny apartment in the burbs. Sydney's expensive. But I have a private terrace with flowering trees between me and the neighbors." He chuckled. "I'm sure that all sounds rather sad to you. You probably have a mansion."

"No, it sounds…idyllic. And I don't have a mansion. Ty and I bought a house in Malibu, but it's not that big. I mean, it's really nice, don't get me wrong. Four bedrooms, and it's right on the water. I know how lucky I am to live there. Although we're hardly ever home since we're on the road so much. Mom didn't see why we couldn't keep living with her when we were in LA. My dad bought their house after the TV show got picked up for season two, and it's not like it isn't big enough. But I just couldn't stay in my teenage bedroom after I turned twenty-four, you know? And Ty was dying to get out. Although maybe he should have stayed at home." He shook his head. "Sorry, I'm babbling."

"I don't mind."

Troy opened a little package of iodine and cotton. "This'll sting." He dabbed it gently.

Brian winced. "Hardly feel it."

"Uh-huh. You don't need to be all tough, you know. It's just me."

"I know." He smiled as Troy taped on a bandage, his tongue between his teeth. "Strange, isn't it?"

"That you took engineering and can barely build a teepee? Totally."

Brian found himself laughing. "*Aeronautical* engineering."

"So you could build us a plane?" Troy teased.

Smiling, Brian nodded. "Better than a teepee, apparently."

"Just messing with you. What were you going to say?"

"Oh, nothing."

Troy poked Brian in the side after patting down the last bit of tape. "Tell me."

"Was just going to say it's strange that I only met you a few days ago."

"I know, right?" Troy packed up the first aid kit. "I read once that trauma can bond people together really quickly. Being scared together and stuff. It's apparently a good idea to go ride huge roller coasters on a first date."

"Makes sense. Where'd you read that?"

"Knowing me? Buzzfeed."

Brian laughed again. "Well, I guess our first date is one for the record books."

"You definitely know how to show a guy a traumatic time." Troy's smile vanished and he flushed, glancing at the cliff. "I'm sorry. I shouldn't joke."

"Gallows humor. It's okay." But Brian felt a rush of guilt as well as he thought of Paula. Had it really only been *days*? Life had taken on an utterly surreal aspect, as if they existed in some twilight zone where the rest of the world had vanished beyond the blue horizon.

"Well, we should finish this." Troy motioned to the teepee. "What do we use to cover up below the blanket? There's still a foot exposed at least."

"I was thinking we could weave together palm fronds around the wood?"

"See? There's that engineering degree in action."

"Yes, palm fronds are often used in aircraft."

Laughing, Brian carefully cut more tape, and they worked together side-by-side as birds sang in the treetops and a gentle breeze came off the waves.

FOR A FEW heartbeats as Troy focused on the white net hanging above him, he had no idea where he was. Then it hit him in a rush—crash, island, teepee, Brian, sand. So much sand, no matter how they tried to brush it away. Acid flooded his gut and he wished there were Tums in the first aid kit.

This was the fourth day now. How much longer would it take the rescuers to find them? How was his family? The band? His friends, the fans. Was Tyson all right? Would this send him on a bender? Did his brother know he loved him? Troy had said it before he left, but did Ty really *know* it?

He reached out his right hand automatically, but instead of finding his phone on the nightstand, his fingers brushed the mosquito net. He'd started each day for years by checking his messages, but now he laid there blinking in the gray light. The large net was designed to be hooked to the ceiling, and they'd rigged a loop of duct tape. The net draped down, which was much preferable to sleeping with it wrapped around them.

Troy shifted, realizing he had morning wood for the first time since the crash. It pushed against the soft material of his boxers, and he automatically skimmed his hand over his belly and through the trimmed hair at his groin to take hold of his dick, tugging and making his balls tingle. With his left hand, he caressed his bare chest and brushed his nipples, and—

Brian shifted and mumbled, and Troy's hands froze, his heart skipping. Brian was a foot to his left, curled toward the other side of the shelter. He breathed deeply and seemed to still be asleep. Feeling like a kid with his hand in the cookie jar, Troy lowered his arms to his sides, shifting and stretching his neck, willing his erection to fade.

On top of the fronds they'd put over the sand, they'd spread out two of the flannel blankets from the plane, keeping one for sitting outside. They had no pillows, but they'd have to deal. Troy's back was sore from sleeping on the ground, but the sand was soft and it could have been worse. There was just enough room to stretch out his arms and legs and not touch the sides of the teepee.

Gray light ringed the bottom of the round shelter where they hadn't finished installing palm fronds yet. It was time consuming, but it was something to do other than obsess about rescue.

Not obsessing was something Troy was failing miserably at in the murky hours of dawn, turning boner-killing scenarios over and over in his mind as his stomach rumbled.

What if no one came? What if they stayed on the island forever? What if they got sick, or hurt? What if Brian died, and Troy ended up alone like that Tom Hanks movie? What if he never saw his family or friends again? What if—

*Stop! Be in the fucking now!*

He shouted at himself in his mind, breathing hard and his pulse humming. He wanted to tear off the net to escape the shelter, but he forced himself to carefully and quietly slip out from under his emergency blanket and the net. The shelter was too low to allow him to stand up straight, and he stooped to edge through the open space they'd left as a door.

It hadn't rained that night, and their campfire still smoldered a few feet away. The bigger signal fire had almost burned out, and he hustled over to stoke it with fresh wood. He mused that they'd have to devise a cover for the wood to keep it dry. Another project to keep them busy that hopefully they'd never really need because they'd be rescued any minute now. Yes, whisked away to the nearest resort with feather beds and hot showers and food, glorious food.

Troy tugged off his boxers before wading into the cool, gentle ocean swells. The parrots would arrive soon, honking over their breakfast, and he was glad to be awake before them. After he pissed, he stood in the chest-deep water and tried to enjoy the peaceful moment and not think about anything else but then and there. He dug his toes into the sandy bottom, feeling the fine, watery grains, and inhaled the salty air deeply.

He touched himself idly, and soon he was hard again. The way the water caressed his skin lit him up, his nipples peaking as he stroked his shaft and toyed with his balls. He breathed shallowly, lips parted. There was something liberating about jerking off in the ocean all by himself. Troy wanted to moan and cry out; he loved being loud during sex. Loved his partners being loud too. Pants and moans and groans heightened the intensity and made his orgasms so much more powerful.

He was close when Brian crawled out of the shelter in his boxers and gave him a wave. Again, Troy whipped his hands away from himself. With a shaky smile, he managed to wave back. He knew his face had surely gone red, but Brian was near the trees. Even with the clearness of the water, he was too far away to have any idea what Troy had been doing below the surface. Had Brian jerked off as well without Troy noticing?

A little ripple of excitement zipped through him, and before he could talk himself out of it, Troy's hand returned to his cock. He backed up until the water was almost to his neck and went to town. The urge to come was overwhelming, even as he watched Brian putter around, gathering wood and kindling.

Realizing it was super weird to be watching Brian while he jerked off, Troy turned and faced the sea. The water flowed around him, between his legs and caressing his sac. He strained for release, staring at the clear horizon as his body tightened. When he came, the wave of pleasure had him gasping softly, and he shuddered, still stroking.

The chorus of honks erupted behind him, and Troy jumped, losing his footing and falling below the surface. Sputtering, he came up and wiped his face, laughing to himself. He turned to spot the swarm of colorful feathers in the trees. Brian stood near them, his head tilted back as he watched. The sun peeked over the other side of the jungle, the sky getting bluer beyond the splash of yellow and orange. Troy wished he could take a picture and upload it to Instagram.

*What if they don't find us?*

"Stop it," he muttered. "They will. They'll find us. Shut up."

Soon, he wore the board shorts, his skin already dry in the growing heat. Brian had put on his cargo shorts before setting more coconut to cook. They sat on the flannel blanket by the fire waiting, and Troy wove together two fronds.

"That's a nice song," Brian said.

Flushing, Troy realized he was humming again. "Oh. Um, thanks." It was the chorus of a song he'd never named. Even after his dad died, he hadn't gone back to the folky guitar-driven music he heard in his head. He'd been too busy, he told himself. Yet here on the nameless island, fragments of the songs he'd written as a teenager echoed once more.

Fortunately, Brian didn't press it. "Definitely need to fish today," he said. "I figure when the tide goes, I can walk out and get closer to the reef. There should be a ton of fish there."

Troy frowned. "Isn't that where those super poisonous sea snakes are too?"

"From what I remember, but they don't usually bite. Of course now I wish I could google it, but alas."

"God, I really, really miss the internet."

Brian laughed. "Me too. Look, I'm sure it'll be fine. Pretty sure it's one of those, 'if we don't bother them, they won't bother us' situations. We need to eat some real food."

"Yeah. I'm starving. Coconut has calories, but it's not enough. The fish aren't poisonous or anything, though?"

"There are some poisonous varieties. From what I recall, they tend to be prickly and spiny. I guess we'll see what we catch. I've seen some TV shows on tropical fishing, so fingers crossed. I know what pufferfish look like, and we definitely won't eat those."

"Maybe we shouldn't risk it."

"We're out of protein bars. We'll be careful. Start with a bite at a time. I don't see what else we can do. We need protein, especially if…"

Troy swallowed hard. "Right. Okay." He rubbed a hand over his stubbly face, thinking about the now. "Oh! Where's the mirror?" Brian passed it to him, and Troy lined up the light through the hole and scanned the horizon.

He took a break from the mirror as they ate their coconut, debating whether the chirruping noise they often heard was some variety of cicada or something else altogether. "Maybe they're nargles," Brian said.

With a big, real laugh, Troy grinned. "I didn't peg you for a Harry Potter fan."

"Sure, why not?"

"I dunno. You're like…a pilot. Who knows all this technical stuff. I guess I never think of people who are pilots and doctors and do important things reading Harry Potter." He raised an eyebrow. "Or maybe you've just seen the movies?" He teased, "Not that there's anything wrong with that. I *guess*."

"I solemnly swear I have read all the books. And am up to no good, of course."

As they discussed random Potter things, it felt good to talk about something normal. Troy could have sat there all day chatting about Hogwarts, but the tide was retreating, and Brian had carved a makeshift fishing pole with clear line triple knotted around the end. He explained the lures and hooks, and they walked out on the wet sand, nearing the reef.

"Wow." Troy squinted at the colorful coral some distance ahead. The water sloshed around his ankles, and he shifted the empty coconut shell he carried from one hand to the other.

"You stay here. Just in case. Have to be careful not to step on any stonefish or eels or whatever else might be down there." Brian had brought the sole pair of flip-flops and slipped them on now.

"Okay." Troy examined the water for any sign of snakes or things that might bite or sting. But all he saw around him was sand.

He waited while Brian carefully picked his way closer to the reef, the water coming up closer to his knees. Brian wore his hat, and Troy was glad he'd put on the orange bandanna. He was used to the sun, but here in the tropics it was much more powerful. He'd already gotten a deeper tan, his skin peeling in places.

"Whoa!" Brian yanked up the pole and grabbed the line. A bright fish flopped around on the hook. "That was quick!" He stumbled a little and regained his balance. "These flip-flops make it too hard to stand. Can't get any grip." He reached down and took them off. "Should be fine if we keep clear of touching the reef. Get near it, but stay in the sand."

Troy came a little closer, watching every step. He thrust out the makeshift pail. "Sounds good."

Brian met him and handed over the flip-flops before carefully taking the squirming fish off the hook and dropping it into the coconut husk. "Let me try for a couple more if they're this quick. Then we'll cook them right away. In this heat, we can't wait long."

It only took five minutes to get two more fish even bigger than the first. Smiling, they splashed back to the beach. "I guess this is what hunters felt like back in the cavemen days, huh?" Troy said. He beat his chest.

Brian's laugh rumbled, a dimple appearing in his cheek. "Definitely. Now let's see about cleaning these. I watched Grandpa do it a million times, but I'm not sure how much I've retained."

"You didn't fish in Australia?"

"No. I guess..." He went quiet, his eyes distant. Finally, he said, "I guess it reminded me too much of him. The things I didn't have anymore."

"I'm sorry. I can do it next time if you want? It looked like shooting fish in a barrel, so I think I can manage."

"It felt good doing it again. We can take turns."

"For now, I'm totally okay with staying well clear of the sea snakes. I know, they could really be anywhere there's water, but just let me believe that all the dangerous things are in the reef."

Brian grinned. "Okay. Now let's clean these. Too bad we don't have a boning knife, but we'll have to make do."

By the time Brian was finished and thought he had most of the bones, his hands were covered in guts and the fish were quite a bit smaller. They laid the pieces of flesh on a flat stone by the fire's edge and waited.

"This is like watching a pot boil," Troy said. "Not that I've done that much. It's like watching a microwave count down."

"It is indeed." Brian poked at a chunk with a stick. "We need a spatula."

"Some lemon would be great."

Finally, they deemed the fish cooked and pushed the crumbling pieces into coconut bowls. Brian took a tentative bite. "Tastes like..."

"Chicken?"

He smirked. "I was going to say fish, actually."

Troy laughed. "Well, that's good, since it's fish and all." He put a chunk in his mouth and chewed slowly, pulling out a little bone and flicking it into the fire. "Yeah, like…fish. Plain fish. Not bad."

"Well, at least we know we can survive on coconut and fish as long as we have to."

"Oh shit." Troy put down his shell and pulled out the mirror. "Almost forgot." He flashed the rectangle rhythmically. "Maybe it'll be today. I think it will be." With hot food in his belly, optimism fueled him.

"Maybe." Brian kept his eyes on his meal, going back to work on the shelter when he was finished while Troy continued with the mirror, waiting to spot salvation.

# Chapter Six

BRIAN SWALLOWED HIS mouthful of crab, roasted coconut, breadfruit, and sweet papaya. The latter two they'd discovered growing on trees farther down the beach and ate daily. The crab had been a lucky grab he'd made in the shallows by the reef, and it was a bitch and a half to kill it, crack it, and cook it. Still, it was a welcome change of flavor.

They sat on their flannel blanket near the campfire, watching the sun disappear, leaving a symphony of red and pink streaking across the sky in its wake.

"They're not coming, are they?"

With a sigh, Brian peeked at Troy next to him. Even though they ate well considering they were on a desert island, Troy's ribs were starting to protrude and shadows darkened his eyes. Stubble covered his face, and they were both tanned and dried out from the sun, never mind the saltwater. In two weeks, Troy looked so much older and wearier than the clean-cut young man who'd boarded the plane in Sydney.

Lying wouldn't help anything, so Brian said, "Probably not."

Troy's gaze remained on the horizon, his dinner untouched in its coconut shell, the makeshift seashell spoon still sticking out of the top. His knees were tucked to his chest. "It's been two weeks. And there's…nothing."

"Search and rescue is very difficult," Brian said quietly. "Especially in the ocean. The vastness…" He rubbed at the thickening beard on his face. "It's hard to comprehend."

Not moving, Troy still didn't look at him. He was defeated in a way Brian hadn't seen before. In a way that made his belly churn. He hated that the optimistic light had faded from Troy's eyes.

"We never even see those white trails jets leave behind. I know they'd be too high up to spot us, but it's like…we're at the end of the Earth. Or like we time traveled, and the rest of the world is just…gone."

Brian tried to think of something—anything—comforting. "But we never know when a smaller plane or ship might spot us."

Troy looked like he needed a hug, but would that be too…weird? Brian tried to think of the last time he'd hugged someone and realized with a pang that it was Paula on her birthday, an awkward press and back pat that had only lasted a moment. He'd isolated himself so much that he second-guessed *hugging*, which was pretty pathetic. He toyed with his coconut bowl, pulling off strands of the coarse husk, wishing he knew the right thing to say and do.

"What if they never come?" Troy whispered.

"Then we survive. They'll find us eventually."

Troy looked at him sharply now. "You don't know that. They probably think we're dead. You said that yourself. It's been two weeks. When planes go missing, it's because they crash, right? How often do they find survivors eating coconuts?"

He took a sip of rainwater, his throat dry. "There are crashes with survivors. That does happen." He scratched the back of his neck, the phantom rush of fire prickling his skin.

"But in crashes like *this*? In the middle of the ocean? Middle of nowhere? Does anyone survive?"

"Not usually, but it's not impossible. In 19—"

"Please don't. No history lesson right now."

"Fine. But we're living proof that it's possible. We're here."

"We're *nowhere*! We might as well be on Mars. The rest of the world is gone. Like they forgot about us." Troy nodded at the signaling mirror where it sat on its designated rock, next to the stone they'd been scratching as a calendar. "We keep flashing that fucking thing around, and no one's there. It's pointless."

"It's not. We never know. There could be a ship that we can't see miles away. A plane."

"But they think we're dead. Wouldn't you?" He jabbed his finger toward Brian. "Wouldn't you think we're dead?"

Brian kept his tone even and calm. "Yes. I would. The search has probably been called off. If we crashed in water and somehow survived, we would have drowned or died of thirst and exposure in a matter of days. With a raft, the odds go up, but are still negligible. And the odds of finding land and making it down safely are ridiculously small. Paula flew the hell out of that plane. It's a miracle, really."

Shoulders sinking, Troy visibly deflated, the burst of fury gone. "A miracle. I prayed for it while we were crashing. Begged God to save us. I don't know if anyone's listening." He blew out a puff of air. "Do you believe in God?"

"No."

Staring up at the stars as they blinked into sight, Troy was quiet for a few moments. "We went to Catholic school before we got the show, and church on Christmas and Easter. I never really thought about it. It was routine, saying the hail Marys and all that. But when you do think about it, it all just seems…"

"Unlikely?"

A faint smile tugged on Troy's lips. "Yeah. I'd like to think it's true. That there's a heaven. I don't know."

"You don't need to know. Not tonight, anyway."

"Guess not." He put his bowl next to Brian. "You can finish mine. I know it's early, but I'm going to turn in. Got a headache."

"You should eat first." Brian handed him the bowl back. "The crab tastes good."

Troy was already on his feet. "Not hungry."

"Troy, come on." Brian thrust out the bowl. "We can't fool around with this. We're both down weight, and with the shape you're in, your metabolism is sky high. Those shorts are hanging off you."

"I'm fine. I told you, I have a headache." He turned toward the teepee.

Brian shot to his feet and blocked the way. "So eat half of it at least."

Rolling his eyes, Troy huffed. "Seriously, dude?"

"Seriously. We cannot afford to get sick. We have enough to worry about without willful malnutrition. We need to eat as much as we can every single day. We don't know if the fruit or fish will suddenly dry up. If the nightly rain showers will stop."

Troy stilled. "You think that might happen?"

"I have no idea. I never thought I'd see a cyclone come out of no-where after the rainy season was over. There are no guarantees." He shook the bowl. "So eat."

With a sigh, Troy took it and sat back down with a thud. Holding the seashell, he scooped up the mash of crab and fruits, chewing silently and staring into the fire. Brian sat next to him and crossed his legs before he finished his own dinner.

A few minutes later, Troy showed Brian his empty bowl. "Satisfied? Can I go to bed now?"

Swallowing his last mouthful along with a spike of irritation, Brian nodded. After Troy disappeared inside their shelter, Brian went to add more wood to the signal fire by the SOS. Uncoiling the pocket chainsaw, he sawed through an uprooted small tree they'd dragged out of the jungle.

The heat of the day lingered in the absence of the sun, and in the light of the stars and fire, he sawed out his frustration. Sweat dripped down his neck, his hair dampening as the pile of wood grew.

When the aggravation with Troy's moping faded, a swell of panic ripped through Brian without warning, the thought of how they might die here filling his mind. He stared at the chainsaw in his hands. How easy it would be to cut himself in a lapse of concentration. Their meager medical supplies wouldn't last. The simplest infection in a wound could kill them. Another storm could come, or one of those sea snakes might bite, and it would be curtains.

He counted his breaths until his heart slowed. Troy was right that the rest of the world seemed a lifetime away. Even Paula's death was distant. Brian thought of her family in Auckland and the parents whose names he didn't remember. Even if he could talk to them, what would he say?

Keeping busy, he carried the wood to the shelter they'd constructed just inside the jungle using fronds and their orange rain ponchos to keep the wood as dry as possible. After he finished stacking and covering, Brian returned to their campfire and gazed toward the shelter.

He hated seeing Troy like this, and was very tempted to try talking more with him, even though Troy clearly wanted some space. Looking up at the stars, Brian told himself sternly to let Troy do his own thing. He barely knew the guy, even if it didn't feel that way. Besides, he should be delighted to have some alone time.

Yet as he sat there by the fire, gazing up at the vast expanse of stars and the waxing moon, he didn't feel the emotional release and recharge of his batteries he normally would being alone after spending so much time with someone.

When he was married to Alicia, it had been a bone of contention that he liked taking walks on his own, or curling up with a book for hours in an empty room. She simply hadn't understood why he'd felt the need, and that it wasn't about her at all.

His girlfriend Rebecca had been a bit of an introvert herself, and maybe that had been part of the problem in the end. *Who am I kidding? I was the problem. She tried to help after it happened, and I wouldn't let her. Wouldn't let anyone.*

Looking back, he could see that he'd gone far beyond enjoying some alone time to basically becoming a hermit once he'd fled to Australia. It hadn't been healthy, hiding away in his tiny apartment and only coming out to work. He flew enough to get by and supplement the generous severance the airline had given for signing a piece of paper promising not to sue.

Leaning back on his elbows, Brian yearned for his Kindle and the escape to another life, another world. But all he could do was worry about Troy.

After another miserable hour, he unzipped the suitcase and uncapped their dozen water bottles, standing them up in the sand. It had rained almost every night, a short downpour that fortunately gave them plenty of drinking water for the time being. They'd found a sad little stream inland but wanted to conserve their water purification tablets.

The deep moat they'd dug around the teepee so their shelter was on higher ground had so far kept them mostly dry, as had the thick orange emergency blanket on top of the structure. Stepping over the moat, Brian stooped and edged through the narrow door.

When he kicked off his cargo shorts and crawled under the mosquito net in his boxers, Troy was curled away from him on his side, unmoving. Pretending to be asleep, since Brian knew that when he slept, Troy breathed deeply with quiet little moans when he shifted. Utter stillness and silence wasn't his MO.

Brian bit back the urge to ask if he was okay. Clearly he wasn't. They were trapped on a desert island. Their future was entirely uncertain. Precarious.

*Life is never certain.*

As memories tore through him, Brian swore he could smell the acrid smoke, feel the heat of the flames and the painful grip of the firefighters dragging him away. He wondered if it would ever stop. And now there were new images of unrelenting rain and the sick swoop of his stomach as the second engine flamed out. Paula's still-warm flesh in his hand, the rest of her gone.

He pressed his lips together, but a little whimper still escaped. In the silence, he heard Troy move.

"Brian?" Troy's voice was hoarse, but concern was clear. He touched Brian's bare shoulder tentatively, his fingers warm.

Part of Brian wanted to unload everything, the urge to talk about it something he hadn't ever really felt before. The airline had forced him to see a shrink, and he'd hated every second of it. But here with Troy in their ridiculous teepee at the end of the world, the words rose up, prickly on his tongue and hot in his throat.

*No.*

It wasn't fair to Troy to dump all this crap on him. Brian was the pilot. The captain since Paula was gone. He was supposed to be in charge. Strong and confident and in control. He cleared his throat. "Hmm?"

"I thought... Never mind," Troy mumbled, pulling his hand back and rolling away.

They settled into silence, and Brian listened to the distant tide returning, sleep not even on the horizon.

BLINKING IN THE pale light, Brian listened to Troy crawl back in under the mosquito net. Troy was usually up first, slipping out while Brian slept until the island's parrot alarm clock system flapped and honked to life. But this morning, Troy had come back. That was strange.

Brian listened, thinking perhaps it was raining again, but he could only hear the gentle breeze rustling leaves and faint chirping as birds awoke. The rain had come after midnight, and when it ended, he'd gone out to cap the bottles and zip up the suitcase to keep bugs and sand out of their water supply. It had become a routine, and since Troy seemed to wake early, Brian didn't mind being the one to get up in the night.

Maybe Troy was just tired. He'd been upset, so likely hadn't slept well. Brian drifted off again, jolting awake what felt like five minutes later when the damn parrots arrived for breakfast. Glancing at Troy, he was surprised to see him still curled up in the boxers that were his now. It was impossible to sleep through the cacophony, but Brian tugged on his shorts and crawled out, leaving Troy to it for a little while longer as he went to organize the fires.

Wearing his flip-flops, he gave the wood shelter a kick and hopped back, waiting to see if anything scurried out. They were getting low, so he made a mental note to gather and cut more wood. Then he scoffed at himself. It wasn't like there were many other activities taking up his precious time, and he wasn't likely to forget. The constant need for firewood, food, and water kept them occupied, at least.

Brian waited for the sun to come over the jungle. With the magnifying glass at just the right angle, smoke wisped from the fronds, the heat building until ignition. They still had the matches safe in a waterproof tube in the emergency pack. He shivered, thinking about how they'd manage a fire once the wet season unleashed. *It's months away. Like Gran said, don't borrow trouble.*

Smiling, he took a few moments to think of his grandmother and her merry wink and cherry smile, lipstick always in her purse along with orange Tic Tacs. At least she'd gone peacefully years ago and wasn't home thinking he was dead.

He peered at the teepee. Still no movement.

After a trip to the jungle toilet, which made him yearn for the comparative luxury of an outhouse, Brian set about slicing a breadfruit. It was roughly the size of a coconut, but at least he could cut open the bumpy, pale green exterior and then quarter and seed it. Once he had long strips, he put them in a wide rectangular breadfruit tree leaf, which was thick and rubbery and held up well to cooking on the flat rock near the flames.

The breadfruit itself was a rather bland, potatoey affair, and he wished the emergency supplies had included salt and pepper. Fortunately, the papaya added a ton of flavor. He cut one open, sucking the juice from his fingers. Next was burrowing a hole in a coconut to drain the juice into a large clam-style seashell, then cracking the fruit open and scraping out the meat to add to the little stir fry.

As the meal cooked, he waited for Troy to emerge. Rubbing his face, Brian sighed, then grimaced. His scruff was out of control. He hadn't worried about it before—surviving and being rescued had certainly taken priority. Still, he had his straight razor, and he hated the way the beard made his face sweat as the humidity rose along with the sun.

Speaking of rescue, he picked up the signaling mirror and caught the sun's reflection, guiding it to the horizon and sweeping back and forth, back and forth. A signal mirror's reflection could be spotted for miles, so they had to keep trying. What he wouldn't give to hear an engine.

But there was only the ocean, the low, constant thrum of the jungle, and a salty breeze stirring the sand from time to time.

When breakfast was ready, Brian returned to the teepee with a frown and edged inside, kneeling. Troy was still under the net, curled into a ball with his eyes shut. He was too rigid to be asleep.

"Troy? You okay?"

After a few moments, Troy answered, his eyes still closed. "Don't feel well. Just going to sleep for a bit longer."

Brian's heart skipped. "What's the matter?" He shoved the net away and pressed the back of his hand to Troy's forehead the way his grandmother had done to him. Troy didn't feel particularly hot. Brian put his hand to his own forehead, and they seemed about the same. "Is it your stomach? Headache? Maybe you haven't had enough water."

"I'm fine. Really." Troy looked at him now, his gaze utterly defeated. "Just…tired. Do you need my help, or is it okay if I sleep?"

"Of course it's okay." Guilt settled in Brian's empty stomach. "Go ahead and rest."

"Thanks," Troy mumbled, closing his eyes again.

"But I'm bringing you food later this morning, and you're going to eat it."

"Mmm-hmm."

Brian knelt there for another few moments, thinking he should do *something* but having zero idea what. Even though the mosquitoes weren't usually around in the day, he reset the net before crawling outside to make himself useful.

BRIAN WAS THERE again.

Stretched on his back, sweat slick on his skin and silver blanket bunched at his feet, Troy kept his eyes closed and his lips slack, feigning sleep under the net. He wasn't sure if Brian was peeking inside the shelter, or if he was just standing outside, but Troy didn't want to talk. It wasn't that he didn't appreciate the concern, but he just…couldn't.

He'd slept off and on, and obediently sat up to drink water and eat the fruit and fish Brian had brought earlier. It was easier not to argue. It had always been that way—just do what his dad and everyone else told him. And he knew Brian was right—not eating was stupid. But the food sat like stone in his belly.

Fabric rustled, and it sounded like Brian was crawling inside. His voice was low. "Troy? I caught another fish for dinner. Nice big one."

At the hopeful tone of Brian's voice, guilt got the better of Troy, and he cracked his eyes open. Brian sat on his heels outside the net on his side of the shelter, peering down at Troy with a furrowed brow and obvious concern. Troy opened his mouth to answer, but his throat was so dry he could only croak, which launched a coughing fit.

Brian rushed outside and returned with a bottle, lifting aside the net to pass it to him. With what felt like a huge amount of effort, Troy propped himself on his elbow and drank. He hadn't realized how thirsty he'd become. After downing half the bottle and swiping his hand over his mouth, he muttered, "Thanks."

"Do you feel sick? Are you congested?" Brian pressed the back of his hand to Troy's forehead as he had that morning, solid and steady.

"No. Just got a little dehydrated in the heat. I'm fine, really." He guzzled the rest of the water.

"Your head hurts?"

"It's not bad."

Brian took the empty bottle and disappeared outside. It was relatively true that Troy's head didn't feel *that* bad. He'd had migraines that were worse than the constant throb and heaviness that accompanied hiding in bed all day. It was too hot in the teepee without the breeze off the water, but he wanted to stay in his little bubble.

With the bottle refilled, Brian returned. "Drink this one too. We've got plenty. The rain last night filled the suitcase and then some."

"Thanks." Troy drank most of it before settling down again, aware of the weight of Brian's gaze on him. "I'm really not hungry. I'll eat in the morning, okay?"

After a few moments, Brian sighed. "Fine, but drink."

Troy nodded and closed his eyes, listening to Brian leave. He shouldn't have been able to sleep, but soon enough he went under, hoping he wouldn't dream.

A RAINDROP SPLATTERED his nose.

Troy wiped at his face. He wasn't sure what time it was, but likely around midnight. That seemed to be when the rain came, and as before, it was a torrent. Their shelter kept off most of it, but some leaked through the sides and low, narrow doorway.

He'd always liked the sound of rain. Like most people, he supposed. Troy wondered if Brian did, and rolled over to look at him in the gloom, hip aching from being on his side for too long. God, he missed his pillow-top mattress. He scratched at an insect bite on his ankle.

The torrent of rain was so loud he couldn't hear if Brian was sleeping or not since he faced the other way. Brian hadn't tried to get him to eat or come out again, and had silently put a fresh bottle of water by Troy when he came to bed several hours earlier.

*At least I'm stuck here with someone cool.*

"Cool" really wasn't the right word, but he didn't know what was. Listening to the thrumming of the rain and watching Brian's shoulder rise and fall as he breathed, a wave of gratitude struck Troy. He wanted to close the distance between them so he could thank Brian.

But he stayed put. When the rain tapered off as quickly as it had started, Brian sat up.

"I'll go," Troy said quickly.

Brian blinked at him in the dark. "I don't mind."

"I have to piss anyway. You can go back to sleep."

After a few moments, Brian stretched out again. "Okay. Thanks."

Troy crawled out into the wet sand. He had sand stuck to him somewhere twenty-four-seven now, and had almost gotten used to it. The fires were out, the wood still smoking in places. The moat around the teepee was full to the brim, and he'd have to dig it a little deeper in the morning.

Because they really weren't coming.

The cavalry he'd somehow expected to materialize despite the odds hadn't found them. This was actually his life now. Maybe forever. So he'd better dig the moat deeper.

A mystery shriek echoed faintly from the jungle, making him jump. They still hadn't figured out which animal made that noise, which only seemed to come after sunset. He thought of that first endless night in the jungle, crammed together into the crevasse, aching and terrified. How had that been only two weeks ago?

As Troy zipped the suitcase and took the bottle caps out of the front pocket, tears overflowed. He screwed on the caps one by one on the dark beach, the stars and sliver of moon twinkling into view as the rainclouds disappeared. Then he walked down to the water's edge and let the cool tide wash over his ankles, snot in his throat and his lungs hitching as he wept.

He cried for his family and friends who thought he was dead. The need to hug his mother and brother and family tugged at him. God, he had to see them again. Smell his mom's sweet perfume and eat chicken adobo and play video games with Ty and get up on stage for thousands of screaming people. He needed to go home.

Troy gazed at the field of stars and galaxies. Was God watching? Was his dad? He could have been the last person alive, utterly alone. But he glanced back at their camp, reminding himself that Brian was inside their nutty, cobbled-together teepee.

After pissing into the shallow water, Troy took a deep breath and returned across the clumpy sand.

Inside the doorway, they kept the T-shirt Troy had been wearing on the plane, using it as a towel to get the worst of the sand off their feet. Troy brushed the cotton over his arches and between his toes, then shimmied under the net, slapping away a mosquito. He got as comfortable as he could on his stomach, watching the faint outline of Brian's profile a foot away. Brian was on his back, but Troy couldn't tell if his eyes were open.

Troy had the sudden urge to grab the flashlight from its spot by the door to make sure Brian was still breathing, panic suddenly gripping him and shaking mercilessly. But no, Brian was fine. Brian was right there. Troy reached out until he almost touched him.

"I'm sorry," he whispered. "For checking out."

"Don't be." Brian's voice was clear and focused; he hadn't been sleeping.

Troy sighed in relief. "I really thought we'd be rescued."

The white net fluttered in the puff of Brian's exhale. "I know. We can't give up hope. We have to believe we'll be found eventually."

"How long is 'eventually'?" He rubbed his puffy eyes. "That's a dumb question. It's not like you have some crystal ball."

"Not enough room in my carry-on. Sorry."

Somehow, Troy found himself smiling. "S'okay. Left mine at home too."

"We're going to get through this. We'll keep using the signaling mirror and start the big fire every day. Someone will spot us. That boatload of your fans, remember? They're out there."

Soft laughter warmed Troy's chest. "Right. With paparazzi in tow." He traced a finger over the flannel blanket beneath him on his bed of fronds and sand. "You're so much better than a volleyball."

Brian snorted. "Thank you. The feeling's mutual. Maybe Tom Hanks can play me in the movie. Although I guess he's too old and has been there, done that with desert islands."

"Maybe...Ryan Reynolds."

Chuckling, Brian said, "That's extremely generous casting. You can play yourself, naturally."

"Dunno. I think I deserve a better actor than me."

They laughed and threw names back and forth until the silences grew longer and Troy's eyes got heavy. He listened to Brian's breathing even out.

When Troy drifted away, he felt lighter, as if the weight lodged against his ribs had shrunk away to hardly anything, at least for the night.

TROY HAD JUST finished jerking off in the gentle ocean swells when the parrots announced their arrival in a flurry of color and piercing cries. Brian crawled out a minute later, his dark hair standing up. He stretched his arms, then idly scratched his bare chest, boxers low on his hips. He was thinner than he had been, skin darker over his lean muscles.

Watching, Troy wondered if the hair on Brian's pecs would feel any different than his own. It was definitely thicker and there was more of it...

Troy's balls hummed with the aftershocks of orgasm, and as Brian's gaze found his, Troy whipped his hand to the surface of the water, not realizing he'd been touching himself again. Brian smiled widely, waving. Troy waved back with his own smile and burning cheeks. He watched as Brian disappeared into the jungle, presumably to go to the bathroom.

When the sun was up over the trees and they were dressed in their shorts, they went to work on the fires. Troy waited for Brian to ask if he was okay and try to get him to talk. But he only handed Troy two coconuts before wading out near the black rocks at the end of the island with the fishing pole.

Smiling, Troy drained the juice from one and drank it before cracking it. Strange how he didn't mind the taste now. His stomach rumbled as he went to work on the second coconut.

Sitting on one of the flannel blankets, Troy was slicing a breadfruit when Brian returned with two fish. Yawning, Troy scratched his chin. "Man, I practically have an actual beard. It's itchy as freakin' hell. Feels so wrong. I guess we'll have to deal with having sweaty lumberjack beards soon."

As Brian scraped the scales off the fish, he smiled softly. "I have a straight razor, actually. I'll get it out after we eat."

"Seriously?" Troy grinned. "Dude, that's amazing. I need to get this crap off my face. Maybe I'm just not used to it, but I hate it. Never had more than a few days' stubble. Of course I wasn't allowed to in the band, but it was fine with me. This feels like I'm growing a wool blanket. Ugh. Too hot."

When their bellies were full, Brian unzipped a leather container and unfolded a straight razor from its dark, protective wooden handle. He held it almost reverently. "It was my grandfather's." He glanced up. "A running theme, I know. But really it's just the hat and the shaving kit. He was a barber, and he taught me how to use this when I started shaving."

"That's so cool. Can you show me?"

"Of course." He hesitated. "Hard without a mirror, though."

Troy picked up the signaling mirror from its place on a rock. "A little small."

Brian chuckled. "How about I give you a shave first and see how it goes."

While Brian fiddled with something, Troy turned this way and that to get the right angle to flash the emergency mirror along the horizon. They had to keep vigilant. *And maybe I'm wrong. Maybe they'll find us any minute.*

Another voice, dark and greasy, hissed: *No one will ever find you. You're going to die here.*

Huffing, Troy shook his head as if to tumble loose his inner Debbie Downer.

Brian sat back on his heels. "What is it? We don't have to do this if…"

"No, no. I was thinking and getting annoyed with my gloomy self. Not with you."

"If you're sure." Brian pulled out what looked to be half a leather belt from his shaving kit. "Can you hold one end of this?"

Troy took the fancy leather strip. "What is this? Oh, for sharpening?"

"A strop." Pulling it taut, Brian scraped the razor up the leather, flipped his hand, and came back down. He quickly repeated the motion over and over. "Stropping aligns the edge of the blade to make sure you get a clean shave. About fifty or sixty strokes. Sharpening is called honing, and it's done on a whetstone. Only need to do that every few months or so."

"Huh. Cool. This stropping business is quite the operation." Troy watched Brian's arm flying with practiced ease. It was somehow soothing.

Brian smiled, his eyes crinkling at the corners. "It's one of my favorite rituals. Feels good to do it again." He ran his fingers over the leather strop, his gaze loving. "Even though Grandpa taught me this when I was a teenager, I usually used crappy disposable razors and cheap shaving cream. Thought this was old-fashioned. Didn't have time for it, you know? Before my first commercial flight as a pilot, I pulled out this kit he'd given me. I don't really know why. But after that, I started bringing it everywhere." He blinked and shook his head. "Sorry. Don't know why I'm babbling."

"I don't mind." On the contrary, it was reassuring to listen to Brian talk about something with that passion in his voice.

Brian gazed around. "Hmm. Usually I'd shower or use a hot towel. Steam opens the pores and all that. Hold on, I know."

He took one of the empty coconut half shells, filled it with ocean water, and set it at the edge of the fire. Hanging the washcloth over a stick, he held it to the steam when it began to rise.

"Obviously wouldn't normally use saltwater for a shave, but I think the steam should be okay. Close your eyes."

Sitting cross-legged, Troy did as he was told. The warm, damp cloth pressed against his face. "That's nice," he mumbled.

After a minute or so, Brian took the cloth away, and Troy opened his eyes. Brian opened a round wooden container. "Shaving soap," he explained. "You know, I didn't even think of this when we've washed up. Coconut oil variety, because apparently we can't get enough coconut here on…whatever this island is called."

"We should name it. Coconut Island? No, that sucks."

With a snort, Brian poured a splash of rainwater into an empty half shell and stuck in his short shaving brush. "I bet there's a Coconut Island already. Some awful theme resort. Not that I would mind being there now drinking piña coladas." He circled the brush in the container of soap for almost a minute, then patted some fresh water onto Troy's face. "Trying to use as little water as I can. I know we shouldn't waste it on silly things like this."

"It's not silly. I mean, I know it's not, like, *essential* to life, but I am so excited to get this sweaty mess off my face. Island spa day."

Brian smiled. "Do you often have spa days?"

"Yeah, probably more often than most people. Have you ever had a hot stone massage? It's heaven."

"I have not. I'll have to look into that." He frowned. "Hmm. Not sure the best way to do this. In the barber shop, you'd be in one of the chairs and it would be reclined. Maybe lie down?"

Troy stretched out on the blanket, brushing sand away. "This good?"

"Hold on." Brian disappeared into the teepee and returned with one of the flannel blankets. He folded it into a square. "Sit up for a sec?"

Once they were settled, Brian sat cross-legged and Troy stretched out, his head pillowed on the blanket in Brian's lap. He rubbed his heels in the warming sand. Tipping his head back, he could see up Brian's nose.

Brian patted more water on Troy's face. "Ready?"

"Yep." Troy closed his eyes and folded his hands over his stomach.

His hip bones protruded, and he scratched at his belly.

"Tell me if anything's uncomfortable, or if I nick you."

"Mmm-hmm."

Brian's chuckle was low and rumbly. "You're not worried?"

Troy cracked one eye open. "Why would I be worried?"

"Because of this?" He held up the razor, glinting dangerously in the sun.

Troy closed his eye. "I trust you."

Brian didn't say anything, and Troy was about to tell him not to be nervous when the warm facecloth pressed against his cheeks again. "A little more steam," Brian murmured.

Troy could hear him lathering a little more, and when the facecloth was removed, the brush dabbed his cheek. The shaving soap felt thick as Brian spread it over his face, and every so often there was a little splash of water. Brian tapped Troy's cheeks or chin when he wanted him to angle his head, and Troy followed his commands, sighing as he listened to the birds chirp and cicadas—or whatever they were—whine. They let the campfire peter out after breakfast since it was too hot to sit near it otherwise, but he could still smell sweet burning wood as the fire died.

When the blade scraped up his neck, he lifted his chin. Brian's exhales tickled Troy's nose as he shaved him with careful, even strokes. Troy dug his toes into the sand, resisting the urge to moan contentedly. Island spa day was a thing that needed to happen on the regular.

Brian's hands were gentle, one of them on the top of Troy's head, holding him still. They must have made quite a picture, and Troy smiled to himself.

"What?" Brian asked, still scraping the blade evenly.

"Just imagining the headlines if the paps were here to snap this photo."

Brian's low laughter puffed over Troy's face. "Desert island gay shocker!"

"Next Up bad boy in gay love nest!"

"We'd sell a lot of papers." Brian dabbed more soap and water onto

Troy's chin. "This cleft is tricky. Hold really still and stop talking."

He did, content to lay there in peaceful silence as Brian navigated the planes of his face. When Brian was finished, he patted Troy's cheek.

"Smooth as a baby's bottom."

Blinking, Troy sat up, running a hand over his face. "Oh my God, that feels so much better. Thank you." He picked up the wooden bowl of shaving soap. "This stuff is amazing. I wonder if we can make coconut oil? I mean, I know there's other stuff in here, but if we had coconut oil we could fry our food with it."

"Good idea. It'll be our new project." Brian held up the signaling mirror. "Look good?"

Troy could only see snatches of his face in the little mirror, since the signaling circle in the middle was fairly big. "Amazing shave. I feel more like myself again." He patted his head. "Man, the salt and sun and no product is drying out my hair big time. This is going to be a curly mess soon."

"I have a vial of hair oil. Another thing my Grandpa taught me. He swore by it."

"I don't mind, actually. Is that weird? I've had to keep my hair short for years because Ty was the one with curls. The cherubic, innocent boy young girls could feel safe loving."

"Because pseudo bad boys don't have curls."

"Nope. But fuck it. I'm letting my hair get shaggy. Well, unless it starts driving me nuts, in which case you're shaving my head."

Brian chuckled. "Duly noted." He rubbed a hand over his face. "Now to see if I can shave myself. That mirror's too small to be any good."

"I can help if you tell me what to do."

"You sure?"

"I think I can fit you into my schedule if we make it snappy."

Laughing, Brian cleaned the razor with a few drops of fresh water. "How about I shave myself and you can tell me when I've missed a spot. Get you used to the process."

Troy put on mock offense. "You mean you don't want me at your throat with a straight razor when I have no idea what I'm doing? *Rude.*"

With a smile, Brian draped the washcloth on the stick again, the dregs of the fire still enough to set the water in the coconut shell steaming. "I'm funny that way. Okay, first lesson: don't cut yourself or anyone else."

Troy nodded seriously. "I'm so glad you're here to tell me these things."

Laughing, they passed the morning shaving, then fished for lunch. They stoked the signal fire and flashed the mirror, and it was a good day. Troy decided to be in the now and enjoy it.

# Chapter Seven

"I THINK I'LL try fishing on the other end of the island. See if we get anything different over there." Brian picked up the basket he'd woven from breadfruit leaves, along with the stick they used as a fishing pole. His belly was still full with—what else—a coconut, breadfruit, papaya, and fish lunch. He could nap, but the lure of alone time beckoned sweetly.

"Cool. Good idea." Troy took a swig of water and hopped to his feet. He squinted down the beach, holding his hand over his eyes. "We should bring extra water."

Brian's heart sank. He tried to stay casual. "I was thinking I'd just go myself. I'll be back in a couple hours."

"Oh." Troy dropped his hand. "You don't want me to come?"

"It's not that. I just…" He attempted a laugh. "Aren't you sick of me? It's been weeks." Twenty days, to be exact, each one a line scratched into the surface of what he thought of as the time rock. Twenty days of not really being alone for more than the time it took to shit. The exception had been the night and day when Troy had retreated into his shell, but he'd been okay again since, much to Brian's relief.

Their routine of fishing, gathering, wood sawing, and fire building now included shaving every few days to alleviate the boredom and keep their faces cool in the unrelenting heat. The shaving soap went remarkably far, but they'd run out eventually and have to find a substitute, which would be a good project.

And then there was basket weaving. Brian was literally *basket weaving*. He needed to change things up and get some space.

But there was no mistaking the hurt that flickered over Troy's face. "No, I'm not sick of you. But clearly the feeling isn't mutual." He hitched his shoulder in a shrug and was suddenly very interested in cracking open a fresh coconut, even though he had to be full.

*Shit.* "Look, don't take it personally. You could be anyone. I just get a little stir crazy if I can't be alone sometimes."

Troy wouldn't look at him. "No, I get it. Cool." He smiled tightly. "Have fun!"

Guilt and irritation curdled into a sludge in Brian's gut. "Well, you don't have to be passive-aggressive about it." He shoved a bottle of water into the pocket of his cargo shorts and slapped on his hat.

"What?" Troy stared up from where he crouched. "I'm not. Look, I said have fun."

"Somehow I don't think you meant it," Brian snapped. "I told you not to take it personally." Ugh, he was being a dick, but he couldn't seem to stop biting out the words. This was what happened when he didn't get the chance to be alone.

Troy went back to bashing the fruit. "Why would I take it personally that you don't want to be in my presence?"

"It's not about you. I just want to be alone for a little while."

"And I said okay." Troy was still focused on the coconut. "Whatever, dude. Go do your thing."

With effort, Brian bit back his response about not needing permission and stalked off down the hot sand. The soles of his feet were rougher every day, and the uncomfortable burning sensation fueled his stride.

Was it such a sin to want a few hours to himself? He'd kill for a good book. He could spend all day reading and walking and not feel lonely at all. Since rescue certainly didn't appear imminent, he had to start getting time to himself or he'd go nuts. God, he'd certainly be sick of himself, so he had no idea why Troy wasn't.

As he marched along, he sighed. Probably because Troy was an extrovert who generally didn't experience the bone-deep urge to be by himself and recharge the batteries—his temporary retreat the week before notwithstanding. Brian and Alicia had had a variation of this snappish fight a thousand times in their doomed marriage, no matter how much he tried to explain.

Brian's steps faltered, the sand uncomfortably scorching between his toes. He should go back and explain properly. He'd been a jerk. Glancing over his shoulder, he was surprised by how far he'd come. Troy was small by their camp in the distance, and Brian couldn't tell if he was still fiddling with the coconut. He didn't want to hurt Troy's feelings, and telling someone not to take something personally was generally a guarantee that they would get their back up.

Sweat trickled down his spine. It was fine; he'd apologize later, hopefully with some fresh fish in hand. First, he needed to take *himself* in hand. He was unaccountably horny, something he hadn't felt in...wow. Months, probably. He'd always jerked off when he couldn't sleep, but that was routine. This was the first time he'd felt truly pent up in ages. It was high time to get off.

Which meant of course that he couldn't.

Well out of sight near the other end of the island, Brian jerked himself, spitting into his palm and stroking roughly. Imagining two women licking each other's tits and pussies, he got hard. *That's it. That's it...*

He leaned against a palm tree, the bark rough against his back and ass, his legs spread and discarded cargo shorts caught around one ankle. His hat rode up where he restlessly rolled his head back and forth, and he tossed it to the sand.

He wanted this. He *needed* this. *Come on, come on...*

Troy invaded his mind, and Brian's hand faltered. No, he had to stop worrying about their stupid fight and come already. This was way overdue. Closing his eyes, he bit his lip and tried to think of the women again, their breathy moans and—

"Fuck!"

He snapped open his eyes. Why was he thinking about Troy and the flash of his white teeth when he smiled? God, this was exactly why Brian had wanted alone time. He was around Troy so much he couldn't even jerk off without thinking about him.

After another minute of concerted effort, his dick started to chafe. Brian gave up, tension in his limbs and a headache brewing as he tugged his shorts back on, muttering to himself. "Might as well go fish. At least that'll be productive."

A couple hours later, he splashed through the shallows of the retreating tide to avoid the burning sand, head down and hat pulled low. He willed the sun to sink below the horizon and bring some relief. Muscles sore, he plodded on, the pole over his shoulder with the empty basket dangling from it.

He'd caught a few little ones, but realized that they could spoil in the sun before he made it back. It wasn't worth the risk, and the whole endeavor had been pointless. If anything, he was more keyed up than when he left.

Lifting his head, Brian squinted toward their camp. Troy must have been napping or going to the bathroom. He snorted. *Bathroom.* It was ridiculous that he still thought of it that way when they were crapping in holes in the ground. Or maybe Troy was jerking off. Brian hoped he had more success.

After putting the pole and basket in their places, Brian took off his hat and wiped his sweaty brow with his arm. Unzipping the suitcase, he refilled his bottle. They were getting low, so he hoped it rained again that night. The warm water was somehow refreshing as he gulped it down, although he would have killed for the glory of an ice cube or five.

He stuck his head into the teepee. Empty. Whatever Troy was up to, he'd be back soon. Brian eyed the tide. In the meantime, he should catch dinner.

He fished for the next twenty minutes as the afternoon waned, glancing over his shoulder every so often with a frown. He finally snagged a nice big fish and hurried back to the beach. At the edge of the jungle, he squinted. "Troy! Everything okay in there?"

Silence. Well, silence but for the opening strains of the chorus of insects that serenaded them each night. He'd stopped wearing his watch but was pretty sure it was just past six. The sun was on its way to the horizon, a ball of fire that sent pink waves over the few clouds scattered in the sky. It would be dark soon.

Brian's heart thumped dully. He cupped his hands to his mouth. "Troy!"

Only the low hum of insects answered.

"It's fine. I'm sure he's fine." And now Brian was talking to himself. Even if Troy was pissed, he surely wouldn't go exploring the dense expanse of jungle as night fell. They'd avoided exploring too far past the beach for a reason.

Pacing back to the smoldering signal fire, Brian threw on a few fresh logs and prodded until they were ablaze. He hadn't noticed the fire had gotten so low. How long had Troy been gone? The nag of worry swelled, flooding his belly with acid as he stared at the shadowy tangle of the jungle, willing Troy to appear.

The setting sun cast the trees in a fiery glow. Brian found himself at the edge of the trees again. "Troy!"

As his pulse thrummed, he peered down the beach to make sure Troy hadn't come out of the jungle farther down. The sand remained empty.

He was alone.

"Careful what you wish for," he muttered, grabbing the flashlight from the teepee. The beam was solid and bright, and he'd have to hope the batteries would last.

At the tree line, he paused, listening. The distant crackle of the signal fire joined the insects' harmony. "Troy!" Could he be hiding close by? Trying to prove some point?

No. Troy wouldn't do that. Brian had only known the guy for twenty days, which seemed utterly impossible, but it didn't seem like something Troy would do. Not given how dangerous it could be in the jungle at night. And how frankly terrifying. The fact that Troy hadn't taken the flashlight indicated he hadn't planned to be in the jungle this long.

Brian's mind raced. Could Troy have gone the other way around the island and be on the opposite side? No, the cliff face and treacherous rocks made passing around this end treacherous unless you swam and—

He inhaled sharply, whirling around to face the placid, retreating water, panic rising like a ringing in his ears. Had Troy gone swimming? What if he'd drowned? *Oh God, please let him be okay. Please, please, please.*

Brian's calves ached as he ran through the sand. In the fading light of sunset, he scanned the ocean's surface. Would a body float? Would it already be gone out to sea on some current? Eaten? What if Troy had gone too far?

His chest heaving, he spun back to face the jungle. There was no sign of Troy anywhere. There was no way to know. But if Troy was in the jungle, Brian could look there. He could at least *do* something.

Sand flying, he rushed back to camp and filled his water bottle before jamming it in his pocket and squinting for his flip-flops at the door of the tent.

*Flip-flops.*

They were missing. Troy had them, which meant he surely went into the jungle. Relief that he wasn't lost in the ocean surged through Brian. *Okay, this is something. This is good.* He tugged on socks and laced up his black leather shoes, swearing as he struggled with the bow. Then he shrugged into his tank top, since it would at least provide some protection from creeping branches.

*Get him. Now. Find him.*

"Troy!" Brian's shout was swallowed by the humid maw of the jungle as he shoved dense foliage aside. The beam of the flashlight only penetrated a few feet. He pushed on, heading first for the little cave where they'd ridden out the storm. It was against the cliff on his left, so he'd search systematically.

It was empty, of course. Keeping the beam on the ground, Brian started toward the right before jerking to a halt. How deep should he go? He and Troy hadn't explored much of the jungle after finding the stream, since it seemed likely full of things that wanted to bite, scratch, trip, and otherwise harm them.

He'd guessed the width of the island was a mile, give or take, which didn't sound like much to navigate until you were in a pitch-black jungle with leaves and branches brushing you, surrounded by the heartbeat of crawling, slithering, flying, living things, musky earth filling the air.

*"Troy!"*

Deciding Troy likely wouldn't have gone too deep, Brian started south, swatting at a vine and trying to ignore the chirps and squawks and periodic rustling. He was profoundly grateful for his solid shoes.

The minutes ticked by, and Brian's stomach churned. Even with the heat of the day dissipating, sweat dripped into his eyes and collected in the small of his back. Troy was okay. He'd find him. Maybe he was worrying for nothing. Troy was a grownup, and he could take care of himself. He was probably back at the beach already, wondering where Brian was. Maybe Brian should return and wait so they didn't miss each other. Maybe he was overreacting.

He stopped and listened. A creature hooted, and blood rushed in his ears. No, something was wrong. He had to find him. *Now.*

The prospect of being alone on the island sent a tremor through Brian as he pushed on through the black. But more than the terror of being truly alone was the thought that Troy was hurt—or worse. Circumstance might have thrown them together, but they were a team. Brian hadn't realized how isolated he'd made himself in Australia. How much he'd missed having a *friend.*

His chest tightened unbearably to think that something had happened. Shit, he should have sucked it up and stayed at camp, and now they'd be sitting around the fire like usual, talking about…what did they usually talk about? Brian didn't even know. Nothing. Everything.

Usually Troy talked and he listened, and God, he'd give anything to do that right now, to hear Troy unconsciously humming as he cracked coconuts, a constant little twinkle of music in the air.

Slapping at mosquitoes, Brian cast the flashlight's beam left and right and all around. "Troy!"

Brian froze in his tracks. Insects whined and something warbled. He listened intently, his mouth dry and heart in his throat. There had been something else...

"Brian!"

*Oh, thank fuck.* With a whoosh, he exhaled and stormed toward Troy's faint voice. "Troy! Where are you?" He stopped again to listen.

"Here!" It was distant, muffled by the damn trees and vines and endless suffocating green.

"Keep talking! I'm coming."

He tripped over something and almost dropped the flashlight, swearing. Troy's voice was thin and reedy, and he repeated Brian's name in hoarse gasps that didn't seem to grow much louder as Brian tried to zero in on him. Finally the light flashed over Troy collapsed on the jungle floor.

"What happened?" Brian sucked in a breath as he dropped to his knees. He shone the light over Troy, whose face glistened with sweat and what could only be tears. He wore the board shorts and black tank top, his hand twisting in the cotton as he trembled.

"It hurts. I don't know what it was. Stinging in my toe, and then it was burning." He gasped. "It won't stop burning!"

Brian whipped the light down. Troy had one knee pulled up and his right leg extended. As the light reached his foot, Brian's breath caught. "Jesus Christ." The words hissed out before he could stop them.

Troy whimpered. "It's bad."

*Bad* didn't begin to cover it. Troy's foot and ankle were a furious red, swollen at least double their size, the flip-flop looking tiny in comparison. He'd clearly been bitten by something. Brian stared at the horribly inflamed flesh and could only imagine how excruciating it must feel.

He fumbled for the bottle of water. "Drink." Inhaling, Brian remembered his pilot training. *Locate, assess, delegate, perform.* He forced his fingers to calmly unscrew the lid and tip the bottle to Troy's dry lips. "There you go. It's okay. You're going to be okay."

After a few gulps, Troy coughed and shook his head. "Must have been poisonous. We don't have any medicine."

"Did you get a look at it?" Although his heart hammered painfully, Brian kept his voice smooth. *Just like on the flight deck. This is your captain speaking. I'm in control of everything.* Because he had to be the captain now.

He'd located the problem: insect or reptile bite or sting causing massive swelling and pain. His assessment was that Troy was in serious trouble. There was no first officer or flight attendant for delegation, so it was up to him to do it all. It was up to him to fix this.

"I saw a flash of something moving away in the dirt, but I don't know what it was. Could have been anything." Troy squeezed his eyes shut, his nostrils flaring. "It burns. Fuck."

"Let's get back to the beach. You're going to be okay." If it had been a poisonous snake, surely Troy would have been dead by now, bloating in the heat, insects descending...

*Stop!*

Shoving the awful images away, Brian refocused. Troy was still alive. He was there, shivering under Brian's touch. Possible suspects tumbled through Brian's mind. Were there scorpions in the Pacific? He knew they lived in the Aussie outback but had no idea where else. Did they only live in the desert? And there were spiders, of course. Hell, it could have been anything. No point in worrying about it now when there was no answer.

Something tickled his calf, and he slapped at it. They had to get out of the jungle. But would moving Troy make it worse? They couldn't stay here. There wasn't enough water, and something else could come along and bite. Dawn was a lifetime away. He had to get Troy on his feet.

Well, foot.

"Hang on to me. Put all your weight on your left foot, okay?" Crouching, Brian stuck the flashlight in one of his pockets and held Troy beneath his sweaty armpits. "On three. One, two—up!" Brian heaved him to standing, Troy crying out in agony.

Troy sucked in a shaky breath, trembling violently. "So afraid I'd die here by myself. I tried to walk. Couldn't."

Without another thought, Brian wrapped his arms around him. "I've got you. You're okay."

Sobbing, Troy clung to him, his tears soaking Brian's neck. "I'm sorry, I'm sorry."

"Don't be." He concentrated on that even, calming tone. "You're going to be okay." He rubbed Troy's back steadily.

"I can't stop crying." Troy hiccupped.

Troy trembled in his arms, and Brian held him close. "I've got you." He wished he could carry him back to their camp, but didn't think he was strong enough. Gently, Brian eased back.

"Let's get your right arm over my shoulders. Use me as a crutch. That's it. One step at a time."

"Which way?" Troy whimpered and tried another step.

*Shit. Great question.* "Uh…" Brian waved the light around. Jungle. Jungle. Jungle. More jungle. Which way had he come from? It all looked the same now. He should have paid better attention, but once he'd heard Troy's voice, he'd rushed forward without thinking.

Looking up, he switched off the light. Oppressive darkness surrounded them. But wait—he could see the odd star through the tangle of leaves. Using the flashlight, Brian found what he hoped was a good climbing tree before maneuvering Troy to lean against the trunk, wishing there was something he could do to take away Troy's pain.

"Just hold on for a minute. Keep your weight off your foot. I'm going to take a look." He shone the light up into the branches, and no yellow eyes flashed back at him. It was as good an invitation as he was going to get.

The trunk grated at his thighs and hands as he climbed. After hauling himself onto a thick limb, Brian picked his way up until there was enough of a parting in the leaves to see the constellations. He turned his head this way and that until he was sure. *Thank God for the Southern Cross.*

He managed to climb back down without breaking his neck, keeping the flashlight pointed west. "Ready?" He slung his left arm around Troy's back.

"Uh-huh," Troy rasped.

They took a few steps, and Troy cried out sharply.

"Lean on me as much as you can. I'm your crutch, remember?"

Troy gripped Brian more tightly and leaned in, his panted exhalations hot on Brian's ear.

"That's it," Brian soothed. "I've got you."

Step by agonizing step, it seemed like hours before they glimpsed the light sand of the beach beyond the jungle's thick leaves. The water bottle was long empty, and sweat drenched them both. Brian's arms ached— one from pointing the flashlight in the right direction, the other from supporting Troy's bulk. Troy had quietened to sharp breathing and the odd cry of agony.

As they finally reached camp, Brian lowered him as gently as he could to the blanket by their campfire.

"We need water," Brian muttered. His throat was like sandpaper. He quickly filled a bottle and helped Troy drink before finishing off the rest. He'd turned off the flashlight when they reached the sand, the stars bright enough even though the moon had waned. He switched on the light now to examine Troy's foot.

*Jesus.*

The red swelling had spread halfway up his shin. Brian crouched and eased off the flip-flops, the one on the swollen foot barely budging. He finally unwedged it as gently as he could. "It still burns?"

Troy nodded jerkily, his lips pressed together and eyes closed. There was something… Brian reached a finger to Troy's face, swiping it across his chin. He flashed the light up, his heart thumping.

*No, no, no!*

Blood dripped out of Troy's mouth. Was he bleeding internally? Was poison slowly killing him? Brian wasn't entirely successful at keeping his voice calm this time. "Let me see your mouth. Open!" He shone the light inside, half expecting to see a rising tide of red in Troy's throat. But it looked normal, so what...

Aiming the light at Troy's lips, he saw the torn flesh. "Stop that!" He squeezed Troy's arm. "Stop biting your lip. Let it out."

Breathing hard, Troy gritted his teeth. "But..."

"Scream! Here, you want me to scream with you?" Brian tipped back his head and let loose a howl of all the tension and fear strangling him. His throat hurt, but it still felt good to unleash it. He realized after a moment that Troy was shouting along with him, and Brian sat beside him, an arm strong around his shoulders as they screamed into the unblinking night.

"AM I GOING to die?"

Troy's scraped-up, barely whispered question hovered in the dank air of the teepee. At Troy's feet, Brian looked up sharply. "No." He put every ounce of assurance and confidence he had left into his next words. "You're going to be just fine."

Troy only murmured.

The mosquito net brushed Brian's back, stretched to capacity where he crouched, trying to avoid even the slightest touch to Troy's swollen foot. He hoped he wasn't making the wrong choice to elevate it, but when his grandfather's congestive heart failure had caused painful edema in his lower body, elevation had been one of the treatments.

Brian had filled the backpack with coconuts and folded his flannel blanket on top for extra cushioning. His kingdom for a few damn pillows.

"Okay, I'm going to lift your leg. I know it's going to hurt, so scream as loud as you want."

Troy nodded tightly, but only cried out weakly as Brian lifted under his knee, trying to avoid the swollen flesh below. As he got the foot settled, Troy panted, every muscle straining.

Brian asked, "How does that feel? I mean, I know it feels hideously painful. But do you want me to adjust the position of the pack?"

Troy shook his head.

"Drink some more. Here." Brian crawled around and tipped a bottle to Troy's chapped, bloody lips. "Is the Advil helping?"

"A little."

Meaning not at all, Brian suspected. Troy settled back down, closing his eyes and shivering, and Brian wondered if he should cover him. He shook uncontrollably, but his skin burned. For now, no blankets. Brian had rinsed Troy's lower leg with saltwater, which had made him spasm. But hopefully the salt would act as an antibacterial.

Poking through the first aid kit again, Brian sighed. Would it help to bandage it? Or just be incredibly painful? Band-Aids, gauze, and tweezers weren't any help. He thought he could see two puncture wounds on Troy's big toe, but it was so swollen it was hard to tell. He'd dabbed the toe with iodine anyway.

After Brian got him to drink more, Troy drowsed restlessly, whimpering. Brian had given Troy an antihistamine along with ibuprofen, and there didn't seem to be anything else he could do. When Brian had sprained his ankle years ago, the doctor had told him to follow the RICE guideline: rest, ice, compression, elevation.

But this was a bite or sting. This was poison. Was elevation just helping it spread through Troy's system faster? Brian had never wanted the internet more than in that moment. They were powerless without information and there wasn't a single thing he could do about it.

# Chapter Eight

G OD, IT BURNED.
Troy hadn't known pain like this existed. He wanted to beg Brian to knock him unconscious, but it was so hard to make words. He whimpered pathetically. So hot, but cold at the same time, and as Brian pressed his hand to Troy's head with deep furrows creasing his face, Troy knew being cold wasn't good.

His whole body throbbed, muscles screaming as the burning seemed to spread. He blinked down at his foot, half expecting to see it engulfed in flames.

"Drink," Brian commanded, sounding far away beyond the rushing in Troy's ears. Troy obediently opened his mouth. The water felt good in his parched throat, rinsing the metallic tang of his blood, but the effort to swallow felt enormous.

At least Brian had found him, and he was here in their teepee. He clung to that comfort. He wasn't sure how long he'd sat on the jungle floor, terrified he was dying, the poison spreading with each frantic heartbeat.

*God, please don't let me die.*

The light touch of Brian's hand brushing back Troy's hair sent a fresh shiver through him. He wasn't alone, and for that he was profoundly grateful. Brian's hand disappeared, and Troy moaned softly, suddenly bereft.

*Brian, don't let me die…*

"Drink."

Blinking in the darkness, Troy drifted back and parted his lips. Had he slept? The flickers of fire outside the tent sent shadows and light over Brian's pinched face, and Troy wanted to say everything would be okay. He wouldn't leave him if he could help it. But all he could do was moan.

Brian brushed a hand over Troy's hair again, this time leaving his palm on the crown of Troy's head. As Troy floated away in the flames, he concentrated on the solid sensation of Brian's hand, an anchor holding him there.

"BRI?" TROY PRIED his eyes open. In the gloom, Brian sat at his side under the net, his legs pulled to his chest. His head whipped up from where it had rested on his kneecaps.

"How are you feeling? Drink." Brian leaned over him and pressed the plastic to Troy's lips, slipping a hand under his head.

It was still hard to swallow, his throat too thick and raw, but Troy drank. He managed to ask, "Time?"

Light flared for a moment. "Two-twenty. I'd ask how you feel, but that's a stupid question."

The back of Brian's hand pressed against Troy's forehead, and Brian mumbled something. Troy tried to keep his eyes open. It was too dark to see his foot, which was still propped on the pack. His back ached and he wanted to curl up, but when he moved his leg so much as an inch, fiery needles shot through his body. He had to bite back a scream, and blood tingled on his tongue.

"Hey, hey," Brian said sharply. "Remember what we said? Don't hold it in."

Troy could only nod. Everything hurt, his muscles begging to be in another position. "Need...sit up."

"Okay." Squeezing his arm under Troy's back, Brian heaved him up and shifted around to kneel behind him.

Troy's head swam, the hot and cold sensations battling. He collapsed back against Brian's chest. His foot was a bulking shadow in the soft starlight peeking in through the low doorway. He didn't know a limb could be that swollen. It felt like some foreign thing taking over his body. Tremors rocked him.

"Let's get you out of this." Brian tugged at the hem of Troy's soaked and filthy tank top.

Lifting his arms was a monumental task, but he managed, barely. It did feel good to have the damp material away from him, even though he shivered in the night.

"Shh, it's okay." Brian rubbed Troy's chest, banishing the goosebumps.

Brian was warm wrapped around him, and Troy was so grateful he wanted to cry. At least if he died, he wouldn't be alone.

But then he thought about what it would be like for Brian if he did die. Brian would be left here, and Troy imagined him alone, day after day, night after night. For how long? Months? *Years?* His throat tightened, eyes overflowing.

"I'm sorry," he gasped.

Brian's voice was low in his ear, his breath warm. "For what?"

"I don't want to leave you alone."

"You won't." It was almost a command. "You're going to be just fine. You're not going to leave me, and I'm not going to leave you."

"Shouldn't have gone into the jungle alone. I was pissed. Restless."

Brian's sigh flowed over Troy's cheek. "It's my fault."

Troy wanted to argue that it wasn't, but more words were too hard. He managed to shake his head.

"Let's have a couple more pills. Open up. And a bit of fruit, hmm? Don't want your stomach to get too empty."

Gulping down as much water as he could, Troy swallowed the pills and let the papaya Brian fed him with a shell spoon slip down his throat. Brian settled him on his back again, Troy's foot still propped. Even a breeze against the swollen skin felt like a cheese grater.

All Troy could do was pray for sleep and that he'd wake in the morning.

THE GASP CAUGHT in his dry throat, and Troy coughed, a sound completely dwarfed by the morning fiesta of the parrots. He opened his eyes to see Brian bolted up beside him, his hair standing up. Brian swore under his breath and blinked at Troy.

"How are you feeling?" He rolled onto his knees by Troy's side, leaning over him to peer at his foot.

In the dawn, it was still twice its size and dark red, but the swelling hadn't progressed past his shin. That was good, right? After a moment, Troy realized he hadn't asked aloud. He wanted to, but his mouth was too dry and he only croaked.

Brian was already uncapping a bottle and lifting Troy's head. "Drink up."

When Troy settled back down, he cleared his throat. "Thank you."

Brian pressed the back of his hand to Troy's forehead. "Feel a little cooler. Hopefully the pills are working. Still cold? You're not shivering the way you were."

His brain muzzy, Troy pondered it. "Little better. Not so cold, and the burning isn't as bad. Had weird dreams."

"I bet." Brian eyed Troy's foot and winced. "I can only imagine how awful it is."

He echoed back Brian's words from after the crash. "Doesn't tickle." Stretching his arms over his head, Troy brushed the mosquito net. "So stiff."

"I know. Do you have to go to the bathroom?"

Amid all the pain, he realized there was indeed pressure on his bladder. "Yeah. Just piss."

"I could get a bottle?"

"No. Need to move."

Of course it was sheer torture, and poor Brian had to bear his weight as Troy hopped outside. It took some doing to stoop through the door. Troy pissed at the edge of the jungle, leaning into Brian with Brian's arm secure around his bare back.

It was a little weird, whipping out his dick and pissing with another guy right there, but it was Brian. *Last men on earth.* Although Troy knew the rest of the world was still out there beyond the sea, it was unreachable. He swelled with another pang of gratitude for Brian's steady presence.

Part of Troy wanted to stay outside, but with the sun coming up, he knew the last thing he needed was to burn his swollen foot. He had more pills and settled back down. If Brian hadn't been there, he'd have had to crawl everywhere.

While Brian got fresh wood and started the fire when the sun topped the trees, Troy dozed. His mind still whirled, images and memories vibrating through him. When fear overwhelmed, he concentrated on the sounds of Brian puttering around outside.

He wasn't sure what time it was when Brian's hand rested on his arm. Troy shook off a dream about being on stage and falling down, not able to get back up. The faint whiff of fruit and fish reached his nose. "Hmm?" The day was hot, and sweat dampened his skin, but not as badly as the night before.

Brian peered down at him, a half coconut shell in his hand. "You need to eat protein. I caught a couple fish." Propping Troy up again, Brian knelt behind and awkwardly fed him with the curved shell. "Come on. You need to eat."

Troy tried his best, but a few bites of chewing the fish felt like a trial. "Enough."

"Nope. Choo-choo's coming, open up the tunnel." Brian pressed the shell to Troy's lips.

The little ripple of laughter felt so *good*. Every pore still ached, and the burning throb of his foot overwhelmed, but at least he could still laugh, even just a bit. Troy opened his mouth and chewed.

When he was resting again, Troy reached out and caught Brian's hand. "Did I say thank you?"

Brian smiled, the worried creases in his face smoothing out for a moment. "Yes. Don't worry about anything."

Doing his best, Troy drifted off again.

"ARE YOU SURE that's okay?" Brian frowned and adjusted the pack under Troy's foot. Was it high enough now that Troy was sitting up? Brian wasn't sure. But at least the swelling had gone down. Not to normal yet and the skin was still red, but hopefully that would fade. "Comfortable?"

Teeth flashing, Troy smiled, gazing up at the stars. "It's perfect. Feels amazing to be outside." He inhaled deeply. "It gets so hot in there. Although the past couple days have been damp as hell." He shifted his butt a little, leaning against the rock pile Brian had created for a seat back and padded with his own blanket. "At least the clouds are gone. That was weird, huh? All that rain?"

"Yeah. Guess that's what it's like in the rainy season. Unrelenting." The thought made Brian's belly tighten. They hadn't had any fire the past couple days, and he'd had to weave another few layers of leaves to cover up their wood store. Wet fronds burned okay, but the wood had to be at least partially dry.

But in rainy season, they might barely have enough breaks in the downpour to get the fires lit. How were they going to cook their fish? The fruit would be fine, but raw fish was asking for bacteria. Their supply of medicine was almost depleted. One little silly infection and…

"Brian?"

"Hmm?"

"I asked what you're thinking about. You're all frowny."

"Sorry. I was just thinking that the lean-to is taking longer than I thought," he lied. There was no sense in worrying Troy when he was just getting his health back. Brian glanced at the half-built structure made of logs duct taped together. Three main supporting beams would hold up a roof slanted down to the ground diagonally. "At least the frame's done. I'll start weaving the roof tomorrow."

"Great. I can help."

Brian sat next to Troy on the blanket, crossing his legs and giving the fire a prod with a long stick. The usual mixture of fish, coconut, papaya, and breadfruit smoked on their cooking stone. "No, you rest."

"Dude." Troy leveled a stare at Brian. "I have been resting in that teepee for days. I cannot rest anymore or I'm going to lose my mind. Besides, it hurts way less. I haven't cried once today." He grinned. "Huge improvement."

A smile ghosted over Brian's lips. "Fair enough. I just don't want you to do too much too quickly."

"I think I can weave. Hell, we should start right now."

"After dinner. We've got to fatten up."

Troy rubbed his face, yawning. "Okay. Can you shave me tomorrow too?" He wrinkled his nose. "Jesus, I stink. I don't know how you're sleeping in there with me."

Brian shrugged. "It's fine." Truth was, Troy was rather ripe, but Brian needed to stay close by. Troy seemed to be recovering, but what if he suddenly took a turn? What if he called for Brian, and Brian didn't hear him? What if he wasn't there?

As they ate dinner, they pointed out the constellations they knew and made up names for the ones they didn't. Brian pointed. "That's the humpback of Notre Dame."

"Is he related to the hunchback?"

Brian laughed. "Humpback, hunchback. You know what I mean. And yes, they're cousins. See?" He pointed. "There's another one just to the left."

"Oh yeah! I see it. We need a beauty to go with the beasts." Troy scanned the heavens. "Hmm."

While Troy searched, Brian found himself watching him in the campfire's orange glow. He'd been frighteningly pale the day after the bite, his tan somehow diminished, especially in contrast to the terrifying red of his lower leg. But now Troy looked much more himself again, and Brian could breathe more easily, the awful weight of fear and regret lighter.

Still, the guilt lingered. He swallowed a bite of fish and took a deep breath. "I'm sorry I took off that day."

Troy tore his gaze from the sky with a frown. "It wasn't your fault. I shouldn't have been a baby about it."

"But I shouldn't have gone."

"Why not?"

Brian raised his eyebrows and nodded at Troy's foot. "Because *that* happened."

"I'm the one who chose to go exploring on my own. This could have happened to either of us anytime. It was bad luck."

"But if I'd been with you, you wouldn't have…" *Been so scared.* "Been alone."

Troy sighed and poked at his dinner with his shell spoon. "Look, it sucked sitting there in the jungle, thinking I was going to die and not being able to do anything about it. But I knew you'd come. I just hoped you'd hurry the hell up, and you did. So stop blaming yourself, okay? And if you want to be alone, you can. I shouldn't have taken it as an insult."

"I didn't explain the way I should have."

"Okay. Explain now."

Brian ate another mouthful and toyed with his makeshift spoon. When he swallowed, he said, "I've always been a bit of an introvert."

"Really? You don't seem shy."

"I'm not. It's like, when you're tired and need to get energy, how do you do it? Some people get it from being around others and engaging with them. But I recharge by being alone. Reading, thinking, just…being."

"Right." Troy nodded, seeming to contemplate it. "That makes sense. I don't mind being alone sometimes, but usually someone's always around. That's one of the great things about being in the band. Always someone to hang with. The guys, or the staff. I guess I do prefer it. But you wouldn't want to be alone all the time, would you?"

"No. I think… In Australia, I was alone too much."

Troy watched him. "Is it a different system down there and you had to train again or whatever? Is that why you were the copilot on my flight?"

The tension was immediate, as always. Brian thought he might snap his spoon in two, so he dropped it in his bowl and put it aside. He wasn't hungry anymore. "No, it was… I liked it better as first officer. I didn't want to be in charge." He could feel the weight of Troy's gaze. "I wanted a change. It could be competitive at the big airlines." It was *a* truth, if not *the* truth.

"Hmm. Yeah, I can see that. You wanted a slower pace."

*I didn't want to be responsible when people died.* "Right."

"I think about that sometimes. We've done four albums and five world tours. It never stops. And I know I really shouldn't complain."

Brian smiled. "You're allowed to complain to me. My tell-all's going to focus on much more salacious details. I won't tell the world how ungrateful you are."

Laughing, Troy slapped carelessly at Brian's arm. "Thanks for that."

"But seriously, I can imagine that must be damn tiring after a while."

"Yeah." Troy's smile faded. "I wonder if they kept going without me." He shook his head. "God, I hope Ty's okay. I hate that I'm not there. That I can't find out." He scrubbed at his face. "It was drugs."

"That's why you and your brother fought?"

"Yeah. Why I left. He's been drinking and doing drugs. It started out as a bit of partying, and I told myself it was normal. He's older now, rebelling. Beer and pot were one thing. Coke and heroin… I just can't. I…" He shook his head, nostrils flaring.

"Hell, I don't blame you." Brian shook his head. "That's scary stuff."

"He promised he'd stop, and I told him if he did that shit again, I was out. So when he did, I had to leave. Or else…"

"Or else it would be an empty threat. Seems like drugs and alcohol are hard to avoid in the music industry. Or Hollywood. Addiction's a powerful thing."

Troy regarded him for a moment. "You sound like you know something about it."

Picking at his coconut husk, Brian shrugged. "Only a little. My mother died when I was seven, and I never knew my father. So it was just me and my grandparents. Gran had an accident when I was about nine. Fell off a step ladder trying to change a lightbulb. Nine times out of ten, you'd be bruised and laugh it off. But she broke her back. It was rough."

Troy winced. "God, that would be awful."

"It was. She was laid up for months. But the real problem came after she was supposed to be recovered. She hid it well, but she'd gotten hooked on painkillers. There were some days when I'd come home from school and she'd be on the couch, out cold. I'd eat peanut butter and crackers for dinner, waiting for her to wake up. Grandpa worked late at the barber shop. Of course I should have told him, but I was scared."

"I'm sorry," Troy murmured.

"It's okay. Wow, I haven't thought about this in a long time. Grandpa did figure it out, of course, and Gran knew she had a problem, and she kicked it. She was a determined woman." He picked up his coconut and fiddled with the spoon, scraping the shell around the edges. "I think you did the right thing. Taking a stand."

Brian's approval was comforting. "Even though it brought us here?"

The idea that he might never have met Troy otherwise was suddenly a rock lodged in Brian's esophagus, and he could only nod.

"I just wish I could talk to them. Send a message in a freaking bottle. Go online and find out how they're doing even if I can't talk to them."

"While you're at it, I have a list of all the things on this island I want to google. Starting with whatever bit you. If it was a snake, it must have been a python or constrictor. They can still bite, but it won't kill you."

"I feel like it was too small. There was something there, but it was…maybe a foot long? I don't know." He gingerly rolled his ankle from side to side. "At least it feels a lot less like burning death."

"I'll drink to that." Brian lifted his water bottle and took a swig. "God, I would kill for a cold beer."

"Also, a Big Gulp Coke with ice would be heaven. I miss processed sugar so much." Troy stared at the gentle swells of the ocean. "Okay, I can't take this." He put down his dinner and hoisted his leg off the pack. "I'm too gross. I need a bath. Can you help me?"

"Why don't we wait until tomorrow when it's light?"

"I can't. Please?"

How could Brian look into those big brown eyes and say no? "Okay, let's get you up."

Once Troy was standing on his good leg—keeping his right foot elevated behind him with his knee bent—Brian swore softly. "Shit. Should have taken your shorts off while you were on the ground. Hold on."

Dropping down, he peeled Troy's boxers over his hips. As his hands skimmed Troy's thighs, brushing over the sparse hair there, Brian's groin tightened, making his heart skip.

*What the fuck?*

They'd been naked around each other before, and Brian had seen a thousand other guys over the years in locker rooms. It had never been anything…*weird.*

But kneeling there in the sand, slipping down Troy's underwear with Troy's hand resting on his head for balance, it was…different. A pulse of heat zipped through him, and he was very aware of the sensation of Troy's flesh under his fingers, his thick cock in the periphery of Brian's vision. Brian kept his gaze zeroed in on Troy's knees.

"Okay, right leg first." Brian's voice cracked, and he cleared his throat as he gently lowered the cotton over Troy's swollen ankle and foot. "Can you put a bit of weight on it?"

"I think so." Troy lowered his foot and tentatively leaned on it. He winced, but lifted his left foot enough for Brian to get the boxers off, leaning heavily on Brian's shoulders now. "Will you be my crutch getting down there?"

"Of course." Brian stood gratefully, trying to shake off his body's strange behavior.

"You're coming in, right?" He glanced down at Brian's cargo shorts.

"Right." With Troy still holding onto his shoulder, Brian quickly unzipped his shorts and stepped out of them and his boxers, keeping his gaze on the pale sand.

He wrapped his left arm around Troy, and they slowly made their way to the water's edge. The skin of their bare torsos and hips stuck together damply, and Troy felt so hot against him that Brian wanted to feel his forehead to make sure a fever wasn't returning. But Troy seemed fine, and Brian was being...he didn't even know what. He shook it off. He was tired and stressed. Whatever. It was nothing.

The water was cool, and Brian sighed as his feet sunk into the soft, wet sand. "This was a good idea."

"Hell yes." Troy lowered his bad foot.

"Feel okay?"

"Salt stings a little, but it's not bad. It feels kind of good. After before, this is nothing." He hopped forward. "Okay, let me get down there." When the water was knee-deep, he let go of Brian and did a little attempt at a dive that was more of a belly flop before rolling onto his back.

"Very graceful. I can tell you're a dancer." Brian gave him a quiet golf clap.

Paddling deeper on his back, Troy flipped him the finger. "I can dance. I'm not a *dancer*. There's a difference. Besides, I'd like to see how graceful you look."

Holding out his arms, Brian splatted into the water, trying to splash Troy as much as possible. So of course Troy splashed him back, and they laughed in the dark little waves under the glittering stars. When they tired of it, they floated on their backs, rocking on the gentle swells.

"I think the beauty's there." Troy pointed. "Near the beasts. That little cluster with a trail behind her. You see?"

"Uh-huh." Brian turned his head to look at Troy. He stuck out his arm, but Troy was beyond his grasp. "Don't float too far. You never know about the currents."

"Mmm-hmm." Troy kicked lazily with his good foot, floating back toward him.

Brian reached out, his fingers brushing over Troy's wrist just to make sure.

# Chapter Nine

"FUCK KATE HUDSON, kill Katy Perry, marry Kate Winslet."

Troy grinned. "Me too! Definitely have to marry Winslet. I met her at a thing once, and she was so nice and beautiful. Not that Katy Perry isn't, because she is. But gotta kill someone. Never met Hudson, so maybe I should switch those. Hmm."

Brian laughed. "Well, I don't have the advantage of having met any of them, so I'm glad I got the 'right' answer."

Stretching out his leg, Troy rolled his ankle. The swelling was finally completely gone, and only the odd red patch remained on his skin.

"Feeling okay?" Brian asked. He wove together the strands of two huge palm fronds. The roof of their rudimentary lean-to was almost finished. Troy wondered what else they could build.

"Good as new."

They stayed close to the fire after the sun was long gone, keeping the bugs at bay. Troy's body ached, but in a good way. They'd worked out that morning before the sun was too hot, doing planks and push-ups. After all those days barely able to walk, Troy didn't want to take his body for granted ever again. He'd started with crunches, and now that the pain and swelling was gone from his foot it felt amazing to tone his muscles again.

He ran a hand over his curling hair. The sun and sea dried it out, and he felt as if a fine layer of sand had become part of him from head to toe. At least his face was mostly smooth, Brian having shaved him a couple days before. He smiled to himself as he thought of the rumble of Brian's voice above him, the hot facecloth pressed to his skin, and Brian's gentle hands. Troy loved spa day.

Something scuttled across the beach nearby. *It's not a spider. Nope. Not a spider.*

"It's just a little sand crab thingy."

Blinking at Brian, Troy wondered if he'd spoken aloud. He didn't think he had. "Even if it's not, just tell me it's a sand crab. Always a sand crab."

His cheek dimpling in the light of the flames, Brian picked up a stick and tossed it over the fire. "Deal."

"Dude, you think you can pick me up a Big Mac on your way back tomorrow?"

"Sure. Milkshake too? Fries?"

"Totally." Troy sighed wistfully. "Or maybe a big juicy steak. Remember steak?"

"I do indeed. I'll see what's open tomorrow."

It was dumb—just their silly little joke. Most days, Brian would go on a walk down the beach at some point to get his alone time. They had a strict agreement that neither of them were to venture into the jungle by themselves farther than it took to have a shit. Troy found he didn't mind the time to himself, even though he missed Brian by the time he came back. It filled him with a warm sort of joy to see Brian returning along the white sand, coming into focus with a smile and wave.

When Brian returned, Troy would ask him what he'd picked up. Some days it was McDonald's, or tacos, or a nice Italian meal of pasta and sourdough. Then they'd eat their fish and fruit and pretend.

They'd brushed their teeth after dinner, taking turns with Brian's toothbrush as usual. The toothpaste was gone, and Troy missed the little burst of mint so much. Sometimes he wondered if perhaps there were different fruits growing in the jungle that could give their food a new flavor, but the thought of going back in there made his heart thump. No, he was happy staying on the beach.

As they sat in comfortable silence, Troy stared up at what he was pretty sure was Orion, a million years away beyond the fire's glow. "You know, it's weird, but…"

"What?" Brian asked quietly.

"Part of me likes being here." He quickly added, "Not that I want to stay forever, obviously. But it's so nice to just…be. Not a little sheep herded around by our agent and manager, and 'people.' I know it's cliché, but there was always someone telling me to do something, or wanting something from me. Even when we had vacations, it took a lot of careful planning to find places where I could have even a bit of privacy. I couldn't just up and go wherever I wanted. Always someone watching. Knowing every person with a cell phone—so, you know, *everyone*—could be taking your picture. To be able to walk around here bare-ass naked with my dick hanging out and not end up all over the internet like Justin Bieber is liberating."

"My tell-all is really going to suffer from the lack of desert island dick pics." Brian's teasing smile faded. "Seriously, though, I don't know how you didn't go crazy."

Troy tossed a hunk of wood on the fire in a shower of sparks. "Yeah, sometimes it really sucked. But I will stop douche whining now about a job that paid me millions and gave me loyal fans."

"You're not a douche." Brian reached out and squeezed Troy's arm, his fingers trailing down before falling away, leaving a shiver in their wake. Troy inched closer to the fire.

"I have no idea what kind of life I'd have if my dad had been some-one different. If we hadn't gotten the TV show. It's weird to think about."

"The road not taken and all that."

"Yeah. Here, I like being able to…" Troy waved his hand around.

"Do what you want for a change?"

"It's not that I don't enjoy singing and dancing and all that. I do. It's fun."

"But?"

He thought of his old guitar, its hollow weight comforting on his leg, the strings putting calluses on his fingers. Troy shook his head. "I don't know. I probably shouldn't attempt any deep thoughts."

"Weren't you the brainy one?"

"No, no, the bad boy." He gave Brian an exaggerated scowl. "Older and dangerous, mysterious and close-lipped. Lock up your daughters."

"Ah. Yes, you're *very* wild. Especially with that hair."

"Shut up." Troy patted down his growing curls and flicked sand in Brian's direction.

Brian flicked some back. "Well, you know what I think?"

Troy waited with a raised eyebrow, realizing he really, really wanted to know.

"You're tired. You've been working nonstop since you were what, twelve?"

"Fourteen, but yeah. I guess I have. First the TV show, and then the band. I kind of love that here, my job is collecting fruit and cutting firewood with a pocket chainsaw."

"We're like those crazy doomsday preppers, living off the grid."

"Minus the collection of machine guns."

Brian leaned back on his elbows, his gaze on the swath of stars. The firelight played over the dark hair across his pecs and around his nipples.

Brian said, "Although a gun might come in handy so we could hunt and not just gather. I'll give the preppers that. But I guess there's nothing to shoot here. Wouldn't want to get lead in our fish."

"Nothing we know of." Troy glanced at the hulking shadow of the jungle. "We'd have seen or heard it by now if there was some-thing...huntable, right?"

"Definitely. These islands are too small. It's just birds and insects and reptiles we don't want to think about."

"Ugh. The birds, I can handle."

"Except those parrots. I wouldn't mind shooting them most morn-ings."

Troy laughed and poked the fire with a stick, making it crackle. The signal fire still burned a little ways down the beach by their fruitless SOS. *What if they never find us? What if we get sick or hurt again? What if—*

He inhaled deeply and counted to five. They were doing everything they could. They'd get through this. They had to. To think they wouldn't wasn't an option.

"What?" Brian asked.

Troy realized his face was screwed up and his hands in fists. He exhaled and unclenched. "Nothing. Like I was saying, I do appreciate the freedom here. But then I feel guilty, or get scared, or… I don't know. My head's a confusing place."

Brian laughed softly. "Yeah, I know what you mean."

"Did it feel good when you went to live in Australia? When you gave it all up?"

He closed his eyes and swallowed, and Troy watched his Adam's apple bob. The sadness that washed over Brian was like a physical thing, and Troy wished he could take it in his hands and crush it. "It felt…like the only thing I could do. It felt better than before, I guess."

Troy wanted so much to ask about the *before*. As he tried to find the right words, Brian spoke, watching the stars again.

"Would you want to do your own music? Instead of being in the band?"

*Yes.* "The thing is, when I write, it never seems to be the right songs that come out."

Brian looked at him. "What do you mean?"

"It's like…this folky stuff. Songs that are stories in a specific way."

"Like the songs you hum?"

Troy blinked. "I don't hum that often. Do I?"

"All the time." Brian smiled. "I like it. What are the songs about?"

"Oh, nothing. I just scribble, really." He waved a hand dismissively. "I've only written bits and pieces of melodies and hooks, parts of lyrics, stories. Not *real* songs."

"Ah." Brian eyed him skeptically, but thankfully didn't press, as usual. He simply said, "Well, I like folk music."

"Thanks." The memory of coming home to find his guitar gone vibrated through Troy's mind. But why hadn't he bought his own in the years since? He was an adult, and Dad was gone. Who would stop him? Why had he stopped himself? Troy wished he had an answer.

After a silence, Brian said, "It's been six weeks, you know. Forty-two days, to be exact."

"Shit. Has it? So weird. When I think about leaving the hotel and going to the airport, it's like a whole other world and we went back in time. If we ever see a ship, I half expect it to have big white sails and pirates on board."

Brian chuckled. "Yes, with eye patches and wooden legs. And God, *parrots*."

They laughed, and Troy said, "Maybe the domesticated kind aren't as loud as these fuckers." A mosquito whined close by and he waved it away. "Guess we should get to sleep. It's pretty late."

"I'll do the bottles." Brian went about unzipping the suitcase and uncapping the bottles to prop them in the sand, the nightly ritual before the usual rain.

Crawling into the teepee, Troy brushed the sand off his feet with the T-shirt by the door and changed into his boxers. He supposed they could have just gone naked all the time, but changing his shorts was a kind of ritual of its own. He hadn't worn his track pants in ages since they were way too hot.

After he was settled under the net with his emergency blanket around his hips, he closed his eyes and listened to Brian putter.

Sometime later, Brian's sigh filled the teepee in an impatient huff. On his side facing away, Troy kept his eyes closed as he asked, "You okay?"

"Yeah, fine." Brian's voice didn't sound sleepy at all. "Sorry."

Troy rolled onto his other side. There was a foot between them under the netting, and in the fading firelight flickering through the entrance, he could make out Brian on his back with his arm thrown over his eyes. "S'okay. Can't sleep?"

"Nope. Could barely keep my eyes open this afternoon, but now—nothing."

"Yeah. I hate that." Troy's skin was tight from too much sun, and he should probably go piss again.

"If I was home, I'd just—" Brian broke off, snorting out a laugh.

Troy asked playfully, "Jerk one out?"

"Yup." Brian lowered his arm, a smile playing on his lips. "Beat the meat."

A laugh bubbled up from Troy's chest. "Buff the banana."

"Choke the chicken."

"Spank the monkey."

"Audition your hand puppet."

Troy scoured his memory. "Celebrate palm Sunday."

"Oh, that's a good one. How about: ride the mayonnaise surf."

"What?" He laughed. "Never heard that one. Okay…oh, I've got it. Crank the love pump."

Brian's shoulders shook. "Yank your plank."

"Tickle the pickle."

"Shuck your corn."

They were both laughing—more like giggling, because they were apparently twelve. "Visit Rosie Palm and her five sisters."

Brian was silent a few moments. "I've got it! Make the bald man cry."

"Shit, I think I'm out." Troy racked his brain. "Oh! Wrestle the eel. Although here on the island, we might actually have to do that."

"Jesus, let's hope not." Brian chuckled and then sighed again. "Christ, I am so horny."

Relief rushed through Troy. It wasn't just him. "Tell me about it."

"I've tried a few times on my walks, but I can't get off." Brian laughed incredulously. "TMI, I know."

Troy laughed too. "It's fine. I can relate."

"It's like being tired and not being able to sleep. Horny and not able to jack off. The universe is clearly punishing me."

"Dude, I hear you." The thought popped into his head and was out of his mouth before he could stop it. "Want me to try?"

In the silence, Troy's cheeks went super hot, and his chest tightened. What kind of weird-ass thing was that to say? Sure, when he was a kid he and his friends had circle-jerk competitions, and sometimes he and Bobby Scully had given each other a hand, but that was just normal boy stuff. As an adult he'd never considered it.

Troy cleared his throat. "I didn't mean...forget it." He watched Brian, who was staring at the ceiling. "I'm not like, hitting on you."

Brian met Troy's gaze in the murk. "I know. Sorry, I was thinking. Guys in prison, or in the navy... They, you know. Help each other out."

Troy exhaled a bit of the tension keeping him motionless. "Yeah. Or boarding school. Nick—he's in the band—he went to one of those fancy prep schools, and he said guys got off with each other pretty much nonstop. And he's a giant pussy hound. But when there are no girls around..."

"Right." Brian's Adam's apple bobbed. "Probably do us good. Relieve tension."

"Uh-huh. Just jerking. It doesn't have to be..." The word hung unspoken between them.

*Gay.*

"Right," Brian repeated.

They stared at each other. Troy's pulse thrummed, blood rushing in his ears. Were they actually going to do this? But why shouldn't they? Who knew how long it would be until they were rescued? What was the harm in relieving stress?

Brian huffed out a laugh. "This is weird. But I don't think any native girls in hula skirts are showing up anytime soon, so what the hell." With a deep breath, he shifted over and shoved his boxers down his hips. Then he licked his palm and spit into it a few times.

Troy's throat was suddenly dry, his nerves jangling as he pushed down his underwear too. He spit into his hand, and he and Brian faced each other on their sides, still several inches apart. *Just do it.* "Tell me if it's too…whatever." He thrust his hand toward Brian's crotch, grabbing his heavy balls by accident.

With a sharp inhale, Brian seized up. "Buy a lady a drink first," he squeaked out.

Laughter loosened Troy's chest, relaxing him a little. "Sorry." He reached higher for Brian's shaft. As he stroked tentatively, Brian's blissful sigh puffed over Troy's face. He was about to ask if it was okay, but then Brian was taking hold of him, and *oh God.*

Troy bit back a low moan, his teeth gnawing into his lower lip. Brian's hand was warm and wet, and it felt *so freaking amazing* to be touched again by someone else. Sex had been fun over the years—sometimes great and sometimes okay, sometimes meaningful and sometimes not. But he'd somehow forgotten how deep-down good it was to be touched by another person. It was like the first time all over again.

Except unlike Melissa Fahey, Brian knew what he was doing, being a guy and all. They didn't look at each other as they stroked roughly; Brian's eyes were closed, and Troy buried his face in the crook of his arm. He summoned his go-to spank bank image—a blond with great tits going cowgirl on him.

But it was distracting, the whole having-another-guy's-dick-in-his-hand thing. It had been one thing when he was in middle school to mess around, but Brian was very much a man. As Brian's cock got hard, it grew longer, and the head dripped.

He was cut, and Troy swiped over the tip and down the ridge on the underside, thinking about what he liked. His knuckles brushed against Brian's thatch of wiry hair on the down stroke.

They were silent, their labored breathing and the sizzle and pop of the fire outside the only sounds. Troy's belly tightened, his dick rock hard now in Brian's grasp, his foreskin pulled back. He pumped his hips, and Brian didn't seem to mind, increasing the tempo of his jacking.

The only parts of their bodies touching were hands on cocks, and Troy missed the sweaty push and pull of sex, the cries and moans and mutters that would usually fill the air. The open-mouthed kisses that felt as necessary as breathing.

He pressed his lips together harder to stop himself from making noise. *Don't make it weird.* It was just giving each other relief. No different really than first aid. Troy thought about Brian's red nipples, and what they'd feel like in his mouth with chest hair brushing his skin.

His breath stuttered, elbow slippery with sweat where he pressed his face. He rubbed Brian faster, trying to keep his mind clear. Fuck, he needed to come. He ached for it, nearing the edge and searching, searching, his legs trembling. His balls tightened, and he bit his arm, thrusting his hips.

The wave of pleasure soared through him, scorching joy flowing to his toes and back again. He spurted, gasping against the soft skin of his inner arm. Brian jerked him loosely, and Troy rode out the aftershocks, liquid pleasure in every pore.

As it faded, he realized he'd stopped the motion of his hand. "Sorry," he mumbled. Without lifting his head, he refocused on his task. Brian's hand fell away from Troy's spent cock, and Troy used more of Brian's precum for lube as he worked him. He hoped Brian was almost there, because sleep was closing in fast.

Fortunately, Brian shot his load a minute later, splashing Troy's arm and hand. Troy stroked him through the aftershocks, liking the way Brian shuddered, breathing hard. *I did that.* Part of him didn't want to let go—wanted to get Brian hard again. Wanted to make him scream this time.

*Super weird, dude.*

Troy let go and rolled onto his back, tugging up his boxers. Scooting down, he grabbed the sand-removal T-shirt by the door and cleaned himself before wordlessly passing it to Brian. They'd have to do something resembling laundry in the morning.

From the corner of his eye, Troy could see Brian shift to his original position on his back. They didn't say anything, and as their breathing returned to normal, Troy wriggled his butt, finding a good spot in the sand under the blanket and floor of palm fronds. He stared at the ghostly licks of orange in the white netting above.

Brian cleared his throat. "Thanks, man."

"Yeah. You too."

Before long, Brian's deep breathing and the distant waves as the tide returned lulled Troy into the best sleep he'd had in weeks.

# Chapter Ten

KAREN. CHRISTINE? NO, wait—*Kylie*. That was it.

As the parrots honked and hooted and obnoxiously celebrated the dawn of another day, Brian stared at the mosquito net draped above him. Troy was already gone, as usual. What wasn't usual was that they'd *jerked each other off last night.*

Brian had slept marvelously, and after cursing the parrots for waking him, his stomach had flip-flopped—and his groin tightened—as it rushed back to him.

Now he was trying to remember the name of the last woman he'd had sex with. Yes, Kylie. He'd been restless and anxious one night, and had gone to the Rocks by the harbor. Plenty of bars there, and he'd never found it difficult to pick up a woman when he wanted. He was handsome enough, but the American accent did the heavy lifting. Would have been even easier if he'd mentioned being a pilot, but he lied and said he was a copywriter. Far fewer questions that way.

He tried to picture Kylie's face. She'd been blond like Kylie Minogue, and he'd made some comment about a resemblance, which she'd laughed off. Were her eyes blue? Try as he might, she remained a vague blur in his memory. When had that been? He thought back. February, and it was June now. *No wonder I was so pent up.*

He sighed. The truth was, he hadn't been horny much at all the past few years. He jerked off when he couldn't sleep, but it was more out of habit as a sleep aid than because he was actually turned on. But the last couple weeks on the island, the old familiar pull of desire had hummed in his veins.

That was why he'd tried to jerk off more than once when he was by himself down the beach. The truth was he'd had to stop not because he couldn't come, but because...

Brian swallowed hard, reluctant to admit it even to himself. He inhaled and exhaled, shuddering.

It was because he'd thought of Troy.

Of course he'd never intended to talk about his horniness, but in the still of the night, there was something about Troy's presence that lulled him and made him want to spill his secrets. Not that he'd told the *whole* truth. Then Troy had made the suggestion to jerk each other, and Brian couldn't believe his ears.

But it was true, wasn't it? Soldiers and sailors and prisoners and boarding school boys got off with each other when they had to. It didn't mean anything. Stress release. They sure as hell had a buildup of stress.

Brian skimmed his hand down his chest. There was a patch of dried semen on his belly that he'd missed, tightening his skin. He traced it with his fingertips, remembering his powerful orgasm and how incredible it had been to be touched again.

He thought of Troy's thumb teasing the head of his dick. Troy's muffled pants. The only time Brian had touched another guy's cock, he'd been a curious kid exploring with his friend at summer camp, and there hadn't been much to it.

Troy's cock was big and thick, whereas Brian's was longer. The heft of Troy's shaft had filled his hand, hot and throbbing and *alive*. He wondered what it would be like to touch more of him, to feel his body hair and powerful muscles, the edges and planes so different from a woman's soft curves.

Sucking in a sharp breath, Brian realized he was getting hard. Over the years, he'd usually woken with a morning hard-on a few times a week, but not every day. He hadn't this morning, and yet here he was swelling, his belly tightening and balls tingling as he thought about another man.

The urge to reach into his boxers and touch himself overwhelmed, and Brian gripped his shaft, bending his legs and spreading his knees as he stroked—as he imagined it was Troy touching him again. Biting his lip, he muffled his moans, getting off in no time like an untrained teenager.

*What the hell is the matter with me?*

Chest heaving, he scrambled to clean himself with the dirty T-shirt by the door. After tugging on his cargo shorts, he crawled outside with the tee in hand.

Troy waved from where he sawed wood some distance away. Brian concentrated on a normal tone. "Morning!" he called.

"Morning!" Troy answered.

There, that was all nice and normal. The sky was blue, the breeze gentle, and it was another day just like the ones before it. But as Brian splashed into the ocean and scrubbed the cum-stained T-shirt in wet sand, his mind raced. Had he ever been attracted to a man before? Was he *attracted* to Troy now? Or was this just a case of biological need? Of…desert island fever?

He'd admired men's bodies before. The rugby players on TV, or particularly buff guys at the gym. He could imagine how much time and effort went into acquiring six-packs and sculpted quads, and he appreciated their forms. But he'd never been turned on by them before.

"Do you want to go try for some fish?"

Brian whirled around guiltily to find Troy a few feet away. "What? Sorry, you startled me."

Troy smiled, which creased his cheeks and accentuated the cleft in his jaw. "Sorry, dude." He looked at the tee clutched in Brian's hands, and his smile faltered. "Everything okay?"

"Yeah, totally. Laundry day. I'll go fish in a minute."

"I can go if you want."

"Nah, it's okay. I don't mind." He wrung out the T-shirt and went to hang it on the rope laundry line before collecting the fishing gear.

*Everything's fine. Everything's normal. BE NORMAL.* "See you in a bit."

"Cool. I'll get the fires going as soon as I can." Troy picked up the signaling mirror from its rock, flipping it over repeatedly in his hands. "I'll do the mirror too, obviously."

"Great. See ya!" Ugh, that had sounded too fake cheerful.

Brian splashed through the receding tide. "Everything's fine," he muttered. "So we got each other off. It's just lending a friend a hand. Keeping ourselves sane. It doesn't mean anything more than that."

*Are we going to do it again?*

Despite himself, desire coiled in Brian's belly, and his breath caught with *want*. He shook his head and muttered, "It's stress relief. That's all."

Squaring his shoulders, he marched on, determined not to overthink it.

"Cool breeze tonight, huh?" Troy asked. As the sun disappeared from view, he followed Brian's lead and pulled on his tank top. Grabbing an extra flannel blanket from the teepee for later, he moved closer to the fire and sat.

"Mmm." Brian chewed a hunk of papaya, then licked the juice off his fingers one by one.

As Brian sucked his index finger and released it with a little *pop*, Troy's dick came to life. Brian licked up the length of his next finger, his pink tongue catching every drop. Troy's nostrils flared, and he jerked his gaze away, drawing his knees up.

*Get a grip, dude.*

He'd seen Brian lick his fingers before. Eating papaya was a messy business, and it's not as if they had napkins. If you didn't get your fingers clean, the sand would stick stubbornly. Brian wasn't doing anything they hadn't both done a hundred times.

Yet now that those fingers had touched Troy's cock, memories tumbled through his mind, sending fire through his blood. It had been so good when Brian touched him. What would his tongue feel like?

*Jesus fucking Christ, stop being a total creeper freak!*

But he couldn't stop wondering the same thing he had all day: Were they going to do it again? Would it become a new nighttime ritual along with uncapping water bottles and double checking the cover on the firewood? Quickly and quietly jerking each other off?

Well, why shouldn't it? They were stuck here for God knew how long, and there was nothing wrong with it. It didn't mean anything. Didn't mean they were gay. Not that he had any problem at all with gay people. He was totally LGBTQ friendly. He'd just always dug chicks.

This didn't mean anything.

Troy chanced a look at Brian a few feet away to find him finished with his dessert and staring out to sea. The waves came in stronger than usual to go with the wind.

Maybe Brian was gay and in the closet? It was hard to say. *Would it bother me if he was?* Troy pondered it. No, it really wouldn't. It wouldn't change their situation, and he trusted Brian completely. He supposed being shipwrecked—well, *planewrecked*—had a way of bringing people together.

"Why'd you break up with your last girlfriend?" *Subtle, Troy. Real subtle.*

Brian shifted to sit cross-legged, his eyes on the flames. He toyed idly with the fraying hem of his tank top. "It just wasn't working out. She couldn't... It wasn't her fault. It was me."

*She couldn't... what? Grow a dick because you realized you liked dudes?* "Sorry, it's none of my business."

"No, it's fine." Brian looked at him then. He took a breath as if to speak and then turned back to the fire.

Troy wanted to shake the words loose, but he thought of how Brian never pressed him and bit his tongue. Yet after the silence stretched out too long, he blurted, "Was it after the thing that happened? The thing that made you run away to Australia?"

"I didn't—" Brian broke off, gripping his hands together in his lap. Finally, he nodded.

"I'm sorry. I know you don't want to talk about it."

"It's been a few years since I've had to tell it. It was one of the reasons I moved down there." He smiled humorlessly. "One of the reasons I ran away. So I wouldn't have to talk about it."

Troy flushed. "I didn't mean to—"

"You didn't." Brian looked at him then, his hazel eyes big and expressive and unbearably sad. "I did run away. I ran away from my girlfriend Rebecca, my friends, my life. The survivors."

Troy's gut somersaulted. "Survivors?"

"They're so grateful, you see? It was a miracle we landed. A miracle anyone made it off before..." He closed his eyes briefly, inhaling deeply.

Troy didn't know whether to say anything or not. The fire crackled, and in the lingering caramel light of sunset as darkness pressed in, he waited for him to speak. As the seconds ticked by, Troy thought maybe he wouldn't, but then Brian started talking.

"It was nothing at first. Nothing. A circuit breaker for the toilet blew. I thought to myself, 'That's weird.' I couldn't remember ever seeing that happen before. But I wasn't concerned. Wasn't even nervous. I thought it was probably a malfunction. Nine times out of ten, that's what it is. An incorrect reading, an alarm on the fritz. In this case, I figured someone had flushed too many paper towels or something. Jammed up the mechanism. We decided to give it a few minutes before turning it back on. My first officer..." Brian swallowed thickly, his voice going hoarse. "Richard." He cleared his throat. "Rich was looking it up in the manual when the smoke alarm in the bathroom went off."

*Oh, Jesus.* Troy breathed shallowly as he waited.

"One of the flight attendants went to check it, and smoke was already coming into the cabin. No visible flames; it was behind the wall. I called ATC right away. Didn't want to risk it. Declared an emergency." He poked at the fire, sending a cascade of sparks into the dusk. "I was the captain, so I took control—said 'My aircraft,' and Rich replied back,

'Your aircraft.' That was the protocol." He closed his eyes for a moment. "I can still hear him say it. *Your aircraft.'* And it was. I was responsible for it all."

Troy wanted to say that whatever had happened, it wasn't his fault even if he was in charge, but he had to let Brian tell it in his own time.

"There were alarms going off all over the place. Rich and I put on our masks and went through our checklist." He smiled faintly. "We called them our Vader masks. We could breathe, but it was a different story in the cabin."

"But everyone had the little yellow masks, didn't they?" Troy had never actually seen them drop down from the ceiling, but he'd idly read the safety card on planes a million times.

"Can't deploy oxygen in a fire. Those are just for a loss of pressurization. Our masks in the cockpit have a separate oxygen source."

"Oh. Right. Wow, I guess I never thought about it. Oxygen and fire don't mix." Troy dug his toes into the warm sand near the edge of the fire pit, flexing and curling, flexing and curling. Acid whirled in his belly.

Brian's faint, humorless smile was haunted. "No. They don't." He stared into nothing, as if his mind was somewhere else even though he was talking. "The nearest runway was too far. The fire behind the bathroom burned through the cables. Our electrical systems failed. It's like dominoes." He flicked with his finger. "One goes, and they all follow. We're left with only the most basic controls. Like you're suddenly flying a WWII bomber but it's sixty tons. We were lucky. Weren't at capacity that day."

A memory flickered through Troy's mind—flopped on the couch in another anonymous hotel room with *Dateline* or something playing. "Wait, you landed in the field! Jesus, that was *you*? You were a hero."

Brian hung his head, wincing as if he was in physical pain. Troy reached toward him, but let his hand fall. He waited.

Head still down, Brian gritted out, "Yes, managed to bring it down in a farmer's field. Landed safely. Stopped safely."

"Well... That's good, right?" Troy tried desperately to remember what else had happened. He knew some people got killed, but couldn't recall the details.

Lifting his head, Brian stared into the night, his fists clenched. "Rich went back to assist with evac right away. Barely stopped before he was gone. Could hear the flight attendants opening the doors, getting people down the chutes. I couldn't move. Had to unbuckle, and I couldn't."

"You were hurt?"

He shook his head. "Exhausted. The level of exertion to keep the plane under control was so much. Took every ounce of concentration and strength. I was barely conscious."

"Superman!" Troy lowered his voice at Brian's wince. "That's what they called you in the press. They said it was next to impossible, what you did."

"I knew I had to get back there and help, but I couldn't. I should have gotten us on the ground faster."

"Brian, it's freaking amazing you were able to land at all."

He breathed shallowly, so distant now, lost in his memories and guilt. "Still should have done better."

Troy kept his voice low. "What went wrong?"

Rubbing his face, Brian shook his head. "I can't. Please."

Troy wanted to give in and stop asking. It hurt seeing Brian tremble, his whole body shivering despite the campfire close by. But he had to get this out. Troy shifted closer and wrapped his arm around Brian's back, needing to touch him.

After sucking in a breath, totally rigid, Brian collapsed against him, the sharp weight of his head finding Troy's shoulder. He was silent for a few ragged breaths.

"When the electrical systems and power go, everything is manual. APU failed too. We still had the engines, but no control." Brian's voice was muffled against Troy's shoulder, the warm moisture of his breath brushing Troy's bare arm.

Troy didn't know what an APU was, but didn't ask since it didn't matter.

"The stabilizer on the tail was set for a cruising altitude. Locked in place, and I had to manually override it. Push against the pressure. God, it was so heavy. Whole body was shaking—burning. It felt like...like I was holding up the weight of the plane myself."

His heart thumping, Troy gently rubbed Brian's arm. "Was the fire spreading?"

"In the body of the plane," he whispered. "Aft. Near the back. The top of the cabin was filling with smoke, and they could smell burning plastic. The flight attendants had everyone breathing through wet seat covers. It was all they could do. Smoke spread into the cockpit. I could barely see out the windshield. ATC gave coordinates for the closest airport, but it was too far. Told them we were coming down. We were over farmland, at least. Had to minimize casualties on the ground."

Troy rubbed Brian's arm steadily. "And you did. You landed in the field."

"Thought we were going to catch a wing and cartwheel. Break apart. But it wasn't over, even when we stopped."

More images from the TV report he'd seen flickered through Troy's mind, details coming back to him: red fire trucks, white foam, orange flames. Black smoke filling the clear sky. "So you were alone in the cockpit. You couldn't move."

"I managed to get the seatbelt off. My mask. Felt like I was miles underwater, like the air was heavy. Then I heard the flashover ignite." He curled into Troy, his knees to his chest, seeming smaller than he was. "Felt the force of it. The heat rushing toward me."

Troy's throat was dry. "The fire spread."

"The emergency doors had been open for almost a minute. Letting in oxygen."

"You had to jump out the cockpit window." He remembered it now—the image of a man diving out the emergency window to the grass below as flames swept through the plane from the rear.

"Knew I was going to die. Guess there was still a tiny bit of adrenaline left in my system, and it got me out the window."

"Must have hurt, falling all that way."

"Didn't feel it. Just my hand." Brian lifted his right palm. "Didn't even scar. Should have."

Left arm still solid around him, Troy reached for his hand. Fresh tremors ran through Brian, and Troy pressed their palms together, threading their fingers. Maybe it was a weird thing to do, but it felt like the right thing. Brian gripped his hand like a lifeline. "You did everything you could."

He shook his head. "Rich died. Chantal, the head flight attendant. They were getting passengers off. They saved so many. Eighty-six on board. Nineteen didn't make it. Should have been twenty."

*"No."* Troy gripped Brian's hand. God, the thought of him being dead... "No," he repeated. "You did everything you were supposed to. It wasn't your fault. You saved those lives. You're a hero."

Tears dampened Troy's shoulder as a jerky sob escaped Brian. "A hero saves *everyone*. It should have been me who died. Not them. Not Paula either."

Useless guilt slashed through Troy. He pushed it away and focused on Brian. "It wasn't your fault. Do you hear me? It wasn't your fault. The people who survived in that field are alive because of you. You saved them." He clutched Brian's hand. "You saved me. I thank God you're here. It's *not your fault.*"

The sobs flowed freely now. Brian turned into Troy's arms, burying his head, his tears soaking the front of Troy's tank top. Troy held him close, rocking him and murmuring soothing noises as Brian let it out.

The fire was fading, and Troy's back twinged dully, but he didn't move. As Brian finally collapsed, his head in Troy's lap, Troy pulled the extra blanket over him and ran his hand through Brian's thick hair. The waves rolled rhythmically into shore, stars filling the clear sky from the horizon all the way to the end of the world. He caressed Brian, lulling him into what he hoped would be a dreamless sleep.

# Chapter Eleven

**B**RIAN OPENED HIS eyes to the pale hush of earliest dawn, the stars receding as the black sky became gray. The fire had burned down to smoldering embers. It hadn't rained. A cool breeze still wafted over the sand. He wasn't cold, though. His heart skipped, and he held his breath. He wasn't cold because Troy was sleeping right behind him. Because Troy was… Well, there was only one word for it.

Troy was spooning him.

His arm rested heavy over Brian's waist, and the puff of his deep, even breaths warmed the nape of Brian's neck. Brian exhaled, not moving. He told himself he should wriggle free or shove Troy away, but he stayed right where he was, with sand stuck to his cheek and Troy's bulk pressed against him. Practically wrapped around him. Their legs touched, and that should have been weird. It was definitely weird that he was struck with the urge to rub his calf over Troy's shin.

He didn't move.

Blankets were twisted under and around them. They hadn't made it back to the teepee, and a hot flush flowed through Brian as he remembered how he'd wept. His eyes felt puffy and were undoubtedly red. His throat was parched, and even though he'd slept at least six hours, he was sure he could still sleep for days.

Listening to Troy breathe, he waited. Waited for the shame and loathing to press down and grind him into dirt. Yet as the world brightened inch by inch, it didn't come. Brian searched for the self-hatred that had simmered deep inside every day since that flight, sometimes boiling over and sometimes only a flicker when he had something to distract him. But always there. Now, Troy's voice echoed in his mind.

*It wasn't your fault.*

Countless people had told him that countless times. He hadn't believed them. Hadn't *let* himself believe them. But now that he'd told the story again, had said it all out loud, his lungs seemed to expand a few more inches. He'd…he'd done everything he could. He truly had.

Brian had hated that they called him "Superman." In the dawn of another day he was lucky enough to see, he knew he wasn't superhuman. But he'd done his absolute best, used every bit of strength he had.

The airline shrink had asked him to come up with another scenario in which he'd done things differently, and how it would have affected the outcome. Brian had refused to answer, retreating into himself, stuck in a mire of self-pity and loathing, PTSD and guilt. He'd quit not long after, stopped answering his friends' calls. Ran away to the other side of the world.

Listening to Troy's soft breathing, feeling the whisper of it across his neck, Brian took a deep breath and ran through the scenarios.

He'd declared an emergency almost right away, so unless he'd psychically known a fire would start, there was nothing he could have done differently there. Once they knew there was a fire, the airport was too far away. If he'd landed earlier, they would have hit the sprawl of a suburb. Not flat enough and too many buildings. Plane would break up, probably explode. Substantial casualties on the ground.

As he spun out the different options, he came back over and over to doing exactly what he'd done. After sucking in a breath, Brian blew it out in a low whistle. It had been the only way.

He ran his fingers through the fine sand and ran scenarios for the flight with Paula—the flight that had landed him and Troy in their predicament. The result was the same: they were going down, and it was either into the water or on the beach. If he'd been in Paula's seat, he'd be dead. It was luck of the draw.

He waited for the guilt to pulverize him, but…it didn't. There was only grief for his friend and the people he hadn't been able to save in that field. He knew it would always be there, but now it didn't crush his lungs and make him want to vomit.

Behind him, Troy mumbled and shifted. He moved closer, holding Brian tighter and sending his pulse skyrocketing. *Was Troy hard?*

Then Troy jerked awake and scuttled back, sitting up. "Um, hey." He rubbed his face and glanced around. "It's early."

Brian sat up too. "Thirsty?" He stretched his stiff limbs and shuffled over to unzip the suitcase and fill a couple of bottles. The water level was getting low, and he hoped it would rain soon.

They went about their morning business in silence—pissing, drinking, and stacking wood and fronds to burn once the sun came up high enough to start the fires with the magnifying glass. It would be at least half an hour, if not more.

As Troy drained a coconut, Brian said, "I'm sorry about all that." From the corner of his eye, he could see Troy look at him, but kept his gaze on the campfire he was building.

"Dude, don't be sorry. You have nothing to be sorry for."

"Well, I'm not usually so…" He waved his hand around. "Weepy."

"Um, do you remember how I was hysterical after that bite?"

"But—"

"But *nothing*. You don't have anything to apologize for."

Brian got the nerve to meet Troy's steady gaze. "You don't…think I'm pathetic?"

Troy screwed up his face. "Why the fuck would I think that? I meant what I said—you're a hero. You're brave."

"Brave?" Brian snorted. "Remember the part where I quit my life and ran away?"

"Survivor's guilt is a hell of a thing. It's completely understandable."

"But…"

"You're not going to win this debate." Troy shook his head. "Nope.

Sorry not sorry."

Brian had to smile, and he exhaled a long breath. "Then I guess I should stop fighting."

"You should. Because the only person you're fighting is yourself."

"You know, a shrink said that to me once."

Troy frowned. "I was wondering about that. Didn't the airline put you in therapy?"

"Oh, yes. Lots and lots of it. But when I quit and moved to Sydney, I never talked about it again. You're the first person I've told. And…" He sliced through a papaya, scraping out the seeds into an empty coconut shell to roast later.

"What?" Troy asked softly.

"Everyone knew what had happened. Telling it to you…I don't know why, but I think it helped. Like it was jammed in there." He inhaled deeply. "Feels better now. Looser."

"I'm glad. And I meant it—none of it was your fault. I'm amazed you could set foot on a plane again after that."

"That never bothered me for some reason." He smiled ruefully. "Figured I'd had my one, you know? The odds of another accident were so astronomical. There are a hundred thousand commercial airline flights a day. Plus cargo and private planes. It really is the safest form of travel. I'm just cursed, apparently."

"Wow. That really is bad luck."

"Or I'm being pun—"

"Dude, shut it. Not even as a joke, okay?"

Brian had to smile a little. "Okay."

"So you weren't afraid to fly again, but you wouldn't be captain."

Shaking his head, Brian quartered a breadfruit. "It doesn't make sense, I know. Completely illogical. But I'd loved flying my whole life, and I kept waiting for it to come back. That rush of elation on takeoff, even on the most routine trip. Making flight plans and calculations—I lived for it. I flew as first officer in Australia to keep the pressure off, but deep down, I was waiting to *love* it again. To love doing it the way I still get excited by the science of it."

"I get it. Sometimes you can't go back."

"Working as first officer, it was…fine. Most of the time on the private jets I was a glorified flight attendant anyway. I wasn't in charge, so I could fly without feeling that pressure. Totally illogical, like I said. First officer still has control of the plane sometimes, but it was different not being captain. When I tried after Wisconsin, they put me on a short hop from New York to Philly. I barely made it. Felt like I was suffocating. I quit after that. But I kept hoping something would change. That some switch in my head would be flipped, and it would be like it was before. That *I* could be like before."

"I wish I could do something to help."

"You help by listening. So thank you."

"Of course." Troy smiled, his teeth gleaming and eyes crinkling.

Brian tore his gaze away and concentrated intently on slicing the fruit.

"I know how hard it can be to let shit go." Troy was quiet for a few moments. "Okay, so I mentioned that my dad died, right?"

"You did." Brian had wondered how, but didn't want to ask.

"Well, my brother's not the only one in the family to have a drug problem. Dad overdosed. He was a user all my life. Booze, drugs—anything he could get his hands on. He was surprisingly functional. I think I told you he worked as our manager, me and Tyson's?"

Brian nodded, wishing he could go back in time and protect Troy from the damage his father had clearly inflicted.

Troy's gaze was distant. "He was a force of nature, my dad. A born salesman. He orchestrated the TV show, and then had the big idea for the band. He held auditions and picked the other guys, shopped us to the label after putting a video on YouTube that went viral. I have to hand it to him, he knew what he was doing. The band's done better than any of us dreamed." His shoulders hitched and his voice went hoarse. "I wish he'd lived to see it."

"Here." Brian passed Troy a water bottle, waiting while he downed it.

"Thanks. So, he was pretty much always on something. I could tell by the way he carried himself. Alcohol had him slouching. Coke was standing up straight as an arrow, and once he started heroin, he was flat on his back. He'd lock himself away for hours. Days, even. We were still doing the TV show, pretending nothing was wrong. We never even talked about it ourselves. We pretended it wasn't happening."

"Your mom didn't try to get him cleaned up?"

"Nope. Not that I know of, at least. Stuck her head in the sand and went on like everything was great." He sighed. "It's not because she didn't care, or didn't want him to stop. But this was her American dream, you know? She came over as a nanny and ended up a hairdresser. Living in a five-bedroom house with a pool symbolized so much for her. We visited her village in the Philippines when I was a teenager. She grew up in a hut. Dirt floor, no plumbing. So I can understand why she didn't want to screw up what we had. It's amazing how people can live in denial for a long-ass time."

Brian sure knew about that. He asked, "Does she have any family in the States?"

"Her three sisters she eventually brought over, and their husbands and kids. But she has four brothers in the Philippines and a huge extended family. The money wasn't just supporting us, but practically Mom's whole village. And once our show was a hit and we moved into that new house in the Hollywood Hills, she'd say, 'Look at the Tanners living in Hollywood!' She was so freaking happy."

"A dream come true."

"Yep. Still, it had been one thing when he was drinking—the heavy drugs were a lot harder to ignore. But I would deal with him when he got bad, so it's not her fault."

Brian hesitated, trying to think of the best way to say: *You were a child and she sure as hell should have protected you from it.* "Well...she's your mom and you love her, but she could have done better. You were just a kid."

Troy shrugged, but the tension in his body was obvious. "She did insist that a big chunk of our money be put in trust funds. Made sure Dad couldn't put all of it up his nose or into his veins."

Brian wanted to reach out the way Troy had done the night before, but in the dawn it seemed harder. "That's good."

Troy pulled at a coconut's husk. "It was when we were recording our first album. Mom was volunteering at the hospital, and Dad hadn't shown up to the studio. Some mornings, I had to haul him into the tub and turn on the cold water to get him up. That day, he'd told us to go on ahead. I didn't like my brother seeing Dad when he was using, so I left while Ty was putting down a solo track. There were still good days, and I figured this was just a bad one."

Cringing, Brian waited. He hated that Troy had gone through this. He wished there was some way he could change it.

"He was in a suit. He always wore suits outside the house. It was like...his signature or something. He'd wear a three-piece to a movie. When I was little I thought it was cool, then embarrassing when I was a teenager. By the time I was twenty, I was just happy if he was acting normal." He went quiet.

"You don't have to tell me."

"I know." He looked at Brian. "But I want to. I want you to know." Troy restlessly tossed aside the fruit and picked at one of his nails, fiddling with a ragged edge. "He was on his back on the kitchen floor. Mom had just had it redone in this black and white tile she loved. He'd puked all over himself, and I remember thinking, 'He's gonna be pissed. He loves that paisley tie.' I never once thought... I'd seen him a mess plenty of times. Dragged him to bed, cleaned him up. Made sure Mom and Ty didn't have to deal with it. I thought this was just another time he overdid it."

After a few moments of silence, Brian murmured, "I'm sorry." He did reach out then, but Troy was already on his feet, busying himself with adding more fronds to the campfire they'd light soon.

"I realized he wasn't blinking—he was just staring at the ceiling. His skin was this pale gray, and his leg was twisted under him. I don't know how long I stood there. Too long. Wanting to wake up and have it not be true. But he was already dead, so I guess it didn't matter. I'd never thought it would happen. No matter how fucked up Dad got, he'd always been able to pull himself together. Flash his smile and charm anyone who needed charming. Never thought he'd actually destroy himself."

"I'm so sorry you had to go through that."

"Yeah. Thanks." With a sigh, Troy looked down and met Brian's gaze. "Guess we both have our crap to deal with, huh?"

"I think it's safe to say." Brian itched to hug him, but he got up and tried for a bad joke. "With all this baggage, it's amazing the jet took off at all."

Troy laughed, and something warm and wonderful spread through Brian. "We have island spa day, and clearly we need therapy day too," Troy said. "We'll take turns being the shrink."

"Sounds like a plan." It was strange how Brian's heart beat too fast. "Thank you for listening."

"You too."

"I guess we should hug it out or something." Brian laughed awkwardly.

Troy was already moving. "Totally." He wrapped his arms around Brian and slapped his back.

Brian slapped his in return, but when they should have stepped away from each other...they didn't. Instead, they hung on tightly. It should have been completely weird, but Brian couldn't seem to care.

It felt so *good.*

He breathed deeply, inhaling sweat and sand and Troy's unique scent. He slowly rubbed his hand up and down Troy's back, the ribbed cotton of the tank top soft. With a little exhale, Troy leaned his head down onto Brian's shoulder.

*This isn't normal. What the hell am I doing? Guys don't hug each other like this. We have to stop, or else...*

His hand was at Troy's neck now, playing with the growing curls there seemingly of its own accord.

*Or else what?*

He held his breath as Troy's hand slid down his back to his waist, where his tank top must have bunched up. A shiver ricocheted through Brian as Troy's fingers brushed over his bare skin. Warm and—

The honking chorus of the parrots going to breakfast exploded from the edge of the jungle, and Brian stumbled back, both he and Troy leaping apart. Troy landed on his ass in the sand, and they stared at the bright swarm of parrots on a nearby tree. They both laughed, Troy's full lips curving up.

Brian reached his hand down, ignoring the flare of heat as Troy took it.

On his feet again, Troy brushed off his shorts. "Looks like the tide is coming in. I'm going to fish for our breakfast."

"Cool. I'll…" He waved his hand uselessly. "See you in a while." Brian busied himself with even more firewood. He'd made things awkward enough for one day.

"Sing something."

With a laugh, Troy turned his gaze from a cluster of stars they'd dubbed "Toucan Sam" to Brian. "What? No!"

"Why not?" Brian was stretched out on a blanket next to Troy's, propped lazily on one elbow, facing the fire and prodding it with a stick. Brian's cargo shorts were low on his hips, his bare chest catching the colors of the flames. He poked Troy's knee with his toe. "Come on."

Laughing, Troy slapped his foot away. "No way." Sitting cross-legged, he chewed on roasted papaya seeds.

"But you're a singer! Come on. Entertain me." Brian's low voice rippled with amusement and teasing, and Troy couldn't help but smile to hear it. Brian was lighter, like he'd popped a blister and now the skin was healing over. Troy felt better himself after telling Brian about his dad. And hugging afterward had been... He didn't know the right word.

"Come on," Brian repeated. "You hum all the time. I know you want to sing."

"Only if you sing along."

"Oh no. Trust me, you do *not* want that. Although it would surely scare away any jungle creatures considering a raid on our camp."

"That bad, huh?"

"Worse." Brian tilted his head. "Come on. What are you, shy? You've performed for millions of screaming girls. Will it help if I swoon and cry?"

Troy shook his head, still smiling. "That won't be necessary."

"So you'll do it?" Brian grinned. "We need some entertainment around here." He tipped his head and motioned to the blanket of stars. "We've tapped out our admittedly limited knowledge of constellations. Need to change things up."

*We could jerk each other off again.*

Troy could feel his cheeks flame. All day he'd been thinking about it. He shouldn't have, but after sleeping with Brian in his arms, he wanted to feel him close. Wanted Brian's hand on him. Wanted to touch Brian. Wanted...

His dick swelled, nipples hardening in the still, humid air. Would Brian notice? Even if he did, he wouldn't know that Troy wanted...

*Things I shouldn't even think about.*

He had to get in control. They'd opened up to each other, and Troy had never felt so close to anyone in his whole life. Even Ty or his mom. It was a different sort of closeness with Brian. But that didn't mean he should want anything...inappropriate. It was probably like Stockholm syndrome or something, minus the captivity. He and Brian were bonding, and it was clearly confusing him.

He wasn't into dudes. The end.

Troy looked up at Toucan Sam. One of the stars glimmered more brightly, and he imagined it was the bird's eye. "Yeah, change things up.

Although the stars are the one thing on this island I don't get sick of."

"Definitely. Wait!" Brian jerked his gaze back to Troy. "The *one* thing?"

Trying to keep a straight face, Troy shrugged. "Well, I guess there's one other thing I'm not sick of."

"I should hope so," Brian said with an exaggerated drawl.

"Fresh papaya. There's nothing better."

Brian kicked at him playfully, and Troy tossed a handful of sand and said, "Oh wait, I forgot getting to swim in the ocean every day. Okay, three things."

They battled with sand for a few more seconds, their laughter filling the night. With a huff and toss of his thick hair that was getting shaggy over his ears, Brian leaned back on his elbow again, giving Troy's hip a final poke with his toe. "You have to sing now that you've hurt my feelings so cruelly."

"I guess I do." Troy still sat cross-legged on his blanket, and he wriggled his butt into the sand, lifting up straighter from his waist and clearing his throat. It was totally dumb, but his chest tightened and he tapped his fingers against his knees nervously. "Um, which song?"

"I dunno. Anything."

He ran through Next Up's catalog in his head. Would Brian like any of those? They were kind of generic, but what the hell. Troy took a sip of water from his battered bottle and closed his eyes. "Angels Everyday" was an up-tempo piece. He launched into the first verse, and God, his voice was out of practice.

The song was basically about nice people doing nice things, and man, it was super lame now that he sang it acoustically and paid more attention to the words he'd heard a zillion times, wondering what Brian would think of them.

He kept his eyes closed, feeling the heat of Brian's gaze on his face, and really, really wanting to stop. But he plowed on through the lilting chorus and second verse, doing the bridge and then cutting the final chorus short. The last note faded away, and he swallowed hard, waiting for the derision surely coming.

"That was lovely."

Troy peeked over, but Brian wasn't smirking. He was still stretched out, regarding Troy seriously. "Really?" Troy asked. "I'm super pitchy."

"I don't think so. Not that I'm an expert, but you sound terrific. You really do have a great voice."

"Eh, it's okay. Serviceable. Ty's voice is way better."

Brian glared. "Would you stop putting yourself down? Sing another one. Please?"

Troy nodded, the tightness in his chest loosening with each verse. By the third song, he'd opened his eyes. He watched the fire, and could see Brian from the corner of his eye, listening intently. Troy's voice was warming up and smoothing out, and joy bubbled through him. He hadn't realized just how much he'd missed it.

Brian applauded at the end of each song and told him how good he was. Even if Brian was only being polite, Troy flushed warm all over. It wasn't thousands of screaming fans, but in a weird way, it was so much better.

He cast about for another song, thinking back to the charity album Next Up had performed on a couple years before. "My Mom loves this one. It's really old, but it's a classic."

"I'm all ears." Brian smiled softly.

The older versions of "Beyond the Sea" were pretty swingy, but Next Up had gone against type and done a slower, pared-down version with only a few instruments. It was romantic and bittersweet, and Troy had loved recording it. He took another swig of water before starting in, keeping his voice low and wistful, a change of pace from the peppier songs.

Flames danced before him as he sang of golden sands and kissing a lost lover past the moon and stars. He spotted movement as Brian sat up, but kept his focus on the lyrics. When he finished the final words, fading out on the last notes, he waited. But there was no applause this time.

*Shit. That must have sucked.*

With a dismissive laugh, he turned to Brian. "I know, that was total-ly lame. I should stick with our pop stuff and leave the classics alone, right?"

Sitting on his blanket, Brian stared at him, the firelight painting his face yellow and orange in the darkness. His lips were parted, and his chest rose and fell faster than usual. Troy frowned. "You okay?"

Brian didn't answer. He shifted closer and went up on his knees, and Troy watched as he reached out a hand. That hand slid against Troy's cheek, Brian's palm hot against his skin. Blood thundered in Troy's ears as Brian's gaze flicked down to his mouth and back to his eyes. Pulse galloping, Troy didn't move—didn't breathe.

Not even as Brian lowered his head and touched their lips together.

As Brian *kissed him.*

Their mouths met, and Brian touched Troy's ear where he held his face. Troy's lungs screamed, his heart beating too hard. They were both frozen, shmushed together, lips pressing. *Kissing. They were kissing.*

Troy's nostrils flared and he pulled back, opening his mouth to suck in a breath. He tingled all over, birds flapping at his ribcage as he met Brian's wide eyes. Brian still held Troy's cheek, gently stroking with his thumb.

"I don't... I'm sorry," Brian croaked. But he didn't let go.

*What are we doing? We can't do this!*

Another voice rose from a whisper to a shout that filled Troy's mind: *Why not? I want this.*

Breathing shallowly, he closed the few inches between their mouths to lick across Brian's lower lip.

If they had been frozen into timid stone before, now they shattered and broke free, tongues meeting. In a frantic haze, they clutched at each other, kissing and groaning. Troy's head whirled, desire burning through him as blood rushed to his dick. He tugged, and Brian pushed him back onto the blanket, sand flying.

A moan tore from Troy's throat, and this time he didn't try to muffle it. Brian was heavy on top of him, his chest hair rubbing roughly against Troy's nipples, and it was *so fucking good.*

He gripped Brian to him, torn between the feel of Brian's chest against his own and wanting to explore it with his hands and mouth. Troy spread his legs, and the way their hips fit felt completely natural.

Completely right.

Rutting together, their teeth bashed as they tried to kiss, licking into each other's mouths desperately, stubble rasping. They tore at their shorts, but couldn't seem to stop touching long enough to get them off. Troy was so turned on he knew he'd blow his load soon, and he didn't care as long as he could kiss and taste and run his hands over Brian's skin.

Jerking his hips up, he shoved his hands under Brian's boxers and gripped his ass, urging him on. Grunting, Brian fucked against him, his hot breath on Troy's face as their kisses got even messier.

Their cocks were out of their shorts, straining and leaking, and the sensation of Brian's dick rubbing against his was the hottest thing Troy had ever experienced.

He'd never needed to come so badly in his life. There was a seashell jammed into his back beneath the blanket, but all that mattered was Brian kissing him and covering him with his weight.

"Brian," he mumbled, digging his fingers into Brian's ass and thrusting up harder.

Gasping, Brian's head shot back, the long line of his neck exposed as he came hot and sticky on Troy's belly. Troy watched, and as he thought about what it would be like to come on Brian's chest, he shuddered with his orgasm, a fiery rush that left him panting and shivery, limbs like jelly.

Brian opened his eyes, and they stared, sticky and slick, glued together from hips to rising and falling chests.

*Oh fuck. What did we just do?*

Troy knew he should have been horrified. He was supposed to be…wasn't he? His throat was like sandpaper, and he swallowed thickly, trying to think of a single thing to say other than *stay* and *please.*

His mouth open, breath coming hard, Brian pushed up to his knees, and Troy whimpered at the loss of contact. He snatched his hands off Brian's ass, waiting for Brian to leap up and leave.

But a moment later, Brian stretched over him again, pulling the other sandy blanket high around them. It blocked the fire's glow, and in the secret shadows, their lips met once more.

# Chapter Twelve

HERE WAS SAND in his ear.

Blinking into the first rays of morning, Brian stuck in his pinkie to dislodge what he could. He was flat on his back, the sky a pale, watery blue that would deepen as the sun continued its journey. Or the Earth, he supposed. Either way, there wasn't a cloud to be seen.

Another day in paradise.

He forced his lungs to expand and turned his head to the right. Troy had spooned him for part of the night, and then they'd separated in sleep, and Troy was on his side facing away. Freckles danced across his shoulder blades, and Brian fisted his hand to keep from reaching out.

The blanket that was tangled around Brian's thighs had slipped down to Troy's waist. Brian assumed Troy's cock was hanging out of his shorts the way his was. He *knew* Troy was also sticky with dried semen.

This was the second night in a row they'd ended up sleeping by the fire and not in their teepee. Insect bites itched near his ankles, and he scratched at a series of red bumps on his arm. And shit, it hadn't rained. A pulse of fear stuttered his heart. They'd have to boil the brackish, muddy stream water from the jungle. *We have purification tablets. It's okay.* But what if the rain stayed away for days? Weeks?

Stomach churning, Brian banished the worry. They'd deal with it. Because right now, he had enough on his plate. Because this morning, instead of waking puffy and drained from sobbing his guts out, he was boneless from...

*Possibly the greatest sex of my life.*

It had been the most intense, that was for sure. Thinking about it sent a shiver of heat through him, his balls tingling, cock stirring. Maybe he was going crazy from being stuck on the island, but if he was being honest... Hell, he'd never wanted anyone so badly. Or maybe he had, and he just couldn't recall the bone-deep desperation?

He pondered it. He and Alicia had had some good sex in their years together, and it was nice with Rebecca and others. Satisfying. He'd never had cause to complain.

But he'd never known it could be like this. He'd never wanted to crawl into someone else's skin.

*Because we're stuck here together without women. We're horny. Troy could have been anyone.*

The lie had barely flitted through his brain when acid flooded his gut. No, the last person Troy could be was *anyone*.

Listening to him sing had been fun at first. But then when he'd done the old song in that clear, rounded voice, sitting in the firelight with the stars looking close enough to touch...

Maybe it was bizarre to think of another guy as beautiful, but Brian had filled with awe and wanting. Wanting that had demanded action, pushing and prodding with hot fingers until he moved. The urge to kiss Troy had been overpowering. The urge to touch—*really* touch him, not just a perfunctory hand job that wasn't supposed to mean anything.

Looking at Troy's back now, Brian wanted to spoon up behind him and kiss the freckles dotting his shoulders. Wanted to nuzzle against his neck and...

Squeezing his eyes shut against the wave of desire, Brian exhaled shakily. Troy was his friend. Hell, here he was the only other person in the world. Of course Brian felt affection for him, and gratitude. Troy was a great guy. Their friendship and horniness were getting confused. It was probably normal.

"So..."

Brian jumped a little as Troy spoke. Watching Troy's back, he held his breath.

"Is this the part where everything's weird and awkward and we pretend nothing happened?" His voice was a little hoarse, and Brian flushed, thinking of how Troy had cried out so loudly while they'd gotten off. Brian wanted to hear that sound again.

Heart thumping, Brian shook his head, then realized Troy couldn't see him. He cleared his throat. "No."

Troy rolled onto his back. They were an inch apart, and Brian could feel the heat of Troy's body, but he stayed motionless. Troy met his gaze. "We're not going to avoid each other?"

"Kind of hard here on... We really need to name this island."

Troy's lips twitched. "We do." He faced the brightening sky, the rays of the rising sun through the trees giving his tanned skin a pink glow. "Hmm. I guess Gilligan's Island doesn't make a whole lot of sense. And there's no giant gorilla, so Skull Island is out."

"Fantasy Island could work. We might see 'da plane, da plane' if we're lucky." At the furrow in Troy's brow, he added, "Never mind—you're too young for that reference. I practically am too, but it was my Gran's favorite. Along with *The Love Boat*. One of the first things I remember is wanting to go on a cruise."

"A plane or a boat would do right now. Hmm. How about Isla Nublar?"

"Because we need a T. rex to come crashing out of the jungle? Pass."

"Good point. And anything related to Dr. Moreau is obviously out."

The line from "Beyond the Sea" popped into Brian's mind. "Golden Sands."

Troy's chocolate eyes met his, and he smiled tentatively. Humming the song softly and horribly off-key, Brian mustered up the courage to roll onto his side, pressing against him. He flattened his hand over Troy's trembling belly and bumped their noses together. Troy sighed into his kiss, and they explored each other's mouths, their stubble scraping roughly.

Brian didn't care that they had morning breath, or that this was undeniably *gay*. He wanted to touch Troy all over and drink him in. Wanted to get lost in him. Wanted…everything.

Breathing hard, he pulled back. Troy's eyes were glazed, and Brian's dick lengthened against Troy's hip. "Have you ever done this before?" Brian asked. "With a guy?" He quickly added, "I don't care if you have. It doesn't matter to me. But I've never done this before."

Troy shook his head. "Me either. Not since I was a kid, just fooling around. All the guys did it. Circle jerks and that stuff. It wasn't real. Not like this." With a shaky breath, he ran his hand over Brian's chest, teasing his hair and nipples. "I like this," he whispered. "Like it with you."

"Me too. Even if I don't know what I'm doing." A laugh tripped out in a nervous tumble.

Troy's smile was sweet. "Me either. Guess it's all pretty much the same when you get down to it."

He supposed it was. Brian stroked his thumb over the cleft in Troy's chin. Then he bent and pressed a kiss to it, caressing Troy's belly with his other hand, earning a shudder. A little voice still shouted that they shouldn't be doing this, but Brian focused on the salt-sweat taste of Troy's skin, and how his nipples hardened when sucked.

Troy's sparse chest hair tickled his nose, and it was different from being with a woman, but…he liked it. And he *loved* how Troy tightened his fingers in Brian's hair and moaned loudly. It was the best sound on the island—no wait, on Golden Sands.

Brian licked and teased as Troy called out, and then they were kissing again and tugging at their shorts, stopping long enough to toss them aside and kick the blanket free, not caring that sand was creeping everywhere. Brian narrowly avoided hitting the smoldering fire with his boxers, and they laughed and yanked the cotton back to safety.

Then the goddamned parrots came out, honking their way joyfully through breakfast, and Brian and Troy laughed harder. Troy rolled on top of him, and Brian groaned at the sensation of being completely skin to skin. They were thin and wiry, all sinew and muscle and bone. Too thin, but they were alive and together, and Brian reveled in it.

Spitting into his palm, Troy took their cocks in his hand. Brian thrust into Troy's grasp, panting. It should have been so weird and wrong to have his cock rubbing against another guy's, but…it was Troy, and Brian couldn't get enough.

Troy's heavy, hairy balls brushed against Brian's thighs, and it was all so desperate and masculine. He didn't have to worry about being too forceful. He dug his fingers hard into Troy's back, and Troy groaned with pleasure.

Sweat bloomed on their skin, the rising sun's heat making itself known. They strained together, panting and kissing, and this hand job was a million times better than the restrained jerking they'd done in the teepee. This was *real* sex, and Brian didn't give a shit what it meant. It was just the two of them, so why not? Why shouldn't they have something so good?

Grunting and striving, stroking their cocks, Troy came, splattering Brian's chest. He slowed down to milk himself, his eyes closed and mouth open, gasping.

*So damn beautiful.*

Brian strained as Troy refocused, propping his weight on his left hand in the sand and jerking Brian mercilessly. It didn't take long for Brian's balls to draw up, and his spunk joined Troy's on his chest, white against hair and sun-kissed skin. The tremors subsided, and Troy flopped down beside him.

After a minute, Troy cleared his throat. "I think I have sand in more crevices than usual."

Brian chuckled. "Me too. Guess it's time for a dip." He dragged his finger through their drying spunk.

"Brian, we…"

"We don't have to overthink it."

Troy exhaled with a smile. "Right. Okay. Cool. We'll be in the now." He hopped up to his feet in a graceful movement that made Brian feel old. "I'm starving. Let's clean off and go fishing." Naked, he extended his hand, and Brian took it.

In the calm shallows, they cleaned themselves, then neared the reef with hooks and lines, still naked. The sun tightened Brian's salty skin, and he knew he should get into the shade of the lean-to before too long. But he stayed put, his gaze sneaking over from spotting fish to the lean lines of Troy's back, dotted with those perfect freckles.

"WHY IS THIS so hard?"

Brian glanced up from where he sat in the shade of the lean-to, weaving a fresh basket to replace one that had gotten grungy. "Because we're not scientists." He scratched at a fly bite on his chest and un-crossed his extended legs, putting the other ankle on top. He poked at a loose button on his cargo shorts. It was hanging by a thread, but clung to life.

Troy snorted. "I don't think you have to be a scientist to figure out how to make coconut oil."

"True. Okay, so we're not chefs. Or even cooks, really."

"That we are not." Sighing, Troy tossed the half coconut aside and picked up the signaling mirror from its rock, performing the ritual. The signal fire burned farther down the beach, and sunlight glinted off the pieces of fuselage scattered through the SOS.

Troy sang softly as he angled the mirror, using *la-la-la* instead of lyrics. Brian recognized the tune as one Troy noodled with frequently. He wondered what the words would be, but didn't push.

When Troy was finished with his sweeps, he joined Brian in the shade. The skin on his shoulders peeled, and he picked at it idly. "It's crazy, isn't it?"

"You'll have to narrow that down." Brian worked free a leaf that had gotten bunched up.

"I mean how it's always the same here." He stared at the calm tur-quoise water. "I never thought I'd say this, but I'm sick of the sun. Even in LA we have a little variety. Hell, I'd take clouds. Here's it's just always…this. We get the showers at night, but I miss rainy days."

After several days of boiling and purifying stream water, the short nightly rains had returned, much to their delight. But Brian still worried about what was to come. "In the wet season, you'll be praying for sun."

Troy smiled faintly. "The grass is always greener, right?" He stretched out his foot, rubbing it along Brian's shin. "When does that start again?"

The motion of Troy's foot sent tingles over Brian's skin. "Around November."

"So still a while away."

"Mmm." It was almost July, and had been forty-eight days on Golden Sands. Thinking of the future, Brian's stomach tightened queasily. Could they stay healthy and uninjured? What if they ate a poisonous fish, or were bitten by something? He shuddered, remembering Troy's cries of agony and the terrifying swelling of his foot. What if one of them were cut on coral and it got infected? What if—

"Brian?" Troy stole his hand onto Brian's thigh, stroking slowly over his worn shorts.

As Troy rubbed, Brian's interest in basket weaving waned quite severely, and the staccato pricks of worry dissolved into sweet, lazy desire. With a shared smile, they kissed, Brian tossing the basket aside. He tore open the Velcro fastening on Troy's board shorts, knowing he'd find his cock thickening for him already.

This was what they did now. Some mornings and afternoons, but always every night. Reaching with hands and mouths, rolling on top of each other urgently, jerking or rubbing until they came, skin to skin. They never talked about it, at least not with words. Instead, they spoke in grunts and moans, sighs and gasps. And in whispers, they spoke each other's names.

"Troy…" Brian pressed him onto a blanket under the lean-to, kissing his neck and licking into the hollow of his throat, tasting salt and sweat and sunshine.

They were naked now, thrusting their cocks together. Brian didn't want to come too soon, so he rolled onto his hip, chuckling at Troy's whine at the loss of contact. Relenting, he gave him a few strokes with his hand. He'd never imagined he could enjoy another man's cock so much, but... Well, this was Troy.

He sucked Troy's nipples in turn, letting his fingertips tease around the creases of Troy's thighs, his bellybutton, and the wiry hair below it. Troy trembled, his eyes closed and red lips parted. Troy had a little mole on his inner thigh, and after tracing it with his finger, Brian wondered if it would taste different than the rest of Troy's skin, and he shimmied lower to flick his tongue over it.

"Oh!" Troy's mouth opened another inch, his chest rising.

Brian's head was in his crotch now, heart galloping as he eyed Troy's cock curving up to his belly. What would that taste like?

Before he could lose his nerve or really even think about it, Brian licked up the side of Troy's shaft, tracing a thick vein there. Troy gasped. Brian's lips hovered by the head poking out of the foreskin. His mouth went dry, and he dared a glance up.

The pure longing in Troy's eyes sent a bolt of fire through Brian, and his breath caught. Troy watched him with lips parted. Then he whispered.

*"Please."*

With that entreaty spoken and a gentle swipe of his tongue, Brian took the head between his lips, tasting a drop of bitter musk. Troy's groan echoed in the afternoon breeze, making Brian even harder. He took him into his mouth clumsily, moving between Troy's legs as Troy spread them wide.

He was sprawled open, his arms out as well, utterly trusting, and a swell of affection burned in Brian's chest. He was actually sucking another guy's dick and liking it. More than *liking*. It did taste different than the rest of Troy's skin. Hotter and wetter like his mouth, although it was Brian's saliva dripping down to Troy's balls as he licked and sucked.

Troy *throbbed* in his mouth, and Brian inhaled forcefully through his nose until he had to pull off and take a deep breath.

One of Troy's hands found Brian's head, running through his thick, too-long hair. Brian had always liked giving oral. Had liked the intimacy of it, the stronger scents and tastes that made sex more primal. Most women he'd been with had hardly had any pubic hair, and instead of being turned off by Troy's, he reveled in it, rubbing his face against the coarse thatch and holding Troy's quivering thighs apart.

He licked Troy's balls, and Troy *screamed*. Brian thought of how Rebecca had done it to him, and after spitting on his finger, he rubbed it over Troy's hole.

"Oh, fuck. Fuck!" Troy's fingers tightened in Brian's hair, and Brian realized he loved hearing the words. He *needed* to hear the words.

As he circled around Troy's hole, Brian licked one of his balls. Voice hoarse, he asked, "You like that?"

"Yes! Fuck, yes. Please."

God, Troy was so gorgeous, splayed and begging. As Brian pushed just the tip of his finger inside and sucked the head of Troy's cock, he wondered what it would be like to fuck him, to fill him with cum. A full-body shudder rocked him, and Brian's dick leaked. Then Troy was coming, and Brian got a bitter taste before he pulled off and watched Troy flush and pant.

Brian's mouth was dry aside from the drops of semen, and he stumbled up, returning a moment later. He stood just outside the lean-to in the hot sand, stretching his body and gulping a bottle of warm water. Troy laid there near his feet, his legs still spread. Jizz splattered his stomach. He made no move to cover himself, and eyed Brian's hard cock.

Brian passed him the bottle, watching Troy's throat work as he swallowed. His dick still achingly hard, Brian reached for it to finish himself off. Troy batted his hand away and pushed up to his knees.

With a rough swallow, Brian ground out, "You don't have to."

At his feet, Troy looked up with those dark eyes, his growing hair a wild halo around his head. "You don't want me to?"

Brian had to laugh. "Of course I want you to."

Troy laughed too, and with a deep breath, he took hold of Brian's cock and swallowed it as far as he could, choking. They both laughed again, and he tried more carefully a second time.

Brian stroked his head. "Easy, easy."

Troy's lips stretched over Brian's dick, his tongue exploring, and Brian knew he wouldn't last long.

"Troy... I'm... Feels so good."

He'd been sucked by plenty of women over the years, women who knew what they were doing compared to Troy's clumsy fumbles. But Brian couldn't remember a blow job ever being like this, as if his heart was being caressed along with his cock. He'd never wanted a man before Troy, but he'd never wanted a woman this much either. Troy's mouth was hot and wet, and he closed his eyes in concentration as he sucked and reached a hand to explore Brian's balls.

Brian didn't manage to get a recognizable word out in warning as the orgasm rocked him on his heels, but he pulled free of Troy's mouth, splashing his face and neck with each pulse. Troy didn't seem to mind, kneeling there and smiling at Brian with satisfaction.

After dropping to his knees, Brian took Troy's face in his hands and kissed him. Troy moaned into his mouth, and when thoughts began to invade Brian's mind—*I just sucked another man's dick, and he sucked mine, and I loved it, and what does that mean?*—he pushed them away, slamming the door and locking it tightly behind him.

They were sticky with semen and sweat, but instead of cleaning off, they rolled back under the shade of the lean-to and kissed and touched until they were ready to come again.

Brian threw away the key.

# Chapter Thirteen

ⓞ🌴ⓞ

"TELL ME ABOUT your songs."

Troy opened his eyes and looked at Brian bobbing beside him. It was still early one morning, and his muscles burned pleasantly from the wood-cutting competition they'd just finished. Since sawing firewood with their pocket chainsaw was such a never-ending chore, they'd taken to racing and timing each other with Brian's watch. Troy had won by three seconds, with Brian vowing to avenge his honor.

Now they floated on their backs, a breeze skimming over the barely cool water. They'd have to get into the shade soon so they didn't sunburn their junk, but they had a few more minutes to loll.

"What about them?" Troy asked.

"I don't know, everything. I know you don't want to, but…please?"

Troy sighed. "It's not like it's *secret*, it's just…embarrassing, I guess."

"Why?" Brian asked quietly, drawing lazy circles in the water with his hand.

"It's super lame. I only write little bits and pieces. Scraps of stories."

"What kinds?"

"I don't know. Different things."

"Well, I like different things."

A wisp of a cloud drifted above, and Troy watched its progress. "One is about a kid living in a small town, and he tries to fix an old windmill. The windmill's a metaphor for his fucked-up family." Troy's cheeks went hot. "Just stupid stuff."

"It's not stupid. At all. I'd listen to it. I love it when you sing."

Troy smiled at the rush of pleasure. "Thank you. I have some in my head—lyrics, I mean. But they don't sound right when I say them out loud. Need to write them down first. Make sense of them."

"You could write them in the sand."

For some reason, the thought left Troy with a bittersweet pang of sadness. "It's not the same. They'd be blown away. Scattered. I'll write them when we get back." It helped to speak of when, not if. "While I guzzle Coke and eat Doritos. And mmm, pizza."

"You know what else I could go for? Ice. Have I mentioned that I'd sign away my first born for a cold beer?"

Troy laughed. "Once or twice, dude. Oh man, can you imagine how good ice cream would taste right now? Haagen-Daz cookie dough. Or mint chocolate."

"Pralines and cream. Followed by beer."

They rattled off the food they were craving the most that day. Troy could feel Brian's eyes on him, and concentrated on the water as he spread his toes wide, flexing his feet, before relaxing them with a little splash.

"I'd like to hear one of your songs one day."

Troy wasn't sure why it made him so uncomfortable. "But it's not the right kind of music."

"Why not?"

"We obviously do pop in the band. Dancey, bubble-gum stuff. Fun stuff. It's not like I can suddenly become a folky songwriter strumming on a guitar."

"Why not?" Brian repeated.

Troy huffed a little. "I just can't. I barely know how to play the guitar anymore."

"Couldn't you learn?"

"Well, I could, but…" He squirmed, paddling with his hands. "Even if I did, it wouldn't sell. No one would want my music."

"That's why you're so afraid to write it?"

"Folk doesn't sell." Troy echoed his father's words.

"So?" Brian quirked a smile. "I'm playing devil's advocate. You've got millions, right? What does it matter if it sells?"

"Of course it matters. It has to be a hit."

"Says who? Your dad?" Brian reached over and smoothed his hand down Troy's arm, leaving goosebumps behind.

"Well...yeah." He shook his head. "Stupid, huh? I'm a grown-ass man, and my dad's dead, and I'm still trying to please him. Why am I doing that?"

"Because you're fucked up."

Laughter burst out of Troy. "Is that your diagnosis, Dr. Sinclair?"

"Yep." Brian laughed too. "Island therapy complete. You're fucked up. I'm fucked up. We're all fucked up."

Smiling, Troy tasted salt as he brushed back his hair. "But would people really want to hear my music?"

"I would."

Troy rolled his eyes. "Of course you would. You're my—" The unfinished thought hung there with the delicate wisps of cloud in the unending blue sky, and his heart thumped. "Friend," he finished lamely.

What else would he be? From the corner of his eye, he could see Brian turn his head to watch him intently.

"We'd better get out before we burn." Troy paddled in, and Brian followed.

They splashed their way out of the water, the fine sand sticking. While Brian took his turn with the signaling mirror, Troy cut up a fresh papaya to share. Juice dripped down Brian's chin, and Troy swiped his tongue over it and then into Brian's mouth. While they shared sweet kisses in the shade, sea water evaporated on their skin, the day growing hotter with each passing minute.

Troy reminded himself that they weren't going to overthink it. They'd agreed, and there was no reason to analyze it. So what if they had fun together trapped here? None of it *meant* anything. Still, the unvoiced word whispered in Troy's mind, low and insistent.

*Boyfriend.*

"Mmm. Yeah, right there."

Troy dug his elbow into the knot under Brian's shoulder blade. "Harder?"

In a breathy, porny voice, Brian begged, "Give me all you've got."

Laughing, Troy swatted Brian's arm. Brian was facedown on a blanket by the campfire, Troy straddling his ass. The cotton of their boxers teased Troy's cock. "Oh, I'll give it to you, baby."

Brian's low laughter settled over Troy like honey. "Come on, big—" He broke off as the sky suddenly unleashed a torrent of rain.

It must have been later than Troy thought, or the rain was early. He supposed it didn't matter as they scurried to uncap water bottles and unzip the suitcase. Then he kicked off his boxers and enjoyed the shower, the rain cool and refreshing. Brian followed suit, and they spread their arms to the sky, the smoke from the doused fire pungent.

It was still raining when they crawled inside the teepee and into each other's arms under the gauzy net. Troy loved the feel of their slick skin sliding together, and he straddled Brian's hips to lean over and rub his cheek against the wet fur on Brian's chest. Brian squeezed and stroked Troy's body.

Then his fingers dipped into the crease of Troy's ass, and Troy groaned. He pushed his knees farther apart, eager for Brian's touch on his hole. He'd been thinking about it since they'd blown each other the day before, wondering what it would feel like to have Brian's whole finger—or more—inside him. He'd played with his ass sometimes when he jerked off, and some of his girlfriends had done what Brian did during blow jobs, but never anything deeper than a fingertip.

Now Troy wanted more. He didn't care if it was crossing some line that made him gay, because what did it matter? He was clearly bi, at least. He'd sucked another man's dick, and he'd liked it. More than liked it, and he wasn't ashamed. This was their little world, and he wanted to feel good. Wanted to make Brian feel good. He'd never craved anything the way he wanted Brian with such a consuming, primal pull.

As Brian's finger found his hole, circling it, Troy's breath hitched. The rain still poured outside in a steady rush, and soon the moat around their teepee would overflow, but he only cared about one thing. Lifting his head, he put his lips to Brian's ear.

"Will you fuck me?"

He felt Brian shudder against him, his finger pressing at Troy's hole.

Troy whispered, "I want to know what it feels like. I want...all of it. All of you." Holding his breath, he lifted his head and met Brian's eyes, barely visible in the gloom. Brian's finger was still on his ass, but he didn't say anything, and Troy's heart skipped.

*Did I cross the line? Is this too gay? Am I a freak?*

With his other hand, Brian reached up to cup Troy's face, his gaze intense. "You want my cock?"

Exhaling in a rush of relief, Troy nodded vigorously. "I want it. Want you to fuck me. Come inside me." He hesitated. "I'm negative. Are you?" He frankly didn't really care. They could be on this island for years. Forever. He needed this.

"I am. God, I want you."

They kissed, a mash of lips and teeth, and Troy rolled his hips, his dick almost painfully stiff against Brian's. He rubbed against it, feeling Brian's length and thickness. He wasn't sure it would fit, but the thought of it inside him opened a well of longing, his balls tightening.

"Please, Brian. Give it to me."

Brian's chest rose and fell rapidly, and he ran his thumb over Troy's mouth. "Don't want to hurt you. You ever been fucked? With a toy, maybe?"

Nerves singing, fire swept over Troy's skin. He shook his head. He'd never been pegged or anything, but holy shit, did he want to be fucked now. "Do it." He attacked Brian's mouth, biting at his lip. "Fuck me."

"We don't have anything to—" Brian gasped softly. "Wait." Urging

Troy off him, he pushed up the net and crawled to his toiletry bag. On his side, Troy watched Brian's pale ass, wondering what it would be like to bury his cock there. He had to grip the base of his dick, squeezing mercilessly until he had control.

Brian returned with a little glass bottle. "Hair oil. Almost forgot I had it."

"Good thing I didn't use it before." Troy smiled, butterflies flapping in his belly as they looked at the bottle and then each other. "So how…"

"I did it sometimes with the ex. Knees and elbows. But you're going to be really tight. How about…" With gentle hands, Brian rolled Troy onto his other side, lifting his top leg and bending his knee. "This good to start?"

"Uh-huh." His ass did feel more exposed, and he breathed shallowly through his mouth as he waited. "It's good."

When Brian pressed a slick finger to his hole, Troy tensed. He felt the soft caress of Brian's lips on the back of his neck, then the puff of his whisper. "Relax. Let me in."

The emergency blanket crinkled under his hip as Troy shifted and forced a deep breath. "Okay," he murmured.

Brian kissed the shell of Troy's ear before sucking the side of his neck as he toyed with his ass, pushing in, then retreating, stretching him bit by bit. When Brian's whole index finger was inside, Troy felt almost unbearably full. There was no way.

But the pain faded, and when Brian withdrew fully, Troy couldn't stop a whine low in his throat.

Brian kissed his ear again with a soft chuckle. "You're doing so good."

Troy preened at the praise, lifting his leg higher and bringing his knee toward his chest. "More."

"You're dying for it, hmm? Greedy for my cock?"

"Fuck yes." They hadn't talked much during sex before, but now they couldn't seem to shut up. "Give it to me. All of it."

"Two fingers first." Brian pushed them past the ring of muscle.

Gasping at the intrusion, Troy seized up. "Fuck," he muttered.

"You're so tight. Jesus." Brian's hot breath fanned over Troy's neck.

"I can take it." He concentrated on his breathing, the burning lessening inch by inch as Brian stretched him. When Brian bent his fingers, Troy just about shot up straight through the mosquito net. "Oh sweet fucking Christ. There. That's...oh fuck." His cock had softened as Brian stretched his ass, and now it throbbed back to life.

"Must be the prostate," Brian murmured, brushing it again.

"Oh my God, don't ever stop."

They both laughed, but soon Troy was moaning, his eyes closed as Brian fucked him with his fingers. "Love the way you sound," Brian muttered. "So hot. Ready for me?"

Troy didn't hesitate, pushing back. "Yes. Now." His nipples tingled and his dick ached, and he was *so ready*.

Until Brian shoved the slick head of his cock inside, and Troy thought he might split in two. It was so hot, like an iron poker. He couldn't even grunt. Sweat broke out over his rain-slick skin.

Brian ran his hand down Troy's arm, murmuring as he threaded their fingers together. "Breathe. You're okay. Tell me if you want to stop."

It was incredibly tempting to shout, *"Yes, stop and never come near my ass again with that thing!"* But Troy worked on his breathing, and the burning began to fade. He squeezed Brian's fingers. "Keep going."

"Let me in." Groaning, Brian thrust. He let go of Troy's hand and pulled open his ass cheek.

Troy had never felt so exposed during sex, but Brian was there, and everything was okay. Everything was *amazing*. Moans grated his throat, gasps flowing off his tongue. "Keep going," he repeated.

When Brian shoved into him, the head finally getting inside and the rest following, Troy felt so incredibly full.

"Bear down," Brian instructed. "Like that. Oh, yeah. So good." He slipped his arm under Troy and looped it around his chest, their damp skin rubbing.

Wiry hair brushed Troy's ass, and he realized Brian was all the way inside. He'd never experienced anything so intense. The sensation of being full was only part of it. It somehow felt like Brian had climbed into his skin—that he was touching Troy everywhere, and Troy's body was expanding in every cell. Troy felt like his guttural groan came right from his leaking cock.

"You're so good," Brian repeated, muttering as he held Troy tightly across the chest and began fucking him in earnest, rocking in and out.

Troy could only moan and cry out, lost in a haze of *want* and *more*. He trusted Brian to take care of him, and he let himself go, taking the thrusts and bolts of pleasure, giving everything up as the sweet tightness in his balls intensified. His skin sang, and when Brian took hold of his straining shaft, stroking it in tandem with the movement of his hips, his cock stretching Troy so *open*, Troy actually saw stars, the orgasm tearing through him.

As he rode out the intense bursts of pleasure, he was aware he was clamping down on Brian's dick. Brian cried out, grunting as he thrust harder, his sweat dripping onto Troy's shoulder. Shuddering, Brian emptied himself.

Knowing Brian was coming deep inside where no one had ever touched him gave Troy a fresh rush of pleasure, and another spurt of jizz dribbled out of his cock. He'd never had sex without a condom before, and this all felt so much messier in the best possible way.

Their harsh pants filled the teepee, and Troy realized the rain had stopped. Brian was softening inside him, and he kissed across Troy's shoulders with sweet little presses before gently pulling out. He released Troy's cock with a tender pat and reached down to his hole, probing lightly. It was oily and messy, and should have been gross, but Troy liked it. It felt...real.

"Okay?"

*Mmm-hmm.*

"Troy?" Brian's voice sharpened, and he pushed up on his elbow, lifting Troy's chin. He peered down anxiously. "Did I hurt you?"

"Huh?" He realized he hadn't spoken aloud before. "No. Feel good."

Brian's brow remained furrowed. "You sure? You'd tell me, right?"

"Uh-huh." He smiled lazily. "I feel fucking amazing. That was…wow."

Exhaling, Brian's shoulders dropped and he kissed him, his fingers still gentle on Troy's swollen asshole. "It was."

"I didn't know it could feel like this."

Brian smoothed back Troy's curling hair before brushing their lips together. "Me either."

As their words hung in the humid air and they moved into each other's arms, the mosquito net enclosing them in their little world, Troy didn't think they were only talking about sex.

# Chapter Fourteen

F ROM THE CORNER of his eye, Brian saw movement as he filled a
coconut with sea water. He'd gone for his walk and was almost done
with their version of laundry, which involved steaming their limited
collection of clothes. From beneath the brim of his hat, he registered the
pale gelatinous shape and stumbled backward in the knee-deep water,
but not quickly enough.

The lash of tentacles whipped across the inside of his left calf, and he
yelped, splashing to safety on the sand.

"Brian?" Troy called.

"I'm fine! I just… Son of a bitch, that stings." He must have looked
ridiculous, hopping around naked with his dick swinging. He folded his
lips together, his nostrils flaring. "Ow, ow, ow."

Troy was suddenly there, naked too, his brow furrowed and arm
around Brian's bare shoulders. "What happened?"

"Jellyfish." Brian winced, tossing his hat aside so he could tug at his
hair. It had always made him feel better somehow to diffuse pain by
causing more of it to distract him. "Son of a bitch."

"Oh shit." Troy's eyebrows flew up. "Wait, you know what this
means, right?"

With a groan, Brian shook his head, but he had to laugh. "I've never
been into golden showers."

Troy shoulders shook. "Me either. But it's supposed to help, right?
Didn't Chandler pee on Monica once?"

"I believe he did." Brian inhaled sharply, the sting burning. "Shit, it really does hurt. Okay, do it."

Troy's arm was firm around him. "Where? I can't see anything."

"Inside of my calf."

"Good thing I have to piss, huh?"

Brian opened his mouth to make some kind of joke, but as the warm urine hit his leg, all he could do was lean into Troy gratefully. He knew it should have been gross, but somehow it…wasn't. He forced in a deep inhale and exhale, pressing his temple to Troy's. The sting wasn't abating yet, but he felt better—safe and protected.

There was something incredibly intimate about it, and Brian shivered from the fiery sting of the jellyfish and something else entirely. Fucking Troy the night before had been amazing—indescribable. It made his belly flutter to think of it, and it was becoming impossible not to think.

Impossible not to question what was really happening, because this had gone past the physical. Miles beyond.

As Troy finished pissing on him, trying to take away his pain, Brian wanted more. He wanted Troy's cum on his skin, and in his body. Brian sought his mouth as Troy wrapped his arms around him, returning the kiss, sliding their slick tongues together.

He wanted to stay right there, tasting Troy's soft lips, feeling the rasp of stubble against his own. Wanted to fuck him again and offer up his own ass. Needed to know what it was like to actually have this man inside him when he felt like Troy was already there.

But shit, fuck, fuck, *ow*. He pulled away with a wince.

"Did it help?" Troy asked, rubbing Brian's back.

He wanted so much to say yes, but couldn't hold back the moan of pain. "Nope. Didn't seem to do anything."

"Shit! Seriously?" Holding Brian's hips steady, Troy crouched to peer at the sting. "I thought that was supposed to work! I think I see something. Let me get the tweezers. Sit down." He helped Brian hobble to the blanket in the lean-to and dashed off to the teepee.

Brian kept his leg outstretched, peering closely at his calf. As Troy hustled back, Brian said, "I think those are tentacles stuck in my leg. Be careful not to touch them."

Kneeling beside him, Troy nodded. "I won't. Just hold still, okay?" He put his left hand on Brian's knee and leaned in with the tweezers.

Brian panted as the burning pain spiked. He pressed his lips together, mumbling curses.

Troy frowned at him. "Scream. Don't hold it in." A little smile lifted his lips. "Want me to scream with you?" He took a breath and bellowed to the heavens.

Half laughing, half yelling, Brian screamed as Troy made quick work with the tweezers. After he'd flung the tentacles back into the retreating sea, he filled a coconut shell with water and knelt by Brian's foot.

"If piss didn't work, you think saltwater will help?"

"Let's try it." Bracing, Brian watched Troy pour water over the sting, which consisted of two short lashes of deepening red. He couldn't imagine how excruciating a full sting would be. The wounds burned so much he expected to see smoke rising. But salt would hopefully disinfect since they were out of iodine.

Troy examined Brian's face. "Shit, it's making it worse?"

"Uh-huh, but keep going."

Frowning, Troy poured the water gently, rubbing a circle on Brian's thigh with his other hand. After making Brian drink a full bottle of rainwater, Troy peered at him carefully, as if examining for symptoms. He pressed the back of his hand to Brian's sweaty forehead.

Brian chuckled. "I'm fine. The thing barely got me. I should finish our clothes."

"You're resting, and that's that. And you need Advil."

"No, we only have a couple tablets left. This isn't that bad." At Troy's skeptical expression, Brian conceded, "Yes, it hurts. But I'll survive. It's starting to fade."

*Fade* wasn't quite accurate, but his calf felt less on fire than it had, so that was something. Brian sighed to himself, watching Troy bustle around. He tracked the flexing of Troy's naked muscles, and loved that he could look all he wanted, and it was okay. Okay to touch too. Troy was all his.

After refilling the water bottle and pressing it into Brian's hand, Troy asked, "What?" He chuckled uncertainly. "What are you smiling about?"

Brian gulped the water and shrugged. "Nothing. Thank you for all of this."

"Of course. You helped me when I was hurt." He grimaced. "You're being much braver than I was."

"Are you kidding? Do you remember what your foot looked like? Hell, your whole lower leg. Because I do, and it was bad. Really, really bad." *I thought you were going to die.* Even remembering the horrible redness and swelling made Brian's heart skip. *What if it happens again? What if he gets hurt?* "This is just a little sting. I'm pretty sure I'll live."

"You'd better." Troy tried to laugh and didn't quite make it. He cleared his throat. "Do you need anything else? Are you hungry? I can—"

"I'm good. Just sit with me? It's too hot to do anything else anyway. Screw the laundry."

With a nod, Troy joined him on the blanket under their lean-to. "You should relax. Come on."

Brian stretched out on his back, resting his head on Troy's muscled thigh. His face was inches from Troy's soft dick, and it should have been weird—shouldn't it? But despite the burning in his calf, sitting together in the shade on another perfectly clear island day was utterly peaceful. Birds chirped, cicadas buzzing. So of course a little voice piped up.

*Am I gay? Is Troy gay? Are we bi? What are we?*

"Bri?" Troy's brow furrowed. "Is it hurting more?"

Making an effort to unclench the muscles he'd subconsciously tensed, he shook his head. He knew they should probably just talk about it, but his stomach flipped at the thought. What if talking made it too weird? What if it ruined everything?

*Don't overthink it. It's just the two of us. Why do we have to be any-*

*thing but happy?*

Troy brushed his fingers through Brian's growing hair, playing with the ends. Looking up, Brian mentally cataloged all the features he loved about Troy's face. The little cleft in his chin and the sweep of his eyebrows. His button nose, although from his position it was Troy's nostrils he could really see. The curls that crept over his forehead. Freckles on his tan skin.

"Tell me something," Brian murmured.

Troy didn't stop playing with his hair. "About what?"

"Anything."

"Okay." Troy was silent for a few moments. "So, the first time I went to the Grammys, I almost threw up on Madonna backstage."

"Seriously?"

"Yup." He shook his head, smiling. "I was so freaking nervous. I mean, *Adele* was there. *Everyone* was there. Including Madonna, obviously. We were waiting in the wings to perform, and I was ready to run away. But I couldn't let Ty and the guys down, or the fans. I realized I was going to puke, and I spun away—just as Madonna came off stage with her award. I missed her stiletto boots by, like, an inch."

"Oh my God. Did she say anything?"

"Nope. She just patted my head and stepped over it like puke backstage was no big thing. She's Madonna. I guess she's seen worse."

Brian whistled. "I guess so. Okay, tell me another one."

As Troy spun out little stories of the rich and famous, a breeze gave relief from the growing heat. Brian's calf still stung, but he couldn't seem to stop smiling.

"You'll never guess what he said next, and remember the mic was still hot."

The low drone of another insect reached Brian's ears, and he idly swept his hand through the air to brush it away. "Okay, I'll never guess. Tell me."

"He was all—" Troy went rigid. "What's that?"

The drone grew louder, and Brian's heart seized as he bolted straight up to his feet, the sting in his leg no match for the onslaught of adrenaline. "Holy shit. It's an engine." He could barely see in the haze of sun reflecting off the sand, shading his hand over his eyes as he scanned the sea and cloudless sky. "Get the mirror!"

Then Troy was at his side, breathing shallowly. "Got it. Do you see it?" He captured the reflection and started sweeping the mirror side to side.

They both searched. The engine was getting louder, but Brian could barely hear it over the pounding of his heart and rush of blood, his ears practically ringing. "There in the sky! Three o'clock."

Chest rising and falling rapidly, Troy aimed the mirror. "Come on, come on…"

"Keep doing that!" Sand flying, Brian raced to throw more wood and leaves onto the signal fire. Then he picked up a piece of fuselage from the SOS and waved it around, barely noticing the pain from the hot metal. This was their chance. This was it. He wanted to shout and scream, even though he knew no one would hear a thing up there.

The little dot came into focus, the thumping of the helicopter's rotors filling his ears. It was getting closer, and he waved and jumped, hearing Troy shout hoarsely. It was close, but was it close enough?

The helicopter flew by in the distance, disappearing from sight beyond the cliff face dominating Golden Sands. Troy raced over, still shouting until he trailed off. The engine's thunder faded.

"Did they… Oh, God. They didn't see us, did they?" Troy's voice broke. "Oh, God."

Hands reddened, Brian dropped the metal. He wrapped Troy in his arms, and they clung to each other. "Shh. It's okay. We're—"

*Thump-thump-thump-thump…*

It was coming back.

When it zoomed overhead in a torrent of wind, seeming to come out of nowhere, Brian and Troy jumped and shouted and waved their arms, still naked. The helicopter flew over the island, then banked into a wide arc, coming back over the reef, the rotors sending churning ripples out over the water in a wide circle. The helicopter door opened, and a figure waved.

A sob ripped out of Brian's throat as he dropped to his knees, sand gritty on his tongue, flying everywhere. "They see us."

"Oh my God." Troy stood there staring at the chopper, his short curls whipping around. "We're going home."

*Home.* Brian's joy was severed by the ache that split him open, deep and hollow as he thought of his shoe-box apartment in Sydney, and days and nights far too alone.

"What do we do?" Troy yelled.

"I guess we put pants on."

If Troy laughed, Brian didn't hear it. They stared at each other and then around at their camp, and Brian couldn't hold back a gasp. The helicopter might as well have been a cyclone, tearing the orange blanket from the top of their shelter and toppling the lean-to.

The clothes that had been steaming were strewn across the sand, coconut shells, woven bowls, and baskets scattered. Everything they'd built together had been destroyed in a blink, and as the helicopter neared, Brian had the absurd urge to scream at it to go away.

Troy was yanking on his sodden and sand-covered board shorts. "We're just…leaving? Right now?"

The scream was still there, clawing at his throat. *No! We can't leave like this! We need more time. One more night.* Brian stared at the hovering helicopter, sand lashing his skin, the jellyfish sting throbbing. He could only nod.

*Move. Get dressed. You're rescued! This is good news.*

Yet as he scrambled to find his cargo shorts, Brian's eyes burned with unshed tears. He blinked them away, distracted by the man being lowered on a winch to the edge of the beach. The sand whipped even more violently, and he and Troy had to duck their heads and turn their backs. Brian kept his eyes squeezed shut until he heard the roar of the engine and rotors retreat, the chopper backing off and the wind calming.

"G'day!" The man who'd been lowered jogged over, wearing an

orange jumpsuit and harness. He lifted off his helmet to reveal a shock of red hair and put his goggles on his forehead. "My word, is the world going to be shocked to see you blokes again!" He stuck out his hand, and Brian shook it automatically, Troy following suit.

"I'm Peter Cade." He frowned. "All right, there?"

Brian could only stare. *Is this real?* But it had to be—his hand smarted from Peter's firm handshake, reddened by holding the piece of sun-warmed fuselage. The sight of someone else on their beach was both miraculous and horrifying. Had it only been minutes ago that they'd lazed in the shade, the two of them in their world? Now a bomb had gone off.

*This is what you wanted! Rescue!*

Yet instead of feeling blissfully found, Brian was sick with the certainty he was losing everything.

"Are you ill?" Peter asked, glancing between them. "Injured?"

Troy was staring dumbly at Peter as well. Brian managed to get out, "Sorry. Just can't believe this is really happening."

Peter relaxed with a smile. "Believe it! You're going home, boys. Gonna get you hooked up and hoisted, then back to the ship."

"The ship," Troy echoed. "From…Australia? Are you the coast guard?"

"Nah, we're private contractors. Working out of Kiribati. Your little brother's paid a pretty penny for these searches. Wouldn't give up, and isn't that a bloody good thing? Can't lie, we thought you were long gone." He glanced around. "Is it only the two of you?"

Brian choked down a swell of bile and the guilt that had lessened, yet he knew would never really go away. "Yes. Paula died in the crash."

"Sorry to hear that, mate." Peter nodded to their decimated camp. "We'd best pack up your gear and get going, hey? I'll put out the big fire. Good job on that, and the SOS. We saw a flash miles away and came closer."

Troy lifted the signal mirror. "We had this."

"That was it for sure, then. Good work." With a nod, he hustled off to the signal fire.

While Peter smothered the big fire with sand, Brian dumped the water out of his suitcase and carefully tucked his shaving kit inside. He and Troy gathered up their wet, sand-covered boxers and worn tank tops. The frame of the teepee still stood, its woven palm fronds mostly torn away along with the orange blanket, which he couldn't see anywhere. Their silver emergency blankets and the torn mosquito net were still inside, caught on the log frame, along with some other fabric.

When his hand closed over the ridge of stars, Brian realized it was his forgotten uniform, which he'd shoved into a corner of their shelter. His stomach rebelled, clenching painfully. Convulsively swallowing the rush of saliva, he crawled out, dragging everything with him.

Troy collected the water bottles and flannel blankets, and they shoved it all inside the suitcase with Brian's leather shoes. He couldn't see the flip-flops anywhere; they were probably buried in the whipped-up sand.

The fishing kit, first aid, laundry rope, and flashlight went into the backpack, and they smothered the campfire. The chopper had come closer again, and Peter motioned them over. Brian and Troy hesitated, sharing a glance.

"I…" Troy opened and closed his mouth. "Brian…"

Brian wanted to say so much, but the roar of the chopper was louder and louder, and there wasn't time. Instead, he forced his lips into a smile and clapped Troy's shoulder when he longed to take his hand.

"Guys, we're burning daylight!" Peter called.

Heads down in the whirlwind, they were across the beach before Brian realized. "My hat!" Ridiculous panic seized him, and he spun around, squinting. He couldn't see it anywhere, but its light color made it hard to distinguish it from the whipping sand. He'd left it on the beach near the water after he'd been stung, and it could have been blown anywhere. He'd kept that little piece of his grandfather safe all these years, and now he'd lost it.

"Shit! I can't see it!" Troy yelled, spinning this way and that.

"Mate, we've got to go!" The chopper had lowered down a stretcher, and Peter had already strapped on their bags, giving a thumbs up to the chopper to hoist it. "Burning fuel. We'll get ya a new one!"

Of course Peter was right, but Brian still wanted to punch his smiling face. Instead, he nodded, and then it was time for the harness. The noise from the rotors was so loud and sand blowing so fiercely that Brian could only stand there with his eyes squeezed shut as Peter strapped a helmet on him and maneuvered him into the gear. The straps of the harness scraped his skin.

Then he was flying, his feet off the ground. He opened his eyes as he was pulled up through the air, watching Troy and Peter shrink. The irrational fear that they'd somehow leave Troy behind struck like a hammer, and Brian stayed glued to the window once he was safely in the chopper, watching with his heart in his throat as Troy was hoisted.

The man working the winch yelled instructions about staying in their seats before hauling Peter up. Brian's head throbbed with the cacophony, and he nodded on cue as Peter came up with grin and shouted a few exuberant things. Brian had no idea what.

He met Troy's shell-shocked gaze and tried to smile reassuringly. Then Peter yanked shut the door and the helicopter zoomed away without any further ado. Brian pressed his forehead to the window.

The haphazard rocks and bits of shiny fuselage making the crude letters of their SOS had all but disappeared in the maelstrom of sand. The fires smoldered, and the shell of their teepee stood barren and listing by the torn-up lean-to.

While their rescuers babbled words he didn't understand, Brian watched Golden Sands fade into the blue as if they'd never been there at all.

# Chapter Fifteen

"HOLD STILL."

Troy tried to bite his tongue, but couldn't keep the frustration from his voice. "I'm fine. I really don't need an MRI."

The technician nodded and spoke with a soothing tone that indicated she was going to ignore his protests. "I understand. The doctor's ordered a full battery of tests for you both just to make sure there are no issues."

"Brian's getting an MRI too?" Troy lifted his head, even though he could only see the bulk of the white machine looming. "Is he here?"

"He's in another exam suite. I'm sure you'll see him soon. Now let's relax and hold still."

When the scan started, the machine erupted with a loud hum that made Troy's ears ring. He cringed. He'd never realized how *noisy* the world was. Since the helicopter had appeared out of nowhere two days before, they'd been shuttled from it to a large boat powering to Kiritimati.

The crew had been welcoming, offering up Troy and Brian their own little cabins. There had been no way to say no; no way to sleep together. Nothing to do but try to smile when Brian gave a little goodnight wave and disappeared behind a closed door.

In the berth that was little more than a closet, Troy had slept fitfully, aching for Brian and their beach. Did Brian feel the same way? Troy kept wanting to reach for his hand.

He stared at the inside of the MRI machine, the noise merciless.

*Am I really here? Is this really happening?*

He wasn't sure whether to be afraid of waking up again under the mosquito net in their teepee, or exhilarated to have Brian's arms around him and the gentle tide returning.

*You're saved! Why aren't you happy?!*

And he was—of course he was. He'd see his family again any minute. He couldn't wait to hug his mother and brother and everyone again, to see them safe and healthy. To tell them he loved them so much and was sorry if he hadn't shown it enough.

But Troy twitched with anxiety, a boulder lodged in the pit of his stomach. All the lights and noise and people, and *where was Brian*? Was he okay? He'd seemed okay on the ship. They'd sat together in the ship's galley, eating chocolate ice cream and sharing a grin even though they both puked it up soon after.

Peter and others had talked at them endlessly, never leaving them alone. He and Brian hadn't touched each other at all, a new awkward distance between them, especially as they'd been interviewed by the US Coast Guard, who'd flown a Hercules plane to Kiritimati to pick them up. Innocent questions about their time on the island seemed…charged. Troy had let Brian do most of the talking, and Brian hadn't said much.

On the bumpy flight to Honolulu, Brian had leaned over and reminded him of the hundred thousand commercial flights a day. Reminded him he was safe. He'd squeezed Troy's forearm briefly with his palm, a flash of warmth and promise that had left Troy desolate.

*What happens now?*

He hadn't seen Brian since they'd been put in separate ambulances at the Honolulu airport, the piercing sirens made all the more ridiculous since they were *fine*. Trapped in the MRI machine, he wanted to either scream or curl up and go to sleep. He didn't have a clue where to start figuring out his feelings. Was it just over? And what was *it* anyway?

The room fell blissfully silent, and the technician's squeaky steps crossed the floor.

"All done. Feeling okay?"

The table he was on slid back out of the machine with a whir. "Yes. I told you, I'm fine."

Her smile didn't falter. "Okay then. Just a few more tests and you can rest. You've had a long journey."

He wanted to stubbornly argue, but she was right about that. He'd barely slept, but he'd relax when he saw Brian again. "Yeah."

"You're remarkably healthy, all things considered." She nodded to his foot, the skin on the end of his big toe scarred a faint red. "Doc said that was likely a centipede? Must have hurt like the devil."

"Uh-huh. It was bad." Memories rippled through him: Brian finding him in the darkness, then always nearby, his voice comforting and touch cool on Troy's fevered skin.

"You must be excited to get back to your life." She pulled over a wheelchair, and he dutifully sat so she could wheel him out and down a hushed hallway past curious glances from other staff and the odd patient.

*My life.* After truly living day to day for the first time since he was a little kid, he had no idea what his life looked like anymore.

WHEN THE DOOR opened, Troy hoped to see Brian but expected to see a nurse. Instead it was his mother, who burst into wailing tears.

"Oh, Bongbong!" Muttering in Tagalog too fast for him to under-stand, she rushed to the side of the bed, throwing herself practically on top of him before he could even sit up. Troy held her tightly, not trying to stop his own tears as he inhaled her flowery perfume. He smoothed his hand over her short, dark curls, his voice cracking.

"Mom. I missed you so much."

Wiping her eyes, she stood, tiny at five foot nothing. Her face glis-tened, eyes roving over him and hands running down his arms as if to check for breaks. There were circles under her eyes, but she still looked far younger than fifty-one. "Too skinny!"

"I'm fine, Mom. We ate pretty well, all things considered."

"We'll do all your favorites when you get home. Chicken adobo and kare-kare."

"That sounds amazing. Mom, I'm so sorry."

"For what? Did you cast a magical spell and make a cyclone?" She smoothed a hand over his hair and kissed his forehead. "I prayed every moment for you. God heard me. Oh, Bongbong." Fresh tears glistened in her eyes. "My brave son."

"But if I hadn't freaked out at Ty and rented the plane—" He looked past her into the empty room. "Where is he?"

Sniffing, she pulled up a chair. "Gosh, so much commotion here, especially with all those clickers outside. Don't know how they got here so fast with their cameras."

The thought of dealing with the paparazzi made him cringe, but he wouldn't be deflected. "Mom, where's Ty?"

Her face tightened, and she looked down at her hands as she clasped them. "Boy is..."

An awful, sickening fear had bile rising in Troy's throat. "Where is he?" He shot up to sitting. "Mom, what happened?"

"Shhh. It's all right. Boy is in a hospital place. Rehabilitation."

Just like Troy was "Bongbong," Tyson had always been "Boy" to their mother and the rest of their family on her side. Nicknames were a Filipino thing he'd never questioned. "He's in rehab?"

She pressed her lips together and nodded.

Troy exhaled and flopped back down to the too-soft mattress. "Oh, thank God."

"You aren't upset he's not here to see you?"

"As long as he's in rehab, that's all I care about. He's really okay?" He brushed his feet rhythmically against the metal frame at the bottom of the bed. How strange it was to be on a proper mattress again. Didn't feel real.

"Yes, really, Bongbong. I wouldn't lie to you."

Troy exhaled with a smile. Growing up, he'd known he was in trouble if she actually called him his real name. "Thank God he finally saw reason."

"Well, your girlfriend was the one who talked him into it, praise the lord."

His stomach dropped. "My girlfriend? Savannah?"

She clucked her tongue. "Who else? She's on her way from New York City. She was crying on the phone. So happy."

"Oh. We broke up before I left."

"A silly fight." His mother waved her hand dismissively. "All in the past."

He wanted to argue, but there were more important things. "Tell me about Ty. He's doing well? Following the program?"

"So they say." Her smile was forced. "After you went away, he was at the rock bottom. The rest of the tour was canceled of course. The authorities said you were dead, but I knew better. I prayed day and night, and God answered." Her eyes welled and she leaned over to kiss his forehead with dry lips. "Oh, Bongbong. I knew you would return."

*After you went away.* His throat thickened. "It's okay, Mom. I'm here."

After sniffling, she cleared her throat. "When they said there was no hope to find you, Boy took it very badly. We all did, of course. I'd come down to Sydney with your Auntie Gloria and Uncle Jojo. We wanted to be close when they found you. But then they said they weren't going to look anymore." She clenched her jaw. "We told them you were alive, but..."

"It's okay, Mom. They were just doing their job."

"Yes, well. Boy went out of control. So angry. Drinking everything, and all the other too."

*The other.* Suppressing a shudder, Troy thought of his father on the black and white kitchen tiles. "But he eventually agreed to rehab?"

She nodded. "Savannah convinced him. She flew home to LA with him. He's been at the center for almost two months now."

"Nick too?"

Muttering a Tagalog curse, she shook her head. "That one says he doesn't need it."

"Idiot. But I'm glad Ty listened." Troy owed Savannah a huge thanks, and probably an apology too. Even if she wasn't the right girl, he cared about her. The words rolled over in his mind, nausea curling through his belly.

*The right girl.* Did he even want a *girl* anymore? His palms got sweaty. Where was Brian?

"Boy sure wouldn't listen to me. And why should he?" His mother's lips trembled. "Why should he listen to me when I did nothing before? When I let your father kill himself?"

"Mom…" Troy grabbed her hand. "Dad made his own choices. It wasn't your fault."

"I should have stopped him. Now look, Boy is poisoning himself too." Her nails dug into his skin. "I pretended your father was okay. I let you deal with too much. It should have been me dealing, not looking everywhere else but at the bad truth." Trembling, her voice broke. "Can you forgive me, Bongbong? I wish I could go back and be different."

After Troy's teenage years of stress and fear, of whispered resentment that she'd let him deal with far too much, far too young, he'd have thought when this moment came, his anger would finally erupt.

But he was *alive* and rescued and holding her hand, solid and warm and real, and that was what mattered now. "Of course I forgive you. It's done. Neither of us can go back. We need to go forward. We have a second chance."

With a sob, she took his face in her hands and kissed him. "A second chance. No more pretending. Never again."

Heart thumping, Troy nodded. *No more pretending.* He had to see Brian. They had to figure out…everything. He swung his legs over the side of the bed. "I have to find—"

"Whoa, whoa, mister." With surprising strength, his mother hauled him back onto the mattress. "The doctors are still running their tests."

He huffed. "I'm *fine.*"

"Yes, you are. But we wait for the tests, Bongbong. No debating."

There was no point in arguing with his mother. "Ty knows I'm okay?"

"Of course. You'll see him soon. He is getting better, and now it's your turn."

"Have they mentioned anything about Brian?"

A tap on the door preceded an employee entering with a lunch tray. She was barely inside when Troy's relatives flooded into the room in a chorus of greetings and tears. Two sets of his aunts and uncles fawned over him, remarking on his tan and how he needed to eat.

The young woman who brought his meal squeezed through the crowd and managed to get his lunch on the tray and swing it over his bed. "There are only two visitors permitted at a time," she said, lost in the cacophony of Tagalog.

Troy smiled at her. "Sorry. They'll leave soon, I promise."

She met his eyes and blushed, smiling and nodding as she scurried away. For a moment, Troy was puzzled by her reaction, and then he remembered. He was famous. He had fans. The life that had become so distant on Golden Sands was his again.

*Where's Brian?*

As his family talked over each other at him, Troy had to smile, affection for them smoothing over the nagging worry about Brian, at least for the moment. He blinked rapidly, keeping tears at bay as he listened to Auntie Thelma and his mother bicker over something to do with food.

"Oh, here he is!" Auntie Gloria threw up her hands.

Troy couldn't see through the crush of bodies in the small room. "Huh? Who?"

"Move, move, move." His mother shuffled everyone aside, and there stood Brian in jeans and a new purple T-shirt that said *Aloha means love*, accompanied by an image of palm trees. Troy's heart flopped like a dying fish. Brian was there. He was okay.

He was freshly showered, but still not shaved. With a deep pang of *wanting*, Troy remembered Brian's head in his lap, and the scrape of the razor over skin, Brian's eyes closed with total trust and a contented sigh on their last island spa day.

"Hi," Troy squawked, his heart thumping.

"Sorry to interrupt." Brian smiled wanly. "I'll come back later."

Troy's argument was lost in a flurry of similar arguments from his family, and his mother caught Brian's wrist as he pivoted in the doorway.

"God bless you for saving my son." She clasped his hand between her own. "God bless you."

"I didn't—there's no need to thank me." Brian smiled at her weakly.

"No need?" She argued this vociferously, Troy's aunties and uncles joining into a chorus.

It was beyond bizarre to see Brian and his family in the same room, and Troy didn't know what to feel. He wanted to rush into Brian's arms and kiss him, but… Taking out the fact this his family would probably pass out in unison from the shock, would Brian even want that? Should Troy want that?

As his mother pledged enthusiastically to fatten him up as well, Brian edged backward with a forced smile. "Okay, thank you. Troy, I'll… I'll leave you with your family. Talk to you later."

"Brian, I want—"

Then he was gone, and Troy's mother and aunties cooed about how handsome he was and what a lovely man. Troy smiled and nodded at the right places, wishing what he wanted wasn't a giant knot to untangle.

AT THE KNOCK, Troy rushed to the door of his hotel room. It had to be Brian, and—

"Oh my God." Savannah stood there, her long brown hair pulled back in a ponytail, tears tracking her pale cheeks, and a little hot-pink suitcase at her feet. She threw her arms around him. "I was afraid to really believe it."

Troy hugged her back, struck by a wave of déjà vu at the press of her slim body and vanilla musk scent. "I'm okay."

She pulled back, still clutching his shoulders and examining him. "You're so thin. Are you sure you're okay?" She hiccupped, tears still falling as she reached up to brush back his hair. "Oh, Troy. I'm so glad you're here. We thought…well, you know what we thought."

"I know. But I'm fine."

"Are you sure? God, I can't imagine what you went through."

"I'm fine."

"I can't believe it's really you. I missed you so much, baby." Savannah leaned up, her lips zeroing in on his.

Troy stumbled back. "It's good to see you too."

Smiling tentatively, she asked, "Are you going to let me in?"

He retreated farther out of the doorway. "Of course." When she'd passed by, he collected her suitcase and closed the door.

Savannah bent and unzipped her black high-heeled boots before yanking them off. "Ugh. I'm retaining so much water after that flight. I must look like crap." She straightened up and shook her head, laughing with a tinge of hysteria. "Not that any of that matters. I'm sorry. I don't know what to say. This is like talking to a ghost, you know?" After taking off her suede jacket and tossing it over a nearby chair, she stood there waiting in her skinny jeans and green silk sweater, vulnerable in bare feet and looking just as beautiful as always. "What was it like? How did you survive?"

Memories of the island and Brian flickered through his mind like a movie on fast-forward. They'd managed to avoid snakes on Golden Sands, but there was a python around Troy's chest now, crushing his lungs.

He had to say something. Anything. "Long story."

She smiled tentatively. "Right. You must be exhausted. Do you want to go to bed?"

Ignoring her question, he tugged at the sleeves of his Henley, then shoved his hands into the pockets of the too-big jeans his mother had brought. "Mom says you got Ty into rehab. Thank you."

"Of course." Her face brightened. "He's doing really well. Have you been able to talk to him?"

"Tomorrow. It was past curfew when I could call. Time difference."

"Right. I have no idea what time it is." She rubbed her face. "Guess it's the middle of the night here."

"You didn't have to come." It sounded harsher than he intended, and the hurt evident in her dark eyes and the downturn of her mouth sent a flare of guilt through him. "I just mean...but it's nice that you did. Thank you."

"You don't have to *thank* me. Of course I'm here." She stepped toward him, her arms slipping around his waist. "My boyfriend just came back from the dead."

Troy sighed internally, bringing his hands to her shoulders. He needed to find Brian, and this was the last thing he wanted to deal with, which was probably pretty shitty of him. He hated to see the tears well in Savannah's eyes.

"I know we had that fight," she said. "I know I screwed up. But come on. You can't seriously still be mad? After all this? When I found out your plane was missing... It was unbearable. I wanted so badly to tell you how much I love you."

"Savannah, I'm not mad."

Her lips trembled. "Then what are you?"

"I don't know." It was the truth, at least.

"I can't believe this." She sniffed, gripping his waist. "I thought..." Shaking her head, she choked on a sob. "I'm such an idiot."

"You're not." All he could do was hold her while she wept against his chest, her tears wetting his shirt. She was small and soft and lovely, but God, it made him ache for Brian.

Her voice was muffled in his chest. "I know I fucked up by not telling you Ty was using."

"It's okay. It doesn't matter anymore." Troy rubbed her back.

She jerked up her head. "How can you say it doesn't matter? Of course it matters! *You* matter to me! Our *relationship* matters!"

Gently, he eased away from her and sat on the closest bed. After a few moments of sniffling and wiping her eyes, Savannah sat beside him. She stared down at her hands, spreading her manicured fingers over her thighs. "I'm so sorry."

"I'm sorry too. But it's in the past now. All forgiven."

Her eyebrows lifted as she looked at him. "Forgiven? But not...not back together?"

"I care about you, and I want us to be friends. I'm so grateful that you convinced Ty to get help."

Savannah's breath stuttered. "Just friends? Troy, we were so good together. I know we could be again."

He tried to think of the best way to say that everything had changed. That the changed thing was *him*, and nothing she did or said would matter.

Then it was too late to say anything because Savannah was straddling his lap and kissing him, pushing him back to the mattress. "Baby, just let me love you. I know you need it."

Her lips tasted faintly of the berry lip gloss she'd always liked, and he was struck by another wave of déjà vu. She was a beautiful woman, kissing and rubbing against him, and it felt good. He could have let her blow him or fuck him or whatever she wanted to do. But it wasn't what he wanted. She wasn't who he wanted.

Taking hold of her shoulders, Troy pushed gently. "Savannah, I'm sorry."

Her eyes welled with fresh tears. "Didn't you miss me at all? You don't even want to screw me? No strings, okay?"

He knew how it would feel to fuck her; knew she could get him off. But God help him, he didn't want it. *Where's Brian?*

After another few moments of conspicuous silence, she jumped off him and dashed into the bathroom. The door was closed before he could manage to call after her. With a sigh, he went to tap on the smooth wood. "I'm sorry. It's not you." He waited. "Savannah?"

Through sobs, she called, "Just give me a few minutes, okay?"

"Sure."

Sitting on the end of the bed closest to the door again, he miserably listened to her cry. Then the tap ran for a while, and finally the door opened. Her eyes were red and puffy and her makeup gone, hair hanging lank around her face. Water had splashed the front of her sweater. She sniffed. "I'll call the desk about another room."

"Don't be silly. It's the middle of the night. There are two beds."

She stood with arms crossed, her gaze on her bare feet. "Are you sure?"

"I'm sure."

She sat on the end of the other bed, not looking at him. "I guess we should get some sleep."

"It's not you, Savannah. It really isn't."

Her chin wobbled, and she looked at the ceiling, pressing her lips together. When she had control, she said, "It's fine. You want to see other girls. I'm sure the line has already started in the lobby. I guess I can't blame you."

"It's not like that."

"Then what's it like?"

He thought of Brian's low laugh, and the feel of his stubble, and the way he listened when Troy sang, smiling as if Troy was an angel. He heard snatches of the new songs running through his mind, waiting to take form. "I'm not the same person. I can't just go back to the way things were."

She ran a hand through her long hair, twisting it into a knot and releasing it. "It's my fault for thinking things would be different. You told me you didn't love me. But I guess I wanted to believe you didn't mean it. That we didn't really break up—we just had a fight, like all couples do sometimes. That you realized how much I meant to you when your life flashed before your eyes." She raised a hand when Troy opened his mouth. "I get it. You can't help the way you feel. Let's go to sleep."

"Okay. I'm going to have another shower." He smiled weakly. "Can't get enough of hot water."

Savannah's smile was equally lackluster. "I bet. Good night, Troy. Enjoy the shower." She hesitated as she unzipped her suitcase. "And no matter what, I'm so glad you're okay. I hope you know that."

He swallowed hard. "I do. And I hope you know I really care about you. I want to be friends. I mean it."

She nodded and busied herself with her suitcase, not meeting his gaze.

Troy escaped to the bathroom, closing the door behind him. The hot shower beckoned, and he avoided looking in the mirror. He knew what he'd see—too many ribs sticking out, skin tanned and peeling, his hair too long and curling. He'd see stubble on his face, and he'd have to shave it off himself.

*Be in the now. There is only now.*

Eyes closed, Troy stood under the thunder of water for a long time.

When he finally emerged, the room was dark aside from the little lamp by the minibar. He tiptoed to the bed by the door, his skin damp and a towel around his waist.

"It's okay, you don't have to be quiet," Savannah said. "Tired as hell, but of course can't sleep to save my life." She was curled onto her side facing the window, and he could only see her back, the straps of her white nightie pale against her tan.

"Sorry."

"Oh, he came by while you were in there. Guess he couldn't sleep either."

Troy's heart stuttered. "Who?"

"Brian Sinclair."

"What did he say?" Troy realized his voice had shot up in volume and also a few octaves. He lowered it. "Did he leave his room number?"

"Uh-uh. Said not to bother you."

Blood rushed in Troy's ears. "What else did he say? What did *you* say?"

Savannah looked over her shoulder with a frown. "Why are you spazzing out? I told him you were in the shower. Asked if he had a message, and he said no."

Heart in his throat, Troy forced a casual tone. "Oh, okay. Cool." He tugged on his jeans and pawed through the suitcase of clothes his mom had brought, yanking out a blue hoodie. He pulled the soft material over his head.

"I'll just go find him," he said. "Can't sleep."

"Troy, what's wrong?"

"Nothing." Barely remembering to grab his key card, he slipped on his favorite Rainbow brand sandals, so familiar and molded to his feet after the years he'd worn them. "Get some rest."

"You're going now? It's the middle of the night."

"My clock's all messed up. We'll have breakfast in a few hours. I'll be back."

The door shut behind him with a quiet *whoosh* and *click*. He stood in the silent hallway. Now what? He barely resisted the urge to start banging on doors to find Brian. Was he on this floor? He could have been anywhere.

Troy strode to the elevator, his sandals silent on the plush carpet. The front desk would know.

*"He's in the shower."*

The girl's voice echoed in every step Brian took. He distantly recalled that Savannah was her name. She'd looked young and beautiful, wearing a silky little white nightgown that barely grazed her thighs. It hadn't seemed to bother her to answer the door practically naked, but he supposed with a body like that, why should it?

He'd glimpsed past her narrow shoulders into the room. The covers pushed down on one of the beds, a pink suitcase open on the other, articles of clothing abandoned on the floor.

*"He's in the shower."*

It shouldn't have hurt. Shouldn't have reached into Brian's chest and squeezed his heart so hard he was afraid it was irreparable. They were back in the real world. Troy's family was here, his girlfriend. His old life. His *real* life.

Walking into that hospital room, Brian had felt like an intruder, and he'd certainly felt it even more acutely when Savannah had opened the door to Troy's room. God, Brian had hoped...

*What? What did I hope for? What did I expect?*

"Sir?"

Blinking, he focused on the young woman behind the counter. "Yes. What was that?"

"Are you sure you want to go to the airport now? It's only three o'clock. Nothing will be open for a couple hours."

"I'm sure. Thank you." The thong of the plastic flip-flops he'd been given rubbed uncomfortably between his toes, and Brian lifted his foot to fiddle with it briefly. "There's a plane arriving for me in a few hours."

She smiled, but it was uneasy. "All right. If you head outside, the doorman will hail a taxi right away."

"Thank you. My airline company took care of the room, yes?"

"They did. Is there any luggage?"

Brian held up his shaving kit. "Nope." He'd taken the kit when they'd insisted on putting him into an ambulance, not willing to part with it. He'd lost his grandfather's hat, but he wouldn't lose this. He didn't know what had become of his suitcase or backpack and didn't give a shit.

"Have a safe trip home, Mr. Sinclair." She smiled kindly, and the other night clerk, a young man nearby tapping a computer and clearly eavesdropping, wished him well.

*Home.*

As Brian pushed open the first set of glass doors, thinking he might puke, Troy's voice rang out.

"Brian!"

Relief, happiness, and dread combined, zapping him with nervous energy. Brian gripped the leather shaving kit, waiting in the vestibule. The door closed behind Troy, shutting out the ambient sounds of the lobby. There was only silence now in the glass rectangle as they stared at each other.

"Are you seriously leaving without saying goodbye?" Troy's curls were wet, his tanned skin somehow pallid in the too-bright lighting.

"You were busy. I didn't want to bother you." It was hollow and inadequate to Brian's own ears, and Troy stared at him incredulously.

"You didn't want to *bother* me? Are you serious right now? After...after everything? That's it?"

"I have to get back."

"To *what?*"

Brian hesitated. "My job. Interviews with the company, the safety board."

"You don't have to run away in the middle of the night!"

Brian was very aware of the desk clerks and the doorman watching them from both sides. He didn't think they could hear them talking, but if Troy kept shouting, they would. "Lower your voice."

"No!"

"We're not alone."

"I—" Troy's nostrils flared, and he glanced left and right. The clerks jerked their heads back to their computers, and the doorman moved to the far end of the front entry, standing near a waiting taxi. Clenching his jaw, Troy spoke quietly. "You don't have to go. You sure as hell don't have to go *right now*."

"I need to get to Auckland."

His brows drew together. "Auckland?"

"Paula's parents live there. George and Maia." His smile was brittle, about to shatter. "I finally know their names."

Softening, Troy sighed. "It doesn't have to be right this second, does it?

"The company's sent a jet for me. I have to see them right away. I have to tell them…" He shook his head. "I don't know what to tell them, but I owe them an explanation."

"Okay. Then what?"

All Brian could do was force his shoulders into a shrug.

"We just got back. I thought we'd…"

Aching all over, Brian swallowed thickly. "What? Troy, it's like you said. We're back. This is all real again. Real lives, waiting to pick up where they left off. Your family and your band. Your girlfriend."

Troy's voice rose. "She's not my girlfriend. I told you, I broke up with her before I left Sydney. I'm not—" He exhaled and whispered, "I didn't sleep with her tonight." He took a step closer. "Is that what you think? Is that why you're doing this? It's over with Savannah."

Brian shouldn't have felt the rush of relief, but it flowed through him sweetly. *It doesn't change anything. One of us has to be realistic.* "No. That's not why. I told you, I have to see Paula's parents."

"Don't use that as an excuse." Troy's eyes glistened. "There's still so much we need to talk about."

Brian yearned to take Troy in his arms and banish his tears. But he remained rooted to the spot, the gleaming marble tiles under his new flip-flops. "What is there to say? We're back. It's over. You have your life, and I have mine."

"And that's it? Separate ways, like it was all…nothing?"

Brian managed to keep his voice even. "I live in Sydney. You live in LA."

"You don't have to live there! I don't have to live in LA! We can do anything we want."

"Troy, you have so much to go back to. What did you expect would change?"

"Everything's changed! And I expected you to still be my friend!" He took a shuddering breath. "If nothing else, I expected that."

Brian knew his protest was feeble. "I am. I'll always care—"

"Stop. Just don't." Troy crossed his arms over his stomach protectively. "I get it. You don't want…this. Me."

Brian's feet moved closer, but he stopped just out of reach. "Listen to yourself," he murmured. "Think about your family and your career. Why would you want to be stuck with a washed-up, screwed-up pilot pushing forty? You're a rock star, remember? Even if you don't like that label, it doesn't make it less true. And now that we're rescued, we're not stuck together. We were the only two people there. Of course we bonded. It was a remarkable, extreme circumstance, and it's over. We have to be realistic about who we are." He lowered his voice even more. "It's not like we're gay now." He tried to laugh dismissively. "We were horny."

*It's what's best for him. I owe him this. I owe him his life back.*

Troy only stared, hurt emanating from his dark eyes. Before he could respond, camera flashes exploded to life outside, and they blinked in the glare as the doorman attempted to wrangle the paparazzi, who must have been tipped off. Troy closed his eyes, his shoulders lifting and lowering as he breathed deeply.

When he opened his eyes, he plastered a smile on his face, so bright and fake it was painful. He stuck out his hand. "Well, thanks for everything. Have a good life."

The flashes were still popping in the night, and Brian had no choice but to take Troy's hand, squeezing his palm. The lump in his throat was choking him, and he couldn't speak. He managed a nod, and then Troy was gone, disappearing toward the elevator bank, his stride forceful.

Tearing his gaze away, Brian escaped into the humid night and a waiting taxi, nodding at the doorman's profuse apologies, flashes still blinding him. At least he had an excuse for blinking away tears as he thought of the last time they'd kissed with hot sand between their toes, not knowing it was the end.

# Chapter Sixteen

"**W**HAT DO YOU mean he's gone?" Lara's voice shot up in concert with her sculpted eyebrows. She nudged Troy's auntie with a tight smile and sidestepped the bed. There were far too many people crammed into Troy's hotel room. All he'd wanted to do was sleep, but it was past noon and his time was up.

"Why aren't you in a suite?" Joe demanded. "Patty, call the desk. We need a bigger room for Troy."

Along with his family and Savannah, who was puffy-eyed and un-characteristically quiet, the band's "people" had arrived. Joe was their middle-aged manager, and he'd given Troy a tearful bear hug, followed by Lara the PR director, Patty the assistant, and Steve and Carlos, whose jobs Troy didn't even know.

Troy appreciated everyone's concern and obviously sincere happiness in seeing him, but now he was backed up near the window, the blinds still tightly shut. He just wanted them to go away. "I don't need a suite. I'm going home tonight."

Lara turned to Joe. "I thought we'd agreed on tomorrow? Give us some time to strategize."

Troy spoke up before Joe could answer. "I booked my own flight. Well, Savannah booked it for me and my mom." The flight hadn't had enough seats left for his whole family, but he'd made sure they could get back ASAP and that it would be charged to his credit card. "I need to see my brother. A two-minute phone call isn't enough. Ty needs me, and he needs to stay in rehab, so I'm going to him."

Lara smiled tightly. "Of course. We all want the very best for him. For both of you." Her power suit looked impeccable, a blue scarf knotted perfectly at her neck and complementing her golden hair. "Now what's this about Brian Sinclair leaving?"

"He left," Troy replied flatly.

"Is he coming back?"

Mouth dry, Troy gulped from a bottle of water. "No."

"But...he can't just *leave*." Lara smiled again. "We have a press conference to do. Can you call him?"

Troy realized with a horrible burst of nausea that he didn't even have Brian's number. "He left."

"But there are so many questions the world wants answered, and it's really best if we control the message and you two are a united front."

Troy's mother squeezed in beside Lara. "The world will have to go jump in the river. Troy's coming home."

"I'm not doing a press conference. Sorry." He shrugged.

Lara glanced down at her tightly gripped phone as if there would be some answer there. Then she met his gaze with calm, practiced understanding. "I know you've been through an ordeal we can't imagine. But we want you to help us understand. There is so much love for you out there, you have no idea. This is a miracle! Let us celebrate you."

In the past, he never would have argued. He'd have gone along with whatever they wanted, carried away in their current. If he flat out refused, he wouldn't have any peace. "I'll give a statement outside the hotel. But no press conference."

"All right," Lara smoothly agreed after a glance with Joe. "Patty?" With a nod to her minion, she turned back to Troy. "We'll craft something for you and have it ready by—"

"I don't need that. I'll figure out what to say."

"Speaking off the cuff is never a good idea, especially when you've been under strain," Lara insisted. "You need—"

"I need everyone to leave me the fuck alone!"

In the sudden hush, Troy's heart thumped hollowly. His mother stared at him with wide eyes, and he waited for her admonishment to apologize and not be rude. But instead, she clapped her hands together sharply.

"You heard him. Leave." As the band's people filed out first, she spoke to the family in rapid-fire Tagalog. Troy only knew as much as a child—questions about being hungry, thirsty, tired, happy—and usually answered in English. She turned back to him, giving his arms a squeeze. "We'll let you rest, Bongbong."

"No, you don't have to go. I'm sorry. I was dying to see you all for so long. I'm just..." He rubbed his face. "I'm sorry."

Savannah spoke from the door. "I'll handle Lara and Joe. Don't worry." She disappeared before he could thank her.

His aunties and uncles followed. "We'll go to the pool," Uncle Jojo joked, patting his broad belly. "Work on our tans." They all smiled and waved and acted like Troy wasn't an enormous asshole.

"You need more rest," his mother said, going for the room phone. "I'll order you food, and then you sleep."

"It's okay. I'm fine, Mom."

She clucked her tongue. "Fine? You were dead, Bongbong." Shaking her head, she muttered to herself, "Okay, let's see if they have anything halfway decent."

Troy didn't argue as she called for room service, ordering far too much. Her voice was even, but when she turned, he could see the tears she refused to let fall. Reaching out, he hugged her. She clung to him, and neither of them said anything for a minute.

When she stepped back, she sniffled loudly. "All right, I'll leave you alone now."

"No. Stay, Mom. Please? We can watch TV. I haven't seen TV in months." He managed a smile. "And you can help me eat all that food."

"All right, if you want."

They settled side-by-side on the bed, leaning against the pillows. It was strange to handle a remote control again, and Troy cycled through the channels almost as if he was seeing television for the first time. It seemed too bright and loud. Then he spotted his own face, and his thumb froze over the button.

"Who cares what they're saying?" His mom reached for the remote. "Let's find a nice movie."

Troy held the remote away, his eyes glued to the screen. "Wait."

There was Brian's picture now, smiling and handsome in his pilot's uniform. No dimples in his cheeks, which meant it wasn't a real smile. Then there he was in the grainy footage of his first crash, diving out the cockpit window as fire tore through the plane.

His mother tsked. "I'm so glad he was with you, Bongbong. Superman, eh? So brave! We're so grateful. And of course that poor woman. How awful for you."

Troy watched the news anchors talking, not hearing the words. There was a new picture now, and his heart skipped. It was from last night, he and Brian downstairs in the glass vestibule, shaking hands, a smile painted on Troy's face. Brian held his shaving kit in his other hand, and Troy thought of the scrape of the blade and the concentration on Brian's face, his breath puffing over Troy's skin.

Brian kissing him, rutting against him, touching him, fucking him. Making him feel more precious and wanted than a million fans ever could. Leaving him without a last kiss.

"He's a very good man, hmm?"

Troy didn't trust himself to speak. He nodded, flipping the channel with pushes of his thumb until he found a *Full House* rerun. The food arrived soon after, and he picked at a too-rich and greasy burger and fries, barely tasting it even when he threw it up later that afternoon.

THE SOUND ON the TV in the private lounge was tinny, but Brian would have known Troy's voice anywhere. He sat on the edge of the plush couch with Joan, the airline rep, watching Troy stand outside the hotel in Honolulu where they'd said goodbye—when? A day ago? Two? He wasn't even sure.

"I wanted to thank you all for your love and support. My family, friends, and fans—I don't know what I'd do without you. I had faith that I'd see you again, and I'm so grateful to be here. And I'm incredibly grateful to Brian Sinclair for saving my life more than once. I know I wouldn't have survived without his bravery and generosity."

Brian couldn't breathe, couldn't move. From the corner of his eye, he was aware of Joan's presence, and he struggled for composure.

Troy looked down for a moment. "And most of all, I need to thank Paula Mercado, who landed our plane against all odds and lost her life. My heart goes out to her family and friends, and I can't begin to tell you how grateful I am for Paula's courage and skill. Thank you."

Then he was gone, whisked into a waiting car so quickly Brian had barely blinked. He sat back on the cushions, exhaling. The reporters were all shouting, and Joan muted the TV.

"Seems like a nice young man."

"What? Yes. Yes, very nice." *Smart, sweet, kind, funny, passionate.*

Joan crossed her legs, the fabric of her pantsuit swishing together. She was an older woman, no-nonsense and efficient, her graying hair in a bun. He'd never dealt with her before and couldn't remember her title at the company although she'd surely told him.

He was extremely glad she was there. She'd arrived with the jet in Honolulu and debriefed him on the way to Auckland. Paula's parents had met them in a private hangar in the airport, and it had been...

Well, it had been torture. Maia had wept, George's stoic facade cracking several times. Brian had assured them Paula hadn't felt any pain, which was the truth at least. There one moment and gone the next. Visibility on the beach had been so poor she probably hadn't even seen the cliff coming.

He didn't tell them about her arm.

Now he was back in Sydney, waiting for entry. His passport and wallet had been in his coat pocket on the plane, but Joan assured him it was being handled. She'd also given him a replacement cell phone, telling him it was all set up with his account. Brian knew he should turn it on and check his messages, but it sat beside him untouched.

Soon, customs officials bustled in, and after perfunctory questions, Brian was cleared and in the back of a Town Car with Joan. She apparently didn't feel the need to fill silence with chitchat, for which he was profoundly grateful.

As they drove to his apartment in Southern Sydney, Brian stared at the passing scenery. It was familiar and utterly foreign at the same time. Joan assured him his apartment and possessions were untouched and his car still parked in its underground spot. He hadn't been officially declared dead yet, so it had all been waiting in limbo.

"How are you for money?" she asked.

Brian stared at a group of kids on the steps of a building, laughing and goofing around. *Money? Oh, right. Money.* "I should be fine. I have some savings."

She nodded. "Shall we stop for groceries on the way?"

"Right. Sure." He'd longed for food so much on the island, but even the prospect of an ice-cold beer left him ambivalent. When he'd imagined eating and drinking all his favorite things again, Troy had been there too.

"Why don't I nip into the store and get you a few things." She spoke to the driver, and Brian tuned out again.

When they turned down his road, he blinked at the mass of people clustered by the three-story apartment building, one of many lining the street along with tall trees Brian didn't know the name of. "Who..." Then he realized it was the media. "Oh."

Joan leaned forward. "Don't slow down," she told the driver. "Make that left, and then another. The manager's meeting us around back." She turned to Brian. "Don't worry. The press will lose interest in a few days. We'll give a statement on your behalf. It'll be standard: gratitude at being alive, condolences to Paula's family, etc. Do you want to approve it?"

223

"No. Say whatever you want."

She nodded briskly and tapped something into her phone. "I'll be back to get you tomorrow afternoon. Sleep in, get acclimated. I know this must be overwhelming."

There was something about her straightforward demeanor and lightly graying hair that reminded him vividly of his grandmother in that moment, and Brian had to swallow hard. "Thank you," he croaked.

Joan smiled then, a sad little movement. "If you need anything, ask me. I mean it. I wish I could give you a few days before we meet with the safety board, but they're chomping at the bit. It'll all be done soon, and then you can rest and...take stock."

The building superintendent waited by the entrance to the underground parking, ushering them inside as reporters raced down the alley, shouting questions Brian wouldn't answer even if he could make them out.

The super chattered about how glad he was Brian had returned, pressing a new set of keys into his hand. Brian nodded and smiled, following him up the stairs to his second-floor apartment. He carried the several bags of groceries Joan had bought, the plastic digging into his fingers.

He couldn't wait to be alone.

THE PARROTS WERE late.

He could tell the sun was up, bright beyond his eyelids. Murmuring, Brian stretched his arms over his head, careful not to tear the mosquito net. Yet his fingers didn't brush the airy fabric. Had Troy—

Gut churning, Brian opened his eyes and stared at the white stucco ceiling. Rays of sunshine streamed through the sheer curtains on the other side of his shoe box, a gauzy film over the sliding glass doors to his little terrace balcony. There was no sand stuck between his toes, and his skin and hair weren't tight with salt and sun.

He wondered how long it would take to remember that he was home, and Golden Sands was lost to him, thousands of miles away. That Troy was too.

*Home.*

He would have laughed if his throat wasn't so dry. His apartment was a simple open space with his bed pushed against one wall, a TV mounted on the other and a beige love seat roughly in the middle. The shallow kitchen stretched along the other side, little more than a fridge, stove, and sink with a few cupboards. The door to the bathroom was just beside it. There was one closet, which Brian's clothes shared with cleaning products shoved in the bottom.

After four days of having his blackout curtains closed to thwart photographers who'd actually tried climbing one of the trees in front of the building, he'd gone to sleep late last night with the sliding door open a few inches and a breeze coming through the screen. Let them take a picture of him sleeping. Fuck it.

Street sounds came into focus. Cars driving by with a low zoom. A bus with brakes that screeched just a little as it pulled up across the road. Beyond the merry chirps of birds were murmurs of conversation, indicating the media was still gathered on the lawn. In the hallway, a door closed, a dog barking a few times before being silenced. The fridge hummed.

This had been his home for three years now. He should have felt comforted to be back within the four cream walls, his one piece of cheap IKEA art—blue flowers in a yellow vase—looking down through freshly Windexed glass. The super had kindly dusted and cleaned, but even with the balcony door open, the musty smell remained.

Brian's bed was soft, pillows positively luxurious in their plain cotton cases (also IKEA). It had to be close to noon, but he was in no rush to move. The duvet was tangled around his legs, but he only idly kicked at the wadded material. He wore boxers that slid down his hips. After three days of interviews with safety board and company officials, he didn't have anything to do.

The screen on his phone on the bedside table lit up with another call. The ringer was off, and he glanced at the number, which had no name attached to it. As he let it go to the voice mail he wasn't checking, the thought occurred.

*What if it's Troy?*

He was reaching for the phone before he could talk himself out of it, pressing the code for his mailbox. He held the plastic tightly to his ear. Of course there was a litany of other messages to get through first. He erased the media calls immediately. They were interspersed with familiar voices, messages from old friends in the States that started the same way.

*"I don't know if this is still the right number…"*

Call after call, the friends he'd cut out of his life too easily wished him well and asked to reconnect. Even Rebecca and Alicia had called, leaving awkward, short messages of support. Alicia hadn't asked to see him again, or for him to return the call, but he hadn't expected it. *"I'm glad you're not dead. Take care and stay that way."*

The voice mail bounced to the menu.

*"You have no new messages. To send a message, press—"*

Jabbing the red end button too hard, Brian tossed his phone to the foot of the bed. He wanted to call people back. He did. But what would he say? How could he explain…any of it? What a shitty friend he'd been, and why he'd run away and let his guilt and self-pity take control. And what if they asked about Troy?

Looking to his love seat, the silver laptop beckoned. Brian ignored it, hauling himself out of bed and into the cramped bathroom. When he came out, his laptop was still sitting on the beige cushion.

Waiting.

With a sigh, he gave in, pulling a beer from the fridge before settling in again, the computer on his knees. He pressed a button, and the screen came to life, the red and white YouTube menu appearing. He scanned the names of the recommended videos.

*Next Up Perform at Brit Awards 2015*
*E! Tyson & Troy Tanner Interview*

*Next Up History Video (Unofficial)*
*BT Best Fanvid*
*Next Up Interview FULL*

Brian clicked on the so-called fanvid. He'd learned that fans and other people referred to Troy as "BT," meaning "Big T." This video was a surprisingly well-edited collection of interview clips from talk shows, some from when Troy had been a gangly teenager on *Rock 'n' Roll Academy,* all long limbs and bright smile. Brian couldn't stop watching, even as the tightness in his chest grew.

When the video ended, another recommendation appeared.

*Next Up Charity Concert Beyond the Sea*

Heart clenching, he slammed down the laptop lid and hurried into the shower, making the water too hot. He scrubbed at his hair, which was still too long and in desperate need of a cut. Yes, that's what he'd do. Treat himself to a shave while he was at it since he couldn't bear to even unzip his grandfather's kit. Everything reminded him of Troy now.

"This is insane. I'm out of my mind."

His voice sounded strange to his own ears in the steamy shower stall, dull and scratchy.

"I'm straight."

They'd had their…whatever it was because they'd been stuck together on a desert island. They did what people do when they're isolated. People have physical needs. That's all it was. He repeated what he'd said to Troy.

"We were horny."

It sounded as hollow now as it had then. It was bullshit.

*I'm not straight.*

He soaped his body roughly under the stream of almost-scalding water. That truth didn't matter. Troy may have seemed like he hadn't wanted Brian to leave, but surely he was glad now. There had been video of him arriving in LA with his mother and Savannah close by his side.

227

Troy had worn sunglasses and kept his head down after waving to fans. He seemed fine. He could get back to his old life. His girlfriend. Once the dust settled, why would he choose Brian?

Surely Troy had snapped out of it. Now it was Brian's turn.

"I'M SO GLAD you called." Kylie's voice was muffled against Brian's chest as she hugged him tightly.

"Me too," he lied, stroking a hand over her golden hair.

"It was so awful to think you were dead. I'd always hoped to hear from you again, you know." She leaned back and gave him a watery smile. "But I know you were busy, being a pilot and all. Imagine my surprise when I saw your face on the telly. Usually blokes lie about *being* pilots, not about *not* being pilots."

"Sorry."

"It doesn't matter now. Come on, let's have some wine." She took his hand and led him to her kitchen, wearing leggings and a flowy blouse that didn't hide her pert breasts or round ass. He'd dressed in dark jeans and a button-down that hung off him. He'd stood in front of the mirror in his bathroom, wondering who he was looking at. Even with the haircut and shave, he barely recognized himself.

He would have gone to a bar, but considering the number of reporters still camped around his building shouting questions about Troy as he'd sped his Honda out of the garage, a bar hadn't been a good idea. Kylie had programmed her number into his phone, and the contacts had all been transferred to his new device.

So here he was at her little house in Parramatta. Brian was pretty sure no one had followed, but Kylie had closed all the blinds in case.

She smiled sweetly and gave him a glass of pinot. "Are you hungry? You poor thing, I can't imagine how you survived."

"I'm fine." He smiled back, because Kylie was a kind woman and she was being far better to him than he deserved.

"There's cheese and crackers and other nibbles. And I can order in if you'd like? There's a terrific Thai place around the corner."

"I'm fine, really." He gulped his wine. "I just need…" *Don't think his name. Don't.*

Kylie smiled slyly. "I know what you need. I'll fix you right up." She put down her glass on the marble island and pressed against him with her softness and glossy lips, her small hands going to work on his fly.

It should have been exactly what he needed. Fuck a hot blond and forget everything else. *Relax. Enjoy it.*

Leaning back against the island, Brian tried to turn off his mind as Kylie slipped her hand into his boxers. But as she kissed him, tasting like red wine and smelling of citrus, her soft fingers teasing his flaccid dick, he knew he could fuck a thousand women—or men—and still want Troy.

Still *love* Troy.

Maybe it didn't make sense, but Brian knew what his heart shouted with each beat. He loved him. He wanted him. Brian couldn't run from it. Wouldn't. Not this time.

Stumbling back, he rammed his hip on the corner of the counter. "I'm sorry. I…"

"You're so tense. Come on, let's sit down and relax. Have more wine. There's no rush, right?" She smiled kindly, which made it worse.

He backed up farther. "I made a mistake. I thought I could…" He shook his head. "I don't know what I thought. It's not you. God, it really isn't. I'm figuring my life out, and I'm a mess."

"Oh." She tucked her hair behind her ear and straightened her blouse stiffly. "Well, then."

"I'm so sorry." He scrubbed a hand over his hair, which felt wrong being short again. "I know this sounds like bullshit, but you're great."

With a sigh, she softened. "You've been through hell. Look, if you want to talk, I can order that Thai food."

"That's so nice of you. But I need to go. Thank you, and…I'm sorry."

Brian escaped to his Honda and slammed it into drive. While he could have talked it out with sweet Kylie, there was no need. He knew what he had to do, starting with visiting the American embassy first thing in the morning to speed through a replacement passport application. There was no time to waste.

He was ready to go home.

# Chapter Seventeen

"**Y**OU'RE STILL THIN."

Troy hugged his brother tightly. "So are you. Besides, I've only been back a week."

"Ten days." Tyson stepped back with a rueful smirk. "Trust me. I'm counting in here."

"Well, it's only been three days since I saw you, and I'm eating as fast as I can." Troy hated not being able to visit every day, but the facility had strict rules.

To the watchful woman in the corner, Ty said, "We're going for a walk."

"Of course," she answered smoothly. "Please return to the greeting center at two-thirty."

"Uh-huh." Tyson led the way from the lobby through glass doors and down a stone pathway to the wide swath of grass and gardens that spread out for at least a mile behind the rehab facility. "Why does everything here have some new-agey name?" he grumbled. "They call the library 'the learning place.' It's so pretentious." He unzipped his hoodie and dropped it on an empty bench.

In his jeans and T-shirt, Tyson did look startlingly thin to Troy's eyes. "I know. But don't let that bother you. Focus on why you're here."

Tyson huffed as he turned down a gravel path surrounded by low sprawls of pink, yellow, orange, white, and purple flowers Troy didn't know the names of. "Can't I bitch without a lecture?"

Troy winced. "Sorry. I just worry."

"No shit, BT." Ty elbowed him playfully, and it was all Troy could do not to hug him again to feel him safe and alive.

Insects whined in the summer heat, and they slowed down to stroll under the shade of leafy trees. Troy was aware of the orderlies stationed around the grounds, well out of earshot but monitoring the handful of patients outside. During his other two short visits, he and Tyson had only been able to talk with a counselor in the room. Apparently Troy's visitor status had been upgraded and they were allowed a bit of privacy now.

Of course he'd been searched thoroughly on arriving—patted down in his shorts and tee, his pockets turned out and sandals handed over for examination. Troy didn't mind the extra vigilance, even though smuggling drugs to his brother was the last thing in the world he'd do.

"Surprised Mom hasn't sat you down and chopped off your hair." Tyson ran a hand over his own buzzed head. "She was pissed when I did this, but fuck it. I don't want to deal with a shaggy mop of curls anymore. I'm not twelve." He smirked. "We can switch styles."

"Deal."

"It's so stupid how Joe and the label wanted us to always have different hair. You're a foot taller than me. No one's going to get us confused."

"I know." He shrugged. "But we went along with it."

"Guess we did. You know what Mom and Dad always said about not causing trouble and following the rules." Ty laughed, a sharp, angry bark. "Pretty rich coming from Dad, huh?"

It was the first time Troy had ever heard Tyson criticize their father. "Ty..." He didn't know what he wanted to say.

"I'm pissed at him. And her for not doing anything."

Troy kicked at a stray stone on the path. "Yeah. Me too." His skin prickled, but not from the heat. "But I should have—"

"You shouldn't have done shit." Tyson's sneakers kicked up gravel as he skidded to a halt. "You were a kid, just like I was."

Shaking his head, Troy insisted, "I was older. I should have done something. I should have…"

"What? Fixed him? You couldn't. Only he could. That's one of the things I'm learning in here: The addict is the only one responsible for their actions. I have to own my truth." He rolled his eyes. "More new-age shit, but they're right."

"I still should have done better. I could have—"

"Troy, stop." Tyson gripped his arm. "Dad made his choices. So did I. You're the best big brother anyone could ever have. You don't know how—" He sucked in a breath, his eyes welling with tears. "When they said you were dead, it was like… Fuck, I hated myself for the shitty things I said. You were trying to help me, and I was such an asshole. You know I didn't mean any of it, right?" His fingers dug into Troy's skin. "You know that?"

Troy pulled Ty into his arms. "Of course. I know. I know."

"I said I didn't need you," Ty mumbled against Troy's chest. "But I need you so much."

Blinking up at the cloudless sky, Troy's eyes burned. "I need you too, okay?"

"Okay." Swiping at his face, Tyson stepped back. "I was so pissed at you for leaving, but you were right. I'm just… Shit, I'm so glad you're here."

"Thanks to you for spending a fortune on a search team."

"I wasn't going to give up," he said fiercely. "No way."

"I'm not giving up on you either. Maybe I should have stayed in Australia, but I thought I was doing the right thing."

"You did." Tyson sniffed and wiped his nose with his wrist the way he'd done since he was little. "My head was so far up my ass I wouldn't have listened to you. When you went missing, I lost it. I'm lucky I didn't kill myself."

Troy shuddered. "Thank God."

"Thank Savannah and the guys. Even Nick got his shit together." He grimaced. "Briefly, that is. He's still in denial. I wish… But I can't be responsible for his choices. I have to focus on my own recovery." Wrinkling his nose, he added, "Their new-agey talk is really rubbing off on me. Anyway, Savannah planned an intervention, and she wouldn't let up about what you would want for me."

"So she guilted you into coming to rehab."

Tyson laughed softly and dropped onto a shaded bench. "Pretty much. But hey, it worked." He was quiet for a few moments. "You know she was really torn up about you. That fight you had." He peered up at Troy. "Are you really not getting back together with her?"

Troy sat on the bench with a sigh. "No. I'm not. I'm sorry to hurt her, but I just can't."

"I don't get it. She's sweet and gorgeous. What's not to like?"

"She's just not who I want to be with. She's not the one."

"Yeah, I guess if you're not feeling it. Well, plenty of other girls out there. You should go hit the town, bro."

Before he could think twice, Troy said, "I don't want other girls."

Ty stared at him blankly. "Huh? Dude, you were just on a desert island for two months. I've been in here a month and I'd give my left nut for some pussy."

"It's not... Never mind." It didn't matter anyway. Brian had made it clear it was over. Whatever *it* had been.

"What's wrong?"

"Nothing." Troy tried to laugh it off. "Come on, let's go check out the fountain." He started to stand.

Tyson pulled him back down to the bench. "Tell me what's wrong, and don't say 'nothing.' I know you. You look like you did when Scrapper died."

"Good ol' Scrapper." Their beagle had lived to thirteen, but it still hadn't been easy to let him go. "Remember when he ate that whole container of Play-Doh?"

"Yeah, it was super gross. Don't change the subject."

Troy sighed. Part of him wanted to spill his guts, and the other half wanted to keep what he and Brian had shared a secret. Something that couldn't be touched. The urge to voice the tangle of feelings jammed inside him won. "I don't want Savannah, or any other girls. I want *him*."

The words hung in the hot afternoon air. For a few long moments, there was only the drone of a lawn mower and the distant tinkle of water.

Tyson stared, his smooth forehead furrowed. "Who?"

"Never mind." Troy shot to his feet. "I don't know what I'm saying." He headed to the fountain at the end of the path, where water flowed over stone dolphins and arced in a gentle cascade.

Tyson hurried to stand beside him. "I'm confused." His eyes went wide. "Wait, are you talking about *him*? The pilot? Brian?"

Troy could only nod miserably.

"Did you...and he...?" He waved his hand in the air. "Holy shit, you *did*!"

"It was just..." *What?* Troy didn't know. They'd agreed not to overthink it, and now he had zero idea how to deal with the confusion and longing filling him so deeply it was hard to breathe. "You can't tell anyone." He clutched his brother's shoulder. "Ty, please."

"I won't. You know I won't."

"Okay." He blew out a long breath. "I know."

"Come on." Tyson urged Troy to sit on the side of the fountain and joined him. "So you guys...messed around?"

"Yeah."

"Well, you were stuck on that island for months. Most people would probably..." He waved his hand again. "You know."

"It started that way, I guess. Kind of. Then it was definitely more. A lot more."

"Did you do it, like..." Tyson dropped his voice to a whisper. "In the butt?"

Troy could feel his cheeks get hot. He nodded.

"Whoa. Were you the pitcher or the catcher?"

He had to laugh, just a bit. "Catcher, but I would have fucked him too. We got rescued before I could."

"Whoa," Tyson repeated. "So...you liked it? Did you go down on him?"

"Yeah, we blew each other."

Ty seemed to ponder this. "Do you want to do that with other guys?"

"I don't know. I don't think so. Maybe? I never have before."

"But with him, you want to?"

Troy nodded. God, he wanted it. A fine mist from the fountain cooled his skin, and he could almost smell the salt of the sea and hear Brian's low, lazy laughter. He cleared his throat, but couldn't get any words out.

"Is he gay?"

"No. At least, I was the first guy he was with."

"And you're not gay either?"

"I don't know. I must be a bit if I want to have sex with another guy."

"Well, everyone's a little bit gay. There's a scale and shit. I did a quiz online once. I'm a three." His tone went wistful. "I miss the internet so much. Sorry, sidetracked. Okay, you want this guy's D, and he wants yours. So what's the problem?"

"Are you serious?" Troy sputtered. "Uh, let's see. Neither of us have ever dated a guy before, and Mom would probably freak, and the fans would *definitely* freak. The media will go crazy, and everyone will have an opinion."

"Fuck 'everyone.' Who cares what they think? And don't give me that about the fans. You know they've been shipping me and Nick for years. There are a zillion Tumblrs dedicated to 'Nickson.' The fans are cool with the gay. You know I am too."

"It really doesn't bother you?"

"Why would it? What am I, some loser homophobe?" He scoffed.

"I know you're not. I just..." Troy took a few breaths. "I don't know how to feel. Am I gay? I guess I'm bisexual. I'm clearly something. Bi makes sense to me. It isn't bad—I just never thought of myself that way.

But now everything's changed. *I'm* changed."

Tyson stood and bent to retrieve a handful of pebbles. He began tossing them into the fountain, one by one. "Why do you need a label? We should be able to feel what we feel without making it some official statement. You like this dude and he likes you. The end. Everyone else can fuck off."

Love for his brother warmed Troy through and through. "That actually makes sense."

"Don't sound so surprised, dick." Ty kicked his shin playfully. "And Mom loves you. We all do. She's so happy you're alive you could bring home a monkey as your date and she'd make it a banana cream pie."

Troy had to laugh at the image, but his smile faded quickly. "It doesn't matter anyway. Brian's back in Australia. He's...not interested." The words scraped out. "It was just temporary."

Tyson threw the rest of the stones into the fountain with a forceful *plop*. "Then he's a fucking idiot, isn't he? He—" Ty sighed wearily. "Shit, time's almost up." He nodded, and Troy turned to see the woman from the lobby holding up her hand with fingers spread. "Five minutes. Better head back. I've got to go share my feelings and take responsibility for my demons. Then we'll probably do a hug circle and trust falls."

"But you're taking this seriously, right?" Troy stood and barely resisted the urge to take his brother's shoulders and shake. "This is your life, Ty. Please."

He snapped, "I'm allowed to bitch, remember?" Turning back along the path, his voice softened. "I'm taking it seriously. I promise. You're back from the dead, and I'm not going to blow it. Got a second chance."

"Okay. I trust you." Troy's shoulders were still up by his ears, and he rolled them restlessly.

"You have a second chance too."

"Yeah." Troy kicked at the gravel.

"Look, I know why you walked away from me. It was the right call, and I don't blame you. But do you really want to walk away from this guy? Don't. Especially if you love him."

Troy could only nod, his throat unbearably tight. Did he love Brian? The unspoken answer was a burning ache from head to toe, expanding and pushing against his ribcage.

*With every bit of my heart.*

"SIR, I'M SORRY to disturb you at this hour, but there's an unexpected visitor." The guard's voice was so clear on the phone he could have been standing beside Troy's bed. It was strange, the little things Troy noticed now that he hadn't before. Surely he'd start taking technology for granted again soon.

He glanced at the green glow of the digital clock. It was past midnight, but he'd only been staring at the ceiling. "It's okay. Are the paps still out there bothering you?" They'd followed him from visiting Ty in rehab, of course. Fans too, but at least most of them had curfews.

"No, they've gone home for the night."

He'd only told his mom he was coming to the Malibu house after visiting Ty, and it wasn't his mom's MO to spring up in the middle of the night. Besides, she was approved for automatic entry to the gated community and had his key. *Please don't be Savannah.* Troy thought they'd parted on a good note, or at least an okay one, but he really wasn't up for dealing with it.

"Who is it?" He'd been ignoring the growing number of messages on his phone, but surely Joe or Lara wouldn't dare show up like this.

"Brian Sinclair."

Heart in his throat, Troy bolted up in bed. "Brian? Are you serious?"

"Yes, sir. That's the name he gave, and I recognize him from the news."

Troy sprang to his feet. "Let him in. Thank you. I, um. Okay, bye." He fumbled the cordless handset into its cradle on the nightstand.

Brian was here. What did it mean? Should he get dressed? Troy glanced down at his faded pajama bottoms. Should he put on a shirt? He raced to the bathroom and flicked on the light, blinking in the glare. His hair was okay, but he had circles under his eyes.

*As if Brian hasn't seen me looking like shit before? What the fuck, dude.*

A vehicle approached, and Troy turned out the light and rushed out of his room to the window at the front of the hall. A taxi appeared around the bend in the long driveway, and he watched, body tingling and pulse ratcheted up so high Troy thought he might explode.

The car stopped, and after a few moments, the back door opened. Brian climbed out, carrying a duffel bag. Brian was really, truly right outside his house, and Troy didn't know whether to laugh or cry.

Instead, he raced downstairs, yanking open the door. Brian glanced back at the taxi as it turned around and retreated in the night, its red taillights disappearing around the curve and beyond a row of hedges.

Troy hadn't turned on the light, so they stood there in darkness but for the moon. He needed to say something. He needed to—

"I'm in love with you," Brian blurted.

Dimly aware that his mouth was open, Troy could only stand there staring.

"Uh… Can I come in?"

Troy managed to jerk out a nod and step back, closing the door behind Brian and turning to face him. "You're in love with me?" His voice was too high.

Brian nodded tightly and dropped his duffel. "Maybe this is crazy, and maybe you don't want this at all anymore after the stupid way I acted, but I had to tell you. Your girlfriend's probably upstairs, and I shouldn't have come, but I had to. I just…had to."

"She's not here. And she's not my girlfriend."

Brian's Adam's apple bobbed. "Okay."

"That's good," Troy said.

Brian hesitated. "What is?"

"That you told me. Because I'm in love with you too, and I hate being away from you, and I don't care if it's crazy because I like who I am when we're together, and I don't want to go back to the way things were before, and—"

It was for the best that Brian strode forward and kissed him, because Troy probably would have babbled for five minutes. It was much, much better to have Brian against him, his lips pressing hard, strong arms wrapping around Troy's body.

They opened their mouths, tongues meeting as Troy staggered back against the front door. He moaned low in his throat when Brian rutted against him, denim rough against the thin cotton of Troy's pajamas and getting him hard already. His head buzzed, heart about to explode.

Brian's mouth tasted like coffee and Juicy Fruit, and his tongue was unrelenting. He pinned Troy against the smooth door, and Troy could have died happy and moaning.

Brian broke the kiss, his eyes wild. "Missed that sound. Missed you so much." He ran his palms over Troy's pecs, circling Troy's nipples with his thumbs and making him gasp. Leaning close, he kissed the little cleft in Troy's chin. Troy shivered, his cock swelling.

With a few tugs, Brian stripped off Troy's pajamas and tossed them aside. Troy had been naked in front of Brian a hundred times now. Yet standing there, with moonlight ghosting over them from the skylight high above the grand foyer and Brian still fully dressed in jeans and a light jacket, Troy felt completely exposed.

But it was Brian. He was safe. Anticipation rippled over his skin like goosebumps.

Brian leaned close to Troy's ear as he reached down to stroke and explore, his breath a hot gust. "Need to taste you."

Troy could only moan and nod and spread his legs wider as Brian sank to his knees. Seeing him there at his feet sent a powerful bolt through Troy, and he ran his hand over Brian's head. *"Please."*

Teasing his fingers over Troy's inner thighs, Brian nuzzled his balls, nosing around and inhaling deeply. Troy thought he'd have to beg, but then Brian took him in his mouth, sucking beautifully, pulling back the foreskin. It was clumsy and messy, but it was *Brian*, and Troy's legs already trembled. Watching Brian's lips stretch around his cock had his head spinning.

The wooden door was smooth against Troy's back and buttocks, ceramic tiles cool beneath his toes. Brian was perfect at his feet, alive and there and *in love with him*. Joy bubbled up in Troy, his balls tightening. As much as he wanted to shoot down Brian's throat and see him swallow it, it was going to happen too soon.

"Wait, wait," he muttered.

Brian let go of his cock with a slick *pop*, looking at up him with wet, parted lips. He was so gorgeous Troy didn't know what to do with himself. When he didn't say anything, Brian frowned. "Is it okay?"

"Yes, yes." Troy caressed Brian's short hair. "But I want to come with you inside me. Will you fuck me again? I tried to fuck myself with my fingers the other night. Pretended it was you, but it wasn't the same, and—"

Springing to his feet, Brian kissed Troy thoroughly. His stubble scraped Troy's skin, sending sparks of pleasure straight to his dick. They stumbled up the curving staircase, and Troy prayed he still had that tube of K-Y in the bathroom drawer. He tore himself away from Brian to fumble for it blindly, half afraid that if he turned on the light, he'd wake up alone.

When he returned to the bedroom, Brian was kicking off his boxers. His cock stood up, his nipples hard, and Troy urged him back onto the king-sized bed, straddling him. After licking his nipples in turn, teasing the little nubs, Troy rubbed his face against Brian's chest hair. He didn't know why it turned him on so much, but he couldn't get enough.

Brian groaned. "You'd better get me inside you soon."

"Mmm. Like the way that sounds." Troy crawled up Brian's body so they could kiss again. "I want to do everything with you."

After licking his finger, Brian reached around to tease Troy's hole. "Thought I could go back to the way things were. The way I was. I can't. Need you."

Troy squirted lube all over his hand—and also Brian's stomach. They burst out laughing, and Troy couldn't remember ever feeling such happiness that it filled every corner of him with each beat of his heart.

*This is what it's like to be in love.*

He realized he'd said it out loud when dimples creased Brian's cheeks and he reached up to caress Troy's face. "It's never been like this before."

Troy really did want Brian to fuck him, so he concentrated on his ass, working himself open with his fingers while Brian stared avidly, licking his lips.

"Jesus. Wish you could see how hot you are fucking yourself. I could come just watching."

"Don't you dare." Scooping up the spilled lube and loving the way Brian's belly fluttered at his touch, Troy slathered it over Brian's cock. Positioning himself over it, he lowered down, the head pushing at his hole. "Oh, fuck," he muttered.

"That's it. You're so good." Brian held Troy's hips, rubbing gently. "That's it," he murmured.

When Troy took the head and sank all the way, his breath froze in his lungs, Brian's grip tight on his hips. His ass burned, but as he adjusted and was able to inhale and exhale, Troy liked the stretch. Scratch that, he *loved* the stretch. There was that incredible feeling of fullness, and the fact that it was Brian inside him made it perfect.

Troy's thighs flexed as he lifted up and started moving. He moaned, shifting his hips as he found a rhythm. Brian was watching him, rubbing his hands up and down Troy's flanks, panting softly.

"Does it feel okay?" Troy asked before he realized that was a pretty stupid question.

But Brian didn't laugh. "Amazing. You feel so good, sweetheart."

The unexpected endearment made Troy's heart stutter, and he leaned down to kiss Brian messily, his hands flat on that furry chest. He rode harder, both of them moaning. "Love having your cock in me," Troy muttered.

"Going to give me yours later?" Brian kissed him, his fingers tight in Troy's hair. "Spread me open and fill me up?"

"Fuck, yes. *Yes.*" Troy strained, his dick rock hard, the head poking out and glistening. "I need...need..."

Pushing up and toppling him over to his back, Brian shoved Troy's legs up and thrust inside him again. Crying out, Troy bit his tongue as his back arched. "Yes! Fuck me hard. Hard. Please, please..."

Troy could hear himself muttering amid his long moans, but the words seemed to tumble off his tongue of their own accord. Brian was heavy on top of him, bending him almost in half, ramming his hole. Troy's cock was caught between them, the hair from Brian's belly teasing it with each thrust.

Troy had thought his sex life was pretty good before he met Brian. But he'd never experienced anything like this—being fucked with such abandon, open and vulnerable, gripping the railing of the headboard as he was pounded. Sweat slicked their skin, their harsh pants and grunts humid puffs of air between them.

He realized the difference wasn't just about Brian being a man. Man or woman didn't matter—it was about trusting Brian with every part of him. It was about being free to finally be himself.

It only took two strokes of Brian's hand on Troy's cock for him to release, his orgasm rushing from his balls and dick, curling his toes. He pulsed all over his chest, Brian encouraging every drop he could.

Shuddering, Troy squeezed Brian's cock, wrapping his legs around his waist. "That's it. Fuck me hard. Fill me up."

After a few more stuttering thrusts, Brian gasped, his head thrown back and mouth open as he came buried inside him. He slumped over, panting and kissing the tender skin of Troy's throat. "Troy," he murmured. "That... I..."

"I know."

# Chapter Eighteen

T HERE WAS NO sand burrowed into the creases of his body. A thick
mattress cushioned his hip where he curled on his side. Yet waves
murmured, and Troy was wrapped around him, his exhalations tickling
the back of Brian's neck. Brian's skin was tight in places, but it was the
remnants of sex, not saltwater and too much sun.

It was getting sweaty where they were plastered together. Brian had
to piss, and his arm cramped where it was stuck under him, but he
didn't move. Not yet.

Seagulls cried plaintively, and he opened his eyes. Last night he'd
barely noticed the house, his focus only on Troy. Troy's mouth and
hands and cock, his ass that was so tight and perfect. Now, Brian looked
around the room, painted in a pale blue with white accents and dark
brown furniture.

He focused on an object sitting on the nightstand. Reaching out, his
fingers closed over the familiar plastic rectangle, the outer shell of the
signaling mirror scratched and battered. He swallowed hard over the
lump in his throat and placed it safely back on the table.

Through the open French doors and balcony beyond, the sky was
the same rich blue, and he imagined the water must be just out of sight.
That it was the same ocean that had lapped at Golden Sands was
somehow a comfort.

"Mmm." Troy stirred, his hard-on nudging Brian's ass. "Morning."

"I keep waiting for those goddamn parrots."

Laughing softly, Troy pressed a kiss to Brian's neck. "Only gulls here. Getting hot. I should shut the doors and put the AC back on. I was listening to the ocean last night, trying to sleep. Trying not to think about you."

"I'm sorry."

"You're here now. That's what matters. It was only what, a week and a half? Felt like years."

Shifting onto his back and giving his arm a shake, Brian kissed Troy's chin. "I knew after a few days it wasn't going to work. Trying to go back to my old life. Trying to stop wanting you."

On his side, Troy drew patterns on Brian's chest. "Why didn't you call?"

"Didn't have your number. But more than that… I was afraid you'd tell me not to come. That you'd have come to your senses."

"Nope. My senses have officially fled." He rubbed his calf over Brian's shin, stroking up and down. "Hey, how did you get my address?"

"Star maps. I bought a PDF online. If you want to drop by and visit Mariah Carey, Michael Keaton, or that prick from *American Idol*, they're just up the road."

Troy laughed. "Good to know. I actually have been to Mariah's place. She has an awesome infinity pool." His smile faded, his chocolate eyes serious. "I'm so glad you're here."

"Me too." Brian brushed back a stray curl from Troy's forehead. "What are we going to do?"

Troy circled his finger around Brian's belly button. "This."

"Not that I'm complaining, but…"

"We don't have to figure it out this morning. Right?"

Brian released the tension that had crept into his muscles. "Right."

"I don't want to get tripped up with worrying about what it all means and what everyone thinks. Ty said we shouldn't worry about labels. Gay, straight, bi. Pan. There are all these different categories."

"Yeah. I always thought of myself as straight, but I'm not. I'll have to google what pan and some of the other terms actually mean. All I know is that it makes me feel alive to be with you."

With a tender expression, Troy caressed Brian's face. "Me too, Bri. I feel like the real me now. Whatever the hell that means."

"Your brother's right—why should labels matter? The only thing that matters is us." He motioned between them. "This. Being together. Being happy. As long as I have you, that's what I care about."

Nodding, Troy let out a deep breath. "Cool. Oh, and just for the record, we're exclusive, right?" He grimaced. "I know it's late to be talking about this when we've already fucked again without condoms. But I haven't been with anyone else, and I don't want to be."

"Me either." Running his fingers over Troy's thick dick, he murmured, "Love doing it raw with you. Don't want anyone else."

Troy's smile beamed. "I'd kiss you, but I think I've got some epic morning breath going on."

Brian kissed him anyway, and they didn't resurface for a few slow, lazy minutes of exploration. He was tempted to roll Troy underneath him and get them off, but they had all day.

As they nuzzled and caressed, Brian asked, "So you told your brother? How's he doing? He's in rehab?"

"Hmm? Yeah, I told him, and he was really awesome about it. He's doing pretty good. Way better than the last time I saw him in Sydney."

"How long's he in there?"

"Another couple weeks. It's a super-intense program. Then he's going to live with Mom for a few months at least. I know she didn't do anything to stop my dad, but she's not going to make that mistake again."

"Glad to hear it. I hope Tyson can make it work."

"I think me kind of dying helped get his priorities straight."

"I would imagine." Brian ran his thumb over Troy's full lips and the perfect cleft in his chin. "It's strange to think about what life would be like if we hadn't crashed. If that crazy weather hadn't come out of nowhere, we would have flown to LA and said goodbye. Routine. I barely would have talked to you. Would have gotten mandatory rest and turned around to fly back. Just another job."

"I can't even... Whoa, man. It blows my mind to think about it. Not knowing you? I can't imagine it."

Brian threaded their fingers together. "Guess life's like this. All these untaken roads we never even know about. All because of chance. Or fate, if you believe in that kind of thing."

Troy smiled softly. "Do you?"

"I don't know. Was it fate that Paula died like that? I tend to think it was just shitty luck for her. For you and me... Well, we'll never know why it happened, but I say we make the most of it."

Squeezing Brian's fingers, Troy said, "I second that motion." With a quick kiss, he added, "Gotta piss."

In the enormous bathroom, they took turns with Troy's electric toothbrush. His mouth full of foam, Troy mumbled, "Isn't toothpaste the *best*?"

Laughing, Brian kissed him again, a minty mess. They managed to get into the shower, a glass-doored stall with enough room for both of them and powerful jets of water coming out of the walls as well as the rainfall shower head.

Brian sighed. "Hot water. I don't think I'll ever get enough of being able to shower again."

Troy held up a green bar of soap. "Irish Spring, like my dad always used." He lathered his hands vigorously. "Soap is amazing. Whoever invented it was a genius."

"Absolutely."

With foamy hands, Troy scrubbed Brian's body. Brian closed his eyes and enjoyed the sensation.

"I watched gay porn the other night," Troy blurted.

Suitably intrigued, Brian opened his eyes, his pulse kicking up. "How was it?"

"At first, it was a little weird, I guess. But dude, it was hot. The guys were really into it." He blushed furiously and lowered his voice, as if someone could overhear. "When I imagined it was you, I got so hard."

"Yeah?" Brian reached down and fondled Troy's cock lightly. "Did you touch yourself? Did you get off on it?"

Nodding, Troy rocked his hips as Brian started stroking.

"What did they do?"

Lips parted, Troy breathed more heavily now in the steamy enclosure. "Blow jobs first. Then the one guy licked the other one's ass. Spread him open and spit on his hole. It turned me on." His soapy fingers found the crease of Brian's ass, rubbing. "Has anyone ever rimmed you?"

Arousal zipped over Brian's skin, making his head a little light in the hot steam. "No. You?"

"This girl I met on tour did it. Felt good." He bit his lip. "Can I lick your ass?"

Brian still had Troy's swelling cock in his hand, and he stroked harder. "I assume this is some kind of diabolical trick question."

A grin lighting up his beautiful face, Troy laughed, and Brian thought his heart might burst. Troy kissed him deeply as his fingers played with Brian's hole. Then he turned Brian to face the wall and dropped to his knees.

And good *God*, then he licked Brian's ass.

His hands planted on the slick tiles, Brian stood leaning with his legs spread and Troy's face buried in his crack. The press of his tongue at Brian's hole, slick yet textured, had Brian's dick leaking. The shower jets in the wall sprayed forcefully, stimulating his cock and balls. His whole body simmered, rising to a boil.

Troy's hands were on Brian's ass cheeks, spreading them wide. His nose bumped as he licked and sucked and poked his tongue into Brian's hole. A constant stream of little sounds escaped Brian's lips—groans, gasps, and high-pitched noises he'd be embarrassed to make in front of anyone else.

But this was Troy. The person who'd held him while he finally cried the tears he couldn't after Wisconsin. The person who'd pissed on his leg to take away his hurt. The person he'd huddled and been hungry with. The person he loved more than he knew was possible.

He came with Troy's hand on his balls and tongue in his ass. Then they switched places, and Brian spit onto Troy's asshole, tasting inside him and wanting more as Troy moaned so perfectly.

Chance may have put them on this road, but Brian was going to drive every inch of it.

"I SEE WHY you like the ritual."

"Mmm." Brian wiped his palm across the steamed mirror, turning his head and pursing his lips as he lathered his face. "You like watching?"

Troy was tempted to leer and make a sex joke, but instead he simply answered, "I do." He was sprawled on the white leather chair in the corner of the bathroom with a plush towel around his waist.

Brian had shaved him first, all gentle hands and stolen kisses, and now he stood naked by the sink, whirling the brush in a new bowl of shaving soap. "I used to watch my grandfather. It was a little more cramped in our bathroom, but I squeezed in and sat on the tub. He'd talk about...I don't know. Whatever was on his mind, I guess."

"Sounds relaxing." Troy brushed his hand over his smooth chin. "I like the lime soap. Smells good."

"I thought a change was in order. Had enough of coconut for a while."

Laughing, Troy nodded. "Fish, coconut, papaya, and breadfruit are off the menu. Not that we really get breadfruit here, but still. It's on notice. Speaking of food, are you starving? I'm starving."

"Now that you mention it, I am." Brian ran the straight razor over his face in a practiced motion. "It made me a little sick at first to eat different kinds of food, but I'm ravenous today." He smiled wryly. "Guess that also has something to do with a huge load of stress being relieved."

"Me too. I have a bunch of leftovers. Had pizza and beer delivered last night and could hardly eat it." Troy grinned. "Feeling a lot better this morning. For reasons."

When Brian was finished shaving, Troy ditched his towel and led the way downstairs, their bare feet slapping on the dark hardwood. Brian whistled softly.

"This is some house you've got."

Troy glanced around at the open kitchen with a wide quartz-topped island in the middle. A dining room they'd hardly ever used was off to one side, a living area with huge TV and wrap-around couch on the other. "I guess it is, huh? Ty and I have barely been here the past year."

Brian stood by the floor-to-ceiling windows that made up the whole side of the house on the first floor, looking out over the wooden deck and the water beyond. Stairs led down to the strip of beach.

"Incredible view," Brian said.

Troy's gaze lingered on Brian's bare ass, pale compared to the rest of his skin. "Mm-hmm," he agreed. Thinking of how he'd licked that ass not long ago, his body tingled anew. He'd always liked going down on girls, but being in love made everything with Brian so much more intense.

*I'm in love. I really am.*

Brian looked over his shoulder. "That's quite a giddy grin." He waggled his eyebrows. "Glad you like the view."

"Oh yes. Only the best here at the Gates of Malibu."

"So I see." Brian joined Troy by the fridge and kissed him. "Is there any ice cream?"

"We'll order groceries. Pralines and cream, right?"

"Pralines and cream, mint chocolate—" He frowned. "Was that...?"

Through the hazy fog of satisfaction, Troy registered that the front door had opened and closed. And that those were quick little footsteps coming toward them, which meant—

"Bongbong? Are you up yet, lazybones?"

He and Brian sprang apart as Troy's mother bustled in wearing capri pants and a floral shirt, her feet clad in the slippers she kept in the front hall. Her eyes widened comically, blinking back and forth between them, and then down. Brian shuffled behind the end of the island.

Someone had to break the silence, and Troy managed to croak out, "Mom. I didn't know you were coming over."

"Obviously. Mr. Sinclair, I didn't expect to see you." She waved her hand in his direction. "Especially not so much."

Brian waved awkwardly. "Hello, Mrs. Tanner."

"You can call me Bea. Seems like formality has gone out the windows here." She hoisted a canvas bag onto the island. "I brought food. I'll go now."

"No, don't go." Troy glanced at Brian. "We'll just...get dressed. Be back in a minute." He went the long way around the island to collect Brian, and they scurried out of the kitchen and up the stairs.

In Troy's room, Brian shook his head. "Oh my God, I feel like a busted teenager," he whispered.

"I know, I'm sorry. It's my mom's specialty, making grown adults feel like naughty kids." He opened a drawer and yanked on underwear and shorts. "Holy shit. I wasn't planning on having this conversation today, but I guess I might as well get it over with."

"Do you want me to be there?" Brian zipped up his own shorts and pulled on a T-shirt.

"Maybe you can go for a little walk, and I'll talk to her alone first."

"Sure. Wait, will the media be out there? Don't really want to deal with them today. Or ever, but especially not right now."

"No, don't worry. It's a private beach a mile in each direction. The security here's great. They even managed to restrict the airspace, so no paps in choppers, and they patrol the water."

"Wow. That's a relief. Okay, I'll head out."

"Wait. You need a hat."

Sadness flickered over Brian's face. "Can I borrow one? Still have to buy a replacement."

"Actually..." Troy picked up a cardboard box from the top of his dresser. "It came yesterday. I ordered it online. Wasn't sure how to send it to you, but…well, here you are." He'd opened the box the night before and run his fingers over the seams of the hat before placing it back inside. He pulled it out now. "It's not exactly the same, but I think it's close?"

Brian carefully took hold of the fabric as if it might break. He stared at the hat in his hands.

"Um, if you don't like it, I can send it back. It's probably all wrong."

"No." Brian cleared his throat. "It's just right." After a shuddering breath, he put it on. "How does it look?"

Troy nodded and echoed, "Just right."

With a little smile, Brian wrapped Troy in a tight hug. "Thank you, sweetheart."

Heart tripping, Troy squeezed him. "You're welcome." He didn't want to let go, but his mother was waiting.

Brian stepped back and raised an eyebrow. "Bongbong?"

Troy had to laugh. "It's a Filipino thing. I'll explain later."

Brian left for his walk with an awkward little wave downstairs, and Troy faced his mom over the island. She hadn't seemed to have moved, still standing there with the canvas bag unpacked. The fridge hummed, and the AC came on with a faint *whoosh*. He tried to think of the right thing to say.

Of course she broke the silence first, her arms folded over her chest. "You two are what? A couple?"

"Yes." Troy's voice sounded distant.

Her face creased in confusion and hurt. "All these years you've lied? Pretended with girls?"

"No! I wasn't pretending. I liked those girls. I did. But now…"

"Now you're homosexual?"

"I think bisexual is a better word. I liked the girls I dated, and now I like Brian. I love him, actually."

Her eyebrows shot up, almost disappearing under her short curls. "Love?" She seemed to ponder it. "And this man loves you?"

"He does. I know it must seem crazy. He's never been with a guy before either. But together on that island, it was us against the world, and I've never felt so close to someone. Never trusted anyone like I trust him. You know what I mean?"

"Hmm." She was silent for a few moments. "I can see this happening in your situation. Stuck together. But now you're home. Now you can have girls again."

"I know. But I want him."

She frowned. "You don't like girls anymore?"

"It's not that." Troy cast about for the right way to put it into words. "It's that I like him more. The most. When we were rescued, I was happy. Relieved, of course. But at the same time, I wanted to stay there with him. I didn't want that part to end."

"And you have the sex?"

"Mom!" His face was so hot he must have been bright red. Troy nodded.

"Hmm." She started unpacking the canvas bag of Tupperware dishes. "Well, if you are happy, I'm happy."

He gripped the side of the counter, barely breathing. "Really?"

"Of course, Bongbong."

"Just like that?"

She raised her hands. "What else do you want me to do? You're my son. Your happiness is the same as mine."

"Thank you. Mom, I… You know how much I love you, right?"

Clucking her tongue, she came around the island and hugged him hard. She barely reached his shoulder, and he ducked his head against hers. "I know, Bongbong. You were always such a good boy."

Tears stung his eyes, and he blinked rapidly as they separated. "How do you think the family will take it? I told Ty, and he's cool."

"They will take it how I tell them to. That's that."

He had to laugh. His mother was the oldest sister and incredibly bossy, but his aunties never seemed to mind. He wondered why his father was the only person she'd never tried to run roughshod over. Maybe he'd ask sometime. But not today.

She opened the fridge and peered inside with a disapproving expression. "Other people will be very surprised, and the clickers will go crazy, but to heck with them." She closed the door and turned to him. "Oh, but have you told Savannah? I know you don't want her now, but she's a good girl. She shouldn't read about it on the TMZ."

Troy nodded, his belly churning at the thought of Savannah finding out from someone else. "I'll call her later today."

"Okay." Hands on her hips, his mother said, "So, this Brian Sinclair. He is a nice man. 'Superman.' Very brave. Very handsome, as I see for myself. Big balls, eh?"

*"Mom!"*

She cackled and came close to pat his cheek. "I just want to see how red you can go."

He pulled her close again. "I love you."

"I love you too." She leaned back a little. "But you know it hasn't been long, Bongbong. You and he might find this fades once life goes back to normal."

The thought made Troy ache to his bones. "I guess we'll see what happens. For now I just want to be with him."

She nodded decisively. "Then that's what you'll do. You both need to put on some pounds, so fetch him while I heat this all up. Will he like kare-kare? Of course he will. It's delicious."

With relief coursing through him like sunshine, Troy went outside and called to Brian, who returned with an apprehensive expression under the brim of his new hat. Troy smiled widely and nodded, and Brian's shoulders lowered.

They sat on stools around the island, and Brian did indeed like the kare-kare, as well as the chicken adobo and sinigang. Troy's mother asked a million questions about Brian's childhood, and when Troy tried to intervene, Brian insisted he was happy to answer.

Troy waited nervously for her to ask about flying, but she didn't. She didn't ask about the band either, and when she announced she had errands to run, he kissed her cheek and told her again that he loved her.

"So." Brian looked around after she'd gone. "What do we do now?"

"Anything we want. Everything we want."

A sly smile tugged on Brian's lips, and he unzipped his shorts. "I'm pretty tired. Ready to go back to bed."

Troy yawned widely. "Yup. Better get back upstairs."

They practically ran.

Soon, they were naked in Troy's bed, the sun through the closed doors warm and perfect, cool air coming through the vents. Troy knelt between Brian's legs, pressing his thighs apart and sucking his big, heavy balls, nosing at the thatch of coarse hair. With slick fingers, he inched in one, then two.

Panting and splayed wonderfully, Brian groaned. "Jesus, that feels…"

Hesitating, Troy asked, "Is it good? Do you want me to stop?"

"Don't you dare stop." He gasped. "Oh God. Right there."

Troy didn't stop.

With Brian's long legs hooked over his shoulders, Troy pushed into him. It was so incredibly tight, and he kissed Brian deeply. He knew how it felt to have Brian's cock inside him, and that Brian was feeling the same thing now made Troy inexplicably elated.

He could hardly keep the smile from his face. Sweat beaded at his brow and prickled the back of his neck. "That's it, Bri. Let me in."

Squeezing his eyes shut, Brian bore down on Troy's cock, and they moaned in unison. "Never knew it could be like this," Brian murmured. "Hurts, but don't stop."

"You're going to come so hard." Troy wrapped his slick hand around Brian's shaft. "Do you want that?"

Opening his eyes, Brian nodded jerkily. "I want to come. Please."

Troy stroked faster, trying to find Brian's sweet spot as he fucked him. They grunted, skin slapping and the headboard creaking against the wall.

Troy muttered, "Going to come for me all over that hairy chest?"

"Yes, yes," Brian panted, clutching at Troy's back and shoulders.

*"Please."*

"Do it. Come for me and I'll lick it up."

Gasping, Brian unraveled, jizz spurting over his chest and belly. Troy milked him, getting every drop. Brian's ass was a vise around Troy's dick, and it only took a few short thrusts before Troy filled his hole with a primal sense of belonging.

The echo of their cries faded to labored breaths, and Troy eased out of Brian gently. He lowered Brian's legs, but stayed between them.

Bending his head, he ran his tongue over Brian's chest, lapping up the bitter, musky semen before it dried. The hair was rough on his tongue, and he loved it. Scooting back, he licked a trail down Brian's belly, making him shiver and tremble. Troy gently sucked at the head of Brian's cock until Brian tightened his fingers in Troy's hair. "Okay, okay."

Troy stretched out beside him, both of them on their backs. With sunlight dancing over their sweaty bodies, Troy was sated in every way possible, except for being rather thirsty. But he couldn't move just yet. "I guess there's one thing we definitely need to do today."

"What's that?" Brian asked lazily, his eyes drifting shut.

"Change these sheets."

Brian laughed, that low rumble that made Troy's toes curl. He rolled over and snuggled up to Brian's side. The water and sheets could wait. *Everything* could wait.

AFTER A DINNER that night of ice cream and more freshly delivered pizza, they went for a walk by the water's edge. One of his neighbors jogged by, and Troy gave him a little wave. The man—a Hollywood lawyer—nodded without breaking stride. That was the great thing about living in a gated community in Malibu. The other residents were so rich and often famous themselves that they didn't give a crap about some boy bander and who he was dating.

He and Brian stood on the wet sand as the sun disappeared beyond the horizon, a wave rushing around their ankles before retreating.

"It's surreal sometimes," Brian said.

"Hmm?"

"Being here. Being rescued even though this is the same sun going beyond the same ocean." Closing his eyes, he inhaled deeply. "I can almost imagine we're back there. Except this time my belly's full with real food and we get to sleep in a bed. No bugs. No parrots." He looked at the orangey-red horizon. "But we still get sunsets."

"Best of both worlds."

Brian smiled. "Lucky us."

"Hey, you know what else I miss? Let's make a fire. We were going to do a bonfire party last winter but it never happened. The wood's still piled up in the shed with the paddle boats and stuff."

So they dug a little pit and made a fire, no need for a magnifying glass or to worry about conserving precious matches. Troy brought down a blanket and a couple of beers in little cozies that stayed in the freezer. He handed one to Brian. "Ice cold beer?"

Brian took it with a grin. "How did you know?"

"Oh, you might have mentioned it a few hundred times. Here, hold mine too." He spread out the blanket and they settled down under the stars, gazing at the Big Dipper this time. Troy sat cross-legged and sipped his beer, his knee brushing Brian's.

"This is still surreal. For the record." Brian drank from his bottle. "Guess it will be for a while yet. Keep wanting to pinch myself. Hard to believe I'm really here. With you."

"You are." Troy leaned over and kissed him softly. "You're really here."

After a minute of content silence, Troy asked, "Have you thought about what you'll do? For work, I mean. Not that you have to work. I have money."

Brian raised an eyebrow. "Are you proposing I be a kept man?"

Laughing, Troy took another sip. "Sure. Works for me."

"It's a tempting offer." His smile faded. "But yes, I've thought about it. I..." He sighed.

"You don't have to talk about it now. I'm sorry. We have time. Don't need to rush anything. Don't need all the answers this minute."

"I know. But I think I already have the answer." Brian stared into the fire with a wistful smile. "I *loved* flying. But after Wisconsin... After Paula..." He went silent.

"It wasn't your fault," Troy said quietly.

"I know." Brian looked at him. "I'm not just saying that. I *know* I couldn't have done anything differently." He picked up a handful of sand and let it run through his fingers. "I can forgive myself, but I still can't forget. That joy is gone. I know I can do it. Could probably captain flights again now without panic attacks. But I don't *want* to. I don't think I'll ever get back the love I had for it." He snorted. "Maybe I just need to get over myself."

"No!" Troy shifted closer, slipping his arm around Brian's back. "You need to do something you love. Something that gives you joy. I really believe that. We both need to find out what makes us happy."

Brian rested his hand on Troy's knee, warm and heavy. "Being your kept man fits the bill."

Troy laughed softly. "The offer stands."

"What about you? The band?"

"I guess I'll have to deal with the consequences of quitting the tour. We were at the end of our contract and in the middle of renegotiations, and I can't see myself doing another album. I was nineteen when we started. After seven years it's time for me to move on." He exhaled, his stomach fluttering. "Wow. That's the first time I've said that out loud. And you know what else? I'm buying a guitar. Working on my folk songs. See what comes of it. Stop worrying about the past and be in the now."

"I love that idea."

"Yeah?"

Brian threw a piece of wood onto their little fire, sending a cascade of sparks into the air. "Yeah."

"I'm used to having a solid, detailed plan. My dad was very big on that."

"My grandparents too." He smiled fondly. "Big planners. But right now, I just want to be with you. Reconnect with some old friends. Go to therapy and actually talk this time."

"That's a good idea. We could both use some mainland therapy."

Brian smiled softly. Peeling at the label on his beer, he said, "When we crashed, I started living again. Before then, I was sleepwalking. You woke me up, Troy. I don't want to go back to sleep."

"Me either."

Troy watched Brian take a long pull from his bottle of beer, his throat working. Desire coiled in Troy's belly, a lazy tendril he knew would spread and grow as the night wore on. He smiled to himself, thinking of how he'd get to spend another night with Brian in his bed. And the next night, and the one after that, for as long as they wanted.

"Sing me our song."

Troy didn't have to ask which one. "It's sad, though. Don't you think?"

"Not when you sing it. There's so much hope in your voice." Brian took Troy's hand, threading their fingers together. "It's perfect."

So Troy sang, and when Brian kissed him with such passion, Troy decided it was perfect indeed.

# Epilogue

"TROY, BRIAN. THANK you so much for being here today. It's such an honor." Anne-Louise Slater smiled beatifically. Not a single tawny hair was out of place, and her lips gleamed dark red.

"Thank you for having us. It's a pleasure to be here," Troy replied.

Brian smiled and didn't say anything. Troy was much better at dealing with the media and sitting there patiently before the cameras rolled as young women powdered their faces, combed their hair, and fiddled with the collars of their buttoned shirts.

Troy was in dark jeans and Brian khaki slacks. Brian had to remind himself not to cross and re-cross his leg anxiously. He folded his hands on his knee in what he hoped was a casual pose.

Brian certainly wouldn't call the interview a *pleasure*—more like a necessary evil. They were in a television studio in LA that had been soft lit with an indistinct background. The network had agreed to their list of no-go topics, including Wisconsin, Paula, flying in general, and Troy and Brian's sex life.

Anne-Louise beamed. "You've been together four years now. This unlikely romance certainly took everyone by surprise."

"Including us," Troy replied with a smile. He pushed back a stray curl.

"A lot of people said it wouldn't last, but here you are." She raised a perfectly penciled eyebrow. "Do we hear wedding bells in your future?"

Brian's laugh was genuine, and he relaxed a few fractions. "You've clearly been talking to Troy's mother. We don't have any plans at the moment since we're honestly too busy. But let's just say it's on our radar."

"Ah, intriguing. Troy, we've heard from you before about what it was like being stranded on the island. Brian, this is actually your very first interview. Did you have anything you wanted to share about that experience?"

"I think Troy's said it all."

"What did you think of him when you met?"

Brian hesitated, thinking of the answer he'd practiced. It was the truth, which made it easier to remember. "That he was surprisingly down to earth. A hard worker. I figured of all the people I could have landed with on that island, I was lucky it was Troy. Now I know just how lucky I was."

"Troy, after you finished Next Up's world tour—which became a farewell tour for the group—you and Brian pulled up stakes and moved to North Carolina. Was it just Brian's new job that brought you there, or were you feeling restless here in LA?"

"Yeah, I think it was both. I was..." Troy paused for a moment. "I was ready for a new challenge, artistically. Ready to expand my horizons."

Anne-Louise picked up a CD. "You certainly have. Your new album, *From Golden Sands to the Top of the World*, sold two hundred and fifty thousand digital copies its first week. It's a real departure for you—very mature, folk-influenced, guitar-driven songs that you've called 'deeply personal.' How rewarding has it been to have this music embraced by the public and critics alike?"

Troy shook his head with a bashful grin. "It's been incredible. Brian encouraged me to spread my wings, and this journey has been so rewarding. And it's not over yet. I'm very excited to start working on my next album."

Anne-Louise said, "Brian, your proud smile says it all."

He hadn't actually realized he was smiling at Troy, and Brian turned his head back to focus on Anne-Louise. "Yes, I'm very proud." *Obviously. God, I hate interviews.*

"And you're enjoying your work as an instructor at the new state-of-the-art pilot training center in Asheville?"

"Very much." She was still looking at him expectantly, so Brian added, "Flight simulators have never been this realistic. It's like being up in the air, but I can stay close to home."

"And your home is in the Smoky Mountains above Asheville? Troy, this is what you refer to as 'Top of the World,' isn't it?"

Troy nodded with a smile. "Yes, it's our little nickname for our cabin. We have a hot tub on the deck, and the view is breathtaking. Some days, it's like being in the clouds."

"Sounds like life couldn't be much more perfect for the two of you. Troy, you're nominated for five Grammy awards this weekend, including album of the year. Are you nervous for Sunday?"

"I am, but it honestly is such an honor just to be nominated." He shook his head. "I know, I know, everyone says that. But the reception this album has received has been beyond my wildest dreams."

"You performed a duet on one of the tracks with your brother Tyson." Anne-Louise put on her serious face. "I think our hearts all broke for him when you went missing and were presumed dead, and it's wonderful to see him healthy and working on his own solo album." She lifted an eyebrow. "You also sang a song with your ex-girlfriend, Savannah Jones, which surprised many people."

Troy shrugged. "We've remained friends, so I'm not sure why it's such a shock. It was great spending time with her in the studio. As you know, she's incredibly talented, and I hope I can work with her again."

Anne-Louise didn't relent. "Well, I think after you left her for a man, it must have been quite a blow for her. She did seem rather heartbroken."

*Here we go.* Brian wanted to tell Anne-Louise Slater to mind her own damn business and stop digging for dirt, but he simply re-crossed his legs and kept a placid almost-smile on his face. Troy could handle it.

"Like I said, we've stayed friends," Troy said.

Anne-Louise smiled when it was clear Troy wasn't going to give her anything else. "That's so...refreshing. It's like you're rewriting all the rules. Neither of you had been involved with a man before you met, yet here you are, going strong all these years later. Does that surprise you, Brian?"

They glanced at each other, and Brian shook his head. "No, it doesn't surprise me. Everyone makes a big deal of gender, but love is love. Troy's the person I want to spend the rest of my life with. We make a great team, and we make each other happy. It's simple, really."

Anne-Louise smiled again. "Well, when you put it like that, I suppose it is."

After a few more questions about the Grammys and Troy's scheduled performance with Tyson, the interview was blessedly over. Brian tapped his foot while an assistant unclipped his mic, and then there were hands to shake and nods and smiles. When they were alone in the back of a limo being shepherded back to Bea's house, Brian exhaled.

"That wasn't so bad, was it?" Troy grinned. "I know, you hated it. I don't love it either, but Lara compromised on a lot."

"It was...acceptable. You'd better win at least one Grammy for all this media stuff we're doing," he grumbled before kissing Troy playfully.

"I'll do my very best," Troy replied solemnly.

"You know I really am so fucking proud of you."

Troy blinked, his face softening. "I know. The feeling's mutual."

They shared a long, slow kiss.

Sighing, Troy leaned their heads together and rubbed his hand over Brian's thigh. "Just think, this time next week we'll be home. In our hot tub. How does that sound?"

"Okay, I guess. If you like that sort of thing."

Laughing, they kissed again, and Troy nuzzled Brian's cheek. "So you're okay?"

"Better than."

With Troy, he was flying.

## The End

## About the Author

Keira aims for the perfect mix of character, plot, and heat in her M/M romances. She writes everything from swashbuckling pirates to heart-warming holiday escapism. Her fave tropes are enemies to lovers, age gaps, forced proximity, and passionate virgins. Although she loves delicious angst along the way, Keira guarantees happy endings!

**Find out more at: www.keiraandrews.com**

Made in the USA
Monee, IL
11 June 2024

59712923R00159